VIRAG

MODERN CL

© Ruth Bernhard

Patricia Highsmith (1921–1995) was born in Fort Worth, Texas, and moved to New York when she was six, where she attended the Julia Richman High School and Barnard College. In her senior year she edited the college magazine, having decided at the age of sixteen to become a writer. Her first novel, *Strangers on a Train*, was made into a classic film by Alfred Hitchcock in 1951. *The Talented Mr Ripley*, published in 1955, introduced the fascinating anti-hero Tom Ripley, and was made into an Oscar-winning film in 1999 by Anthony Minghella. Graham Greene called Patricia Highsmith 'the poet of apprehension', saying that she 'created a world of her own – a world claustrophobic and irrational which we enter each time with a sense of personal danger', and *The Times* named her no.1 in their list of the greatest ever crime writers. Patricia Highsmith died in Locarno, Switzerland, in February 1995. Her last novel, *Small g: A Summer Idyll*, was published posthumously, the same year.

Novels by Patricia Highsmith

Strangers on a Train
Carol (*also published as* The Price of Salt)
The Blunderer
The Talented Mr Ripley
Deep Water
A Game for the Living
This Sweet Sickness
The Cry of the Owl
The Two Faces of January
The Glass Cell
A Suspension of Mercy (*also published as* The Story-Teller)
Those Who Walk Away
The Tremor of Forgery
Ripley Under Ground
A Dog's Ransom
Ripley's Game
Edith's Diary
The Boy Who Followed Ripley
People Who Knock on the Door
Found in the Street
Ripley Under Water
Small g: A Summer Idyll

Short-story Collections

Eleven
Little Tales of Misogyny
The Animal Lover's Book of Beastly Murder
Slowly, Slowly in the Wind
The Black House
Mermaids on the Golf Course
Tales of Natural and Unnatural Catastrophes
Nothing that Meets the Eye: The Uncollected
Stories of Patricia Highsmith

A SUSPENSION
OF MERCY

Patricia Highsmith

Introduced by Joan Schenkar

virago

VIRAGO

This paperback edition published in 2014 by Virago Press
First published in Great Britain in 1965 by William Heinemann Ltd

3 5 7 9 10 8 6 4

A CIP catalogue record for this book
is available from the British Library.

ISBN 978-0-349-00457-0

Typeset in Goudy by M Rules
Printed and bound in Great Britain by
Clays Ltd, St Ives plc

Papers used by Virago are from well-managed forests
and other responsible sources.

MIX
Paper from
responsible sources
FSC
www.fsc.org   FSC® C104740

Virago
An imprint of
Little, Brown Book Group
Carmelite House
50 Victoria Embankment
London EC4Y 0DZ

An Hachette UK Company
www.hachette.co.uk

www.virago.co.uk

To B.J.C.

INTRODUCTION

2.30 a.m. My New Year's Toast: to all the devils, lusts, passions, greeds, envies, loves, hates, strange desires, enemies ghostly and real, the army of memories, with which I do battle – may they never give me peace.

Patricia Highsmith, 1947

Well, she's back.

Just when we thought she'd settled down to a quiet Afterlife, too.

But here she comes, The Dark Lady of American Letters, frowning and smiling and blowing her smoke rings of misdirection at us through the slow, insidious pull of her novels on the gravitational field of modern fiction.

She's back and she's putting the frighteners on again.

Oh, it's Patricia Highsmith all right. I'd know those cloven hoof-prints anywhere. She sidles into your sentences, hacks your *aperçus*, drunk-dials your dreams. Scatters her props and propensities all over your imagination, then shatters your sense of self with her secret plans for sharing: 'What I predicted I would once do, I am already doing[;] that is, showing the unequivocal triumph of evil over good, and rejoicing in it. I shall make my readers rejoice in it, too.'

Here are her maps, her charts, her obsessive little lists. Her art-loving psychopaths and lovesick stalkers. The minds marred by murder, the ambitions cleft by failure. The ice-cold blondes, the amnesiac alter egos. The beer-stained, tear-stained love notes on napkins. The traces of blood at the corner of her smile.

An outsider artist of gravelled gifts, savage talents and obsessional interests, Mary Patricia Highsmith (1921–1995) wrote some of the darkest, most delinquently original novels of the twentieth century. She is responsible for inserting an adjective ('Highsmithian'), a proper name ('Tom Ripley'), and a phrase ('strangers on a train') into the language, but her best books are still corralled in categories which cannot account for their depth, their dazzle or their direct attack on her readers.

'Crime' and 'suspense' are the classifications to which her work is most often relegated, but her novels and short stories splay across genres, interrogate genders, disrupt the idea of character and offer the most thorough anatomy of guilt in modern literature. Patricia Highsmith isn't a crime writer, she's a *punishment* writer.

Born in her grandmother's boarding house in Fort Worth, Texas, rooted in her family's unreconstructed Confederate past, raised in Greenwich Village when it was 'the freest four square miles on earth', Pat Highsmith was a paradox from birth. She was both 'legitimate' and 'born out of wedlock' nine days after her artist mother divorced her illustrator father. She grew into her contradictions.

High art was always her goal, but in the 1940s she had a secret seven-year career as the only woman scriptwriter for Superhero comics.* Proustian in her innumerable love affairs and desired by many, she brought a headsman's axe to all her relationships. She

* It was Pat's anonymous writing for comic-book superheroes and their mild-mannered second selves that gave her an early (and unacknowledged) opportunity to explore her affinity with alter egos and double identities. 'My obsession with duality saves me from a great many other obsessions,' is how she put it.

'worshipped' women, preferred the company of men and cloaked her narrative voice in another (but not exactly opposite) gender. She is as unconscious a 'gay male novelist' as Ernest Hemingway, and as gifted an anatomist of male sexual anxiety as Norman Mailer. Murder was always on her mind, and she usually confused it with love.

'Murder,' she wrote, 'is a kind of making love, a kind of possessing,' and nearly every Highsmith novel is organised around the reverberant psychologies of a homicide. Although love was her lighthouse and she lived for its illuminations, she couldn't live *with* it. So she killed for it over and over again in her writing. A Freudian in spite of herself, she murdered her fictional victims at Greenwich Village addresses where she made love in life.

At twelve, Pat knew she was 'a boy born in a girl's body'. At sixteen, writing was for what she *wished* would happen: she turned her urge to steal a book into a short story about a girl who steals a book. 'Every artist,' she said, 'is in business for his health.' At twenty-one, her focus was fixed: 'Obsessions are the only things that matter. Perversion interests me most and is my guiding darkness.'

Her turbulent love–hate relationship with her erratic mother sundered her psychology and spawned all the Noir bitches in her writing and most of the heartbroken blondes in her bed. Her sentiments for her mild-mannered stepfather were simpler: she wanted to kill him and said so. She grew up to occupy both sides of every question.

In adolescence, Pat began 'double-booking' herself with *cahiers* (notebooks) for her novels, short stories and essays, and with diaries for her love affairs with the beautiful, intelligent women who were her Muses – and the few good men who were not. These lifelong journals – like conjoined twins arising from the vapours of her youthful fascination with doubling – embezzled each other's materials, rehearsed her obsessions before she published them, and gave her the opportunity to renew her vows to the only lasting love match she ever made: the union that joined her intense rushes of feeling with her compelling need to commit them to paper.

At twenty-nine, she published her sensational debut novel, *Strangers on a Train* (1950). The 'deal' at its dark heart – an anonymous exchange of homicides – set up the quintessential Highsmith situation: two men bound together by the stalker-like fixation of one upon the other; a fixation which always involves a murderous, implicitly homoerotic fantasy.* *The Price of Salt* followed in 1952, and its richly figured language borrowed elements from *Strangers* and subdued them to the subject of requited lesbian love – the only 'crime' Pat left out of her other fictions. Published anonymously for forty years, *The Price of Salt* (now reissued as *Carol*) sold hundreds of thousands of copies and made its author uneasy all her life.

Highsmith's industry was staggering. Five to seven neatly typed pages of finished fiction rolled from the platen of her coffee-coloured 1956 Olympia Deluxe portable typewriter each day, followed by book themes, articles, lists of every description, short-story ideas, and four or five personal letters in her oddly impersonal prose. Her thirty-eight writer's notebooks and eighteen diaries were written in five languages, four of which she didn't actually speak. She drew, she sketched, she painted; she made sculptures, furniture and woodcarvings. The simple savageries of gardening – who lives? who goes to the compost pile? – appealed to her American Calvinism, and she took up her secateurs with a will.

Out of her great divide (and in the acid bath of her detail-saturated prose), Patricia Highsmith developed a remarkable

* Alfred Hitchcock's wonderful (if skewed towards normality) film version of *Strangers on a Train* (1951) revived his directing career. Raymond Chandler, on the other hand, said that working on the film script drove him crazy.

image of an alternate Earth: Highsmith Country. Its shadow cabinet of homicidal alter egos, displaced guilts, and unstable identities convenes in permanent session in the Nightmare Alley just behind the American Dream. And the deep psychological partitions its citizens suffer (as they count up their culpabilities or slip into measurable degrees of madness) come from its author's unblinking examination of her own wayward tastes:

I can't think of anything more apt to set the imagination stirring, drifting, creating, than the idea – the fact – that anyone you walk past on the pavement anywhere may be a sadist, a compulsive thief, or even a murderer.

Pat's Suffolk period was the first creatively settled interval in her long, strange European expatriation. And England was ready for her. She had loyal English publishers and agents. Francis Wyndham's crucial survey of her dark materials (part of an extended review of *The Cry of the Owl* in the *New Statesman* in 1963) had provided the public with an elegant introduction to her work: '[T]he reader's sense of satisfaction,' he wrote, 'may derive from sources as dark as those which motivate Patricia Highsmith's destroyers and their fascinated victims.' London-associated writers as diversely distinguished as Julian Symons, Brigid Brophy, Graham Greene, Arthur Koestler, Sybil Bedford, and Muriel Spark admired her writing.* And *The Two Faces of January* (1964) would win the CWA's Silver Dagger Award in 1965.

But it was love alone – and in a magnitude she hadn't yet experienced – that brought the talented Miss Highsmith to Suffolk. In late 1962, domiciled in America, but travelling widely

---

* Muriel Spark adopted Highsmith's favourite cat, Spider, the dedicatee of *The Glass Cell*, when Highsmith moved to England from Italy. Spider, Dame Muriel said, 'brought a bit of Patricia Highsmith with him'.

and restlessly, Pat fell in love ('like being shot in the face', is what she said – still mixing up love and murder) with a cultured, attractive, solidly married Londoner. Obsessed by this woman 'as never before' and so 'killed by pleasure' that she couldn't continue the novel she'd started about a good man wrongly imprisoned (*The Glass Cell*), Pat 'cleared her complicated decks' in America and made her way to Europe and thence to Suffolk, to be nearer (if not closer) to love's inspiring shocks.

Stalking her London romance – but keeping her distance from it, too – Pat wrote most of *The Glass Cell* (1964) in Positano and Rome, and then revised the manuscript extensively in Aldeburgh. Finally, in 1964, she settled in Earl Soham in Suffolk in what had been two country cottages, now knocked together as one dwelling: Bridge Cottage.

The double structure of Bridge Cottage suited her psychology as much as the ambiguities of a love affair with someone else's wife suited her temperament. Lush productivity and plain prose were the results, punctuated by an invigorating volley of complaints. English weather, 'dreary' English pubs and too-infrequent meetings with her English lover encouraged her natural negativity, but only an English Christmas could raise it to the level of simile: 'The holidays here exhaust one, creeping through closed windows like a poisonous gas,' she wrote, sounding just like a Highsmith character.

In fact, Pat was having a better time in Suffolk than she admitted. Enlivened by her new surroundings, she very quickly began to write *A Suspension of Mercy* (1965), and then found a collaborator with whom to plot out a possible television script. She made fast friends with Ronald Blythe, at work on his Suffolk book *Akenfield*, and they gossiped for hours and toured the Suffolk churches. And James Hamilton-Paterson, future author of *Gerontius* and *Cooking with Fernet Branca*, won her heart by walking out on her when she burst into tears. 'I don't blame him,' said Pat, who would have done the same thing herself, 'give him my love.'

Although each of the three novels Pat completed during her Suffolk period was set in a different place (New York, Suffolk, Venice), Highsmith Country is their one, true home.* The first of them, *The Glass Cell*, was sourced from Pat's detailed correspondence with an American convict who wrote to tell her how much he'd enjoyed *Deep Water*. ('I don't think my books should be in prison libraries,' said Pat – and made the convict give her the particulars of prison life.) As always, she followed her unruly feelings in reversing her new novel's line of logic. Philip Carter is a classic Highsmith 'criminal-hero' – with his orphan background and professional training; his high culture and low behaviour; his sluggish libido and ambiguous affections. In *The Glass Cell*, his punishment has been enacted *before* he commits a crime. He is unjustly accused, wrongly imprisoned, physically tortured, and entirely innocent.

Philip Carter and his prison mate Max (a forger who dies in a prison riot) approach intimacy and practise French, and Max seems 'more real' to Carter than his own wife. Carter reads Swift, Voltaire and Robbe-Grillet (and keeps the complete Verlaine in his cell), murders his wife's lover when he's released (guiltlessly and with a piece of classical statuary), and weeps while listening to Bach. He lies to everyone, forces 'guilt' and 'innocence' to change places and exchange definitions, and knows the police will follow him for ever. Still, murder has made his life better: 'Everything was going to be all right now,' he thinks.

* Tom Ripley, the 'criminal-hero' of Pat's best-known work *The Talented Mr Ripley* (1955), is Highsmith Country's most prominent ambassador. A socially sinuous, fragilely gendered serial killer, forger, fraudster, and identity impersonator, he is also Highsmith's darker emissary to herself; her *semblable*. It was Ripley, Pat said disconcertingly, who wrote that novel; she was merely taking dictation. And she added Ripley's name to her Edgar Allan Poe award.

But in *The Glass Cell*, the push-broom of Pat's paragraphs sweeps the detritus of confinement steadily before it, trailing strings of objects or mundane actions or simple thoughts in a dogged accumulation of detail as dispassionate as that found in most prisons – or most pornographies. Her gut-punch prose – she's the court recorder here, not the judge, but her style (as spare as a prison bunk) is convincingly mimetic – suggests that Carter has carried his private incarceration (his 'glass cell') into the world with him. The world is his prison now, nor is he out of it.

Nothing if not practical, Pat liked to furnish her houses of fiction with the large and small irritants of her daily life. In *A Suspension of Mercy*, the only novel she both wrote and set in Suffolk, she used her circumstances to make a work at war with itself – a comedy of terrors – and lent her 'criminal-hero' more of her own qualities than even she imagined.

Sydney Smith Bartleby, a young American novelist displaced to Suffolk by his upwardly mobile English marriage, is beginning to chafe. He's in a situation not unlike his author's – and he's burdened with most of her local irritations, too: a collaborator on a television script; a frustrated desire to see a body carried out in a carpet (a gambit Pat considered for other works and parodied in this one by leaving the body *out* of the carpet); a partner in absentia (Sydney's would-be painter wife is taking a holiday from their marriage and its meannesses); some difficult writing to get on with; and an imagination unable to refrain from replacing the dullish realities of his life with the homicidal narratives he wants for his work.

Sydney's names, yoked together by violence, are clipped directly from the baptismal rolls of Highsmith Country. 'Sydney Smith' was the wit, writer and clergyman on whom Jane Austen is said to have based the attractive protagonist of her Gothic satire *Northanger Abbey* – while 'Sir Sydney Smith' was Edinburgh's renowned forensic expert on methods of murder. And 'Bartleby' is Herman Melville's inscrutably persistent Wall Street scrivener. The ways in which Pat uses *A Suspension of Mercy* to juggle these contradictions and toy with the conventions of crime and suspense are both experimental *and* satirical – though the smiles are properly constrained and the laughter suitably stifled.

As Sydney relaxes his ability to distinguish between the fantasies he's staging in his head and what he'd really like to do about his absent spouse, he begins to rehearse the actions, the feelings, and the false identity of a guilty wife-killer; falling under suspicion for his wife's murder after she disappears. In the course of his games, the principles of Highsmith Country, greatly exhilarated by his masquerades, come out to play: deeds before motives, effects before causes, punishments before crimes – and Sydney unintentionally frightens a suspicious neighbour to death, then languidly commits a murder which is both there and not there.

For this ostensible murder – and for his accidental one, too – Sydney feels no guilt. He looks forward to recording what he's just lived through in his writer's notebook. It's a brown notebook, we are told quietly; the same colour as the writer's notebooks Patricia Highsmith used all her life.

Strictly speaking, there is no homicide in Pat's third Suffolk novel, *Those Who Walk Away* (1967). Once again, a murder is there, and not there – and Pat began to imagine the novel's rapid reversals and deep disruptive shocks late in 1966 on a trip to Venice: a city whose end-stopped streets and serpentine canals might have been designed for the psychological volutes of a Highsmith novel.

Pat's first intention for *Those Who Walk Away* sounds like something out of *Sunset Boulevard*: 'A suspense novel from the point of view of the corpse'. But the suicide of the painter Peggy Garrett, wife and daughter, respectively, of the two male protagonists (one of whom, an artist, blames the other, a gallerist, for her death), predates the novel's first page, pervades the work, and tries to pass itself off as the trigger for the purest expression yet of Highsmith Country's 'infinite progression of the trapped and the hunted'.

The dead woman's husband, Ray Garrett, is pursued by Ed Coleman, the vengeful painter who is her father. Ray starts a game of hide and seek with his potential murderer, chasing his own death by following Ed to Venice after Ed tries to shoot him in Rome. Filled with the inspiration of art and artists, Ray seeks what all Highsmith males look for: total oblivion through the dissolution of his burdensome identity.

Just like wrestlers unable to leave the mat, Ray Garrett and his father-in-law try out different holds and postures on each other, different ways of winning and losing, different means of being brutal and being passive. But there is no death in Venice, and Ray and Ed are both caught in the mantrap Highsmith's imagination first sprang in *Strangers on a Train* – and then prised open again in *The Talented Mr Ripley* (1955).

In *Those Who Walk Away*, Pat Highsmith, always a little more frightening than any of her characters, imagines a 'reality' built around the *whole* of the hunt: the hunter, the hunted, their constant exchange of roles, and the terrible necessity of the pursuit itself. Someone as creatively caught up with hunting as Pat was could never choose the hunter over the hunted – or vice versa. Hence her constant shifting of roles and shuffling of identities: a compellingly forceful premise in her fictions – and a cruelly exhausting one in her life.

With her usual discipline, Pat continued to write in Suffolk as her London relationship slowly, then rapidly, declined. She began 'a religious television play' based on a Jesus-like character – and put it to perverse use as a frame for *Ripley Under Ground* (1970). She finished her second snail story, 'The Quest for Blank Claveringii', wrote a 'ghost' tale, 'The Yuma Baby', and in a single month completed a short, artistic autobiography disguised as a handbook for would-be writers: *Plotting and Writing Suspense Fiction* (1965). From Earl Soham she travelled to Hammamet in Tunisia for weeks of immersive research for *The Tremor of Forgery* (1969), another book about another American writer losing his sense of moral balance in expatriatism. Back at Bridge Cottage, she finished a film script for her novel *Deep Water* (1957). She never stopped working.

She went on drawing and sketching too, and jotted down little inventions and quirky ephemera in her notebooks: 'The Gallery of Bad Art', a 'sweating thermometer', some free-form 'lamp-shades'. Her 'strychnined lipstick' expressed her feelings for women just as much as her idea for a cookbook, 'Desperate Measures', represented her response to food. The best that can be said of her scheme for the global deployment of children (as tiny territorial ambassadors) is that it adds a new terror to child development.

The final breakdown of her English love affair – she described it as 'the worst time of my entire life' – swept her across the Channel to France and Switzerland, where she moved from region to region, relationship to relationship, and drink to drink. She went on writing as though her life depended on it (it did); monitoring her thoughts the way a searchlight sweeps a prison yard for escaping convicts. And she continued to curate her expatriate's museum of American maladies.

The pearl of a girl from mid-century Manhattan turned into an embittered old oyster in her last home, her Fortress of Solitude (a modernist citadel with jutting twin wings) in a sunny canton in Switzerland: the country, as Scott Fitzgerald wrote, where many things end and few begin.

Even the manner of her dying sustained that volatile attachment to duality which haloed her life and allowed all her contradictory emotions to meet and mate and ignite into art. For Patricia Highsmith – she could have written this ending for herself and perhaps she did – expired of two competing diseases. Her doctors said they could not treat the one without exacerbating the other.

Welcome to Highsmith Country.

Joan Schenkar, 2014

I

The land around Sydney and Alicia Bartleby's two-storey cottage was flat, like most Suffolk country. A road, two-laned and paved, went by the house at a distance of twenty yards. To one side of the front walk, which was of slightly askew flagstones, five young elms gave some privacy, and on the other side a tall, bushy hedge provided a better screen for thirty feet. For this reason, Sydney had never trimmed it. The front lawn was as untended as the hedge. The grass grew in tufts, and where it didn't, fairy rings had eaten circles exposing green-brown earth. The Bartlebys took better care of the ground behind the house, and they had besides a vegetable and flower garden an ornamental pond some five feet across that Sydney had made with a cemented pile of interesting stones in its centre, but they had never succeeded in keeping goldfish alive in it, and two frogs they had put there had decided to go somewhere else.

The road led to Ipswich and London in one direction and towards Framlingham in the other. Behind the house, their property trickled off vaguely, bounded by nothing visible, and beyond lay a field belonging to a farmer whose house was out of sight. The Bartlebys were supposed to live in Blycom Heath, but Blycom

Heath proper was two miles away towards Framlingham. They had had their house a year and a half, almost as long as they had been married, and it was mostly a wedding present from Alicia's parents, though she and Sydney had contributed £1,000 towards its £3,500 price. It was a lonely neighbourhood from the point of view of people and neighbours, but Sydney and Alicia had their own pursuits – writing and painting – they had each other's company all day, and they had made a few friends who were scattered as far away as Lowestoft. But they had to drive five miles to Framlingham to get so much as a shoe repair or a bottle of Chinese ink. It was the loneliness of the neighbourhood, they supposed, that kept the house next to theirs empty. The sturdy, two-storey house with its facing of flintstone and a pointed gable window was in better shape than theirs to look at, but they had heard that there were all sorts of things to do on the inside, as it had not been occupied for five years, and then by an ageing man and his wife who hadn't had the means to put in any improvements. The house stood two hundred yards from the Bartlebys', and Alicia liked looking out a window now and then and seeing it, even if it was empty. Sometimes she did feel geographically lonely, as if she and Sydney lived at some deserted pole of the earth.

Through Elspeth Cragge, who lived in Woodbridge and knew Mr Spark, a real estate dealer there, Alicia learned that a Mrs Lilybanks had bought the house next door. She was an old lady from London, Elspeth said, and expressed her regret that it couldn't have been a young couple who might have been more fun as neighbours.

'Mrs Lilybanks moved in this afternoon,' Alicia said brightly one evening in the kitchen.

'Um. You get a look at her?'

'Not any more than I did before. She's rather elderly.'

Sydney knew that. They had both had a look at Mrs Lilybanks

a month ago, when she had come with the rental agent. For more than a month, workmen had been prowling over the place, hammering and banging, and now Mrs Lilybanks had moved in. She looked about seventy, and she would probably write a short note of complaint if they had any noisy parties this summer in the back garden. Sydney carefully made two martinis in a glass pitcher and poured them.

'I would've gone over to see her, but she had a couple of people with her and I thought they might be staying the night.'

'Um,' Sydney said. He was making the salad, which was his usual job at dinner. He braced the metal cabinet with his hand automatically before jerking open the sticky door to get the mustard. Then, forgetting, he raised straight up and hit his head on a slanting rafter. 'God's *teeth*!'

'Oh, darling,' said Alicia absently, checking her steak-and-kidney pie in the oven of the Baby Belling. She wore pale-blue narrow slacks, made like blue jeans, but with a V slit in the cuffs. Her shirt was of blue denim, the real McCoy sent by an American friend. She wore her streaky blonde hair carelessly and it hung almost to her shoulders. Her face was slender, well-bred and pretty, her eyes wide-set and blue-grey. A smudge of darker blue paint streaked half across her left thigh, still there after many washings. Alicia painted in an upstairs back room of the house. 'Tomorrow, though, I probably will,' Alicia said, still going on about Mrs Lilybanks.

Sydney's mind was miles away, back on his afternoon with Alex in London. He resented the third intrusion of Mrs Lilybanks. Why didn't Alicia ask him about his afternoon, about his work, the way any wife would have done? Sometimes she deliberately hung on to subjects that she knew bored him. Therefore Sydney didn't answer now.

'How was London?' Alicia asked finally, when they were seated at the table in the dining-room.

3

'Oh, the same. Still there,' Sydney said with a forced smile. 'Alex is just the same, too. Meaning no new ideas.'

'Oh. I thought you were hammering out one today.'

Sydney sighed, vaguely irritated, yet it was the only subject he wanted to talk about. 'We were going to. I had an idea. It just didn't get off the ground.' He shrugged. The third serial that he and Alex had doped out – mostly he had doped out, Alex simply wrote it in television form – had been rejected last week by the third and last possible purchaser in London. Three or four weeks of sweat, at least four sessions in London with Alex, a complete detailed synopsis and Instalment One of one hour written, neatly bound and dispatched to one, two, three possible buyers. All that down the drain now, and add today also. Seventeen shillings for the day-excursion fare from Ipswich to London, add eight hours' time and a certain amount of physical energy, add the frustration of watching Alex's big, dark face grow cloudy with thought and dense silence, followed by, 'Ah, no, no, that won't do,' and the result was a day that would make a man tear his hair out, throw his typewriter in the nearest creek, then jump in himself.

'How was Hittie?'

Hittie was Alex's wife, a blonde, quiet girl totally absorbed in the care of their three small children.

'As usual,' Sydney said.

'Were you talking about your new idea, the one about the man on the tanker?' Alicia asked.

'No, darling. That was the one that just got rejected.' How could she forget that, Sydney wondered, since she'd read the instalment and the synopsis? 'My new idea, I don't know if I mentioned it, was about the tattoo. The man who has a tattoo faked to resemble the tattoo of a man who's supposed to be dead.' He hadn't the energy to launch into the complicated story. He and Alex had a sleuth-hero named Nicky Campbell, a young fellow with an ordinary job and a girl friend, and Nicky kept running

4

into crime and solving mysteries and capturing crooks and winning fistfights and gunfights and the stories kept not getting bought. But Alex was sure they would make it one day, and then they'd both be set. Alex had had one television script accepted two years ago, and since then had written five or six that hadn't been accepted, but they had been straight hour-long dramas, and Alex was confident that what television needed now was a good serial. Fortunately for Alex, he had a steady job in a publishing house. Sydney had no job, and hadn't succeeded in placing his last novel, though he had had two novels published a few years ago in the States. As a reliable income, he had about a hundred dollars a month which came in four times a year from some stocks an uncle in America had bequeathed him. On this and on Alicia's more substantial fifty pounds a month, they lived, buying oil paint and canvas, typewriter paper and ribbons and carbon paper, the tools of their trades that returned them so little. Alicia's income to date from painting was five pounds, though she didn't take painting so seriously as a money-making activity as Sydney did his writing. They bought nothing in the way of luxury items but drink and cigarettes, though since these items were so costly in England, buying them at all seemed luxury to the point of madness, cigarettes being like rolled up ten-bob notes going up in smoke and drink molten gold. They had not bought a new gramophone record in months. Their television set was rented from a Framlingham shop. Most English rented their sets, since new models appeared rapidly, and a set that one bought was soon out of date. Sydney reasoned that he needed a television set for his work with Alex.

'Are you going to keep on trying with Alex?' Alicia asked, her last bite poised on her fork.

'What else? I hate to waste days in London like this one, but if it breaks for us, it breaks.' A sudden anger swept over him, a hatred of Alicia and the house, and he wanted to drop the

5

subject, wished that he could erase every word and thought of today, of Alex, of their damned plots. He lit a cigarette, just as Alicia passed him the salad, and mechanically he helped himself to a little. Tomorrow would find him tackling his synopsis anew, trying to incorporate or improve on the flimsy ideas Alex had come up with today. After all, he was supposed to think up the stories, he was the mainspring.

'Darling, the garbage tonight. Don't forget,' Alicia said with such gentleness, Sydney might have laughed if he had been in a better mood, if there had been other people present.

Alicia probably meant him to laugh, or smile, but he only nodded absently and seriously, and then his mind focused on *garbage*, as if it were a vital and very large problem. The dustmen came only once a fortnight, so it was a serious matter if they forgot to put all the garbage out at the edge of the road. Their one dustbin of inadequate size was always at the edge of the road, and into this went tins and bottles only. Papers they burnt, and vegetable and fruit parings they threw on their compost heap, but since orange juice and tomatoes and lots of other things came in cans and bottles, this department was always bulging at the end of two weeks, and a couple of cartons stood full in the toolhouse for days before the dustmen arrived. Usually it was raining on the eve of garbage day, so Sydney had to carry the cartons out across muddy ground, drop them by the dustbin, and hope they would not dissolve by morning.

'It's annoying that one has to feel ashamed of having garbage in the English countryside,' Sydney said. 'What's so abnormal about having garbage, I'd like to know? Do they think people don't eat?'

Alicia calmly girded herself for the defence of her country. 'It's not shameful to have garbage. Who said it was shameful?'

'Perhaps it isn't, but they make it so,' Sydney replied just as calmly. 'By taking so long between collections, they focus people's attention on it – rub it in their faces, practically. Just like the drinking hours. You find a pub door locked in your face, so you want a drink more than ever and drink two or three the next chance you get.'

Alicia defended the pub hours on the grounds that it cut down drinking, and the infrequent garbage disposal on the grounds that more frequent disposal would put up the rates, and so this discussion, which they had had before, went on for about two minutes more and left them both in a rather irritated mood, as neither had convinced the other of his point.

Alicia was less irritated, and in fact her irritation was mostly a pretence. It was her country, she liked it, and often it crossed her mind to say that if Sydney didn't like it, he might leave, but she had never said this. She loved teasing Sydney, even on the delicate subject of his writing, because the answer to his problem seemed so simple to her: Sydney should relax, be more natural, more happy, and write what he pleased, then it would be good and it would sell. She had said this to him many times, and he came back at her with some complex and masculine answer, upholding the virtue of hard thinking and of aiming at markets. 'But we decided to live in the country just so we *could* relax,' she had said to him a few times, but this was like oil on the fire, and Sydney would really flare up then, asking her if she thought living in the country with a million bucolic chores was more conducive to relaxing than a flat in London, however small. Well, rents in London were high and getting higher, and if she pinned Sydney down, he didn't want to live in London really, because he preferred a country landscape and preferred to wear chinos and shirts without a tie and old plimsolls, and he actually liked mending a fence occasionally and pottering around in the garden. What Sydney needed, of course, was either to sell a serial with Alex or sell his novel, *The Planners*, that he was still tinkering with. Alicia thought he had tinkered with it enough, and that he ought to

7

show it to every publisher in London, if necessary. He had shown it to six here, including Nerge Press, where Alex worked, and to three in the United States, and they had all turned it down, but there were a lot more publishers, and Alicia had heard of books that had had thirty or more rejections before they were finally accepted.

As she washed the dishes, she looked out now and then at Sydney, prowling about in his plimsolls that he had put on as soon as he got home. He had carried the garbage cartons out, and now he was looking at the garden in the dusk, bending now and then to remove a weed. The lettuce had just come up, but nothing else so far.

Sydney kept glancing at the solitary light in the back upstairs corner of Mrs Lilybanks's house. An early retirer, he supposed, or very economical with the electricity. Probably both. It was strange to have another person living so close to them, able to look out now, for instance, and see him vaguely at least, walking around in the back yard. Sydney didn't like it. Then he realized he was not glancing at the lighted window to see Mrs Lilybanks, about whom he was not at all curious, but to see if she were looking at him. But he saw absolutely nothing at the window except two vertical yellowish curtains, almost closed on whatever was going on behind them.

2

At that moment, 9.17 p.m., Mrs Lilybanks was not thinking about going to bed in spite of the strenuous day she had had. She was arranging her night-table in the most convenient position beside her bed, and debating whether to hang her painting of Cannes (done nearly fifty years ago on her honeymoon) over the fireplace, or a still-life of apples and wine bottle that her friend Elsie Howell (who had died twelve years ago) had painted especially for Mrs Lilybanks's London flat to which she had moved when her husband Clive Lilybanks had died. Mrs Lilybanks moved slowly, putting her sewing basket into a top drawer, straightening her silver-backed comb and brush on the top of the chest of drawers, aware that she was so tired she was no longer being very efficient, but she felt particularly happy and content, and wanted to stay up a little longer to enjoy it. It was strange, she thought, to be fixing up a house – Mrs Lilybanks had fixed up at least twenty houses in her long life, because her husband's work had caused them to travel quite a bit – a house that would definitely be the last house she would ever bring into order, because in all probability, she was not going to live two more years. Mrs Lilybanks had a bad heart, and had already had two strokes. The

9

third would kill her, her doctor told her quite frankly. Mrs Lilybanks appreciated frankness, even in such matters. She had enjoyed life, quite a long life, and she was ready for the end when it came.

Mrs Lilybanks turned down her bed, which Mrs Hawkins had made up for her that afternoon, went into the bathroom and took her two pills, a ritual before retiring, then went downstairs, holding firmly to the banister as she descended. She turned on some more lights, sliding her hand along unfamiliar walls until she found them, took her torch and went out into the small and now unkempt front garden and picked a few pansies. She put them in a small plain glass and carried them upstairs and put them on her night-table. Then she brushed her teeth, which were still her own teeth, complete in front, though six molars had been drawn. She had had her bath earlier in the day at her Ipswich hotel.

But she did not get to sleep immediately. She thought of her daughter Martha in Australia, of her granddaughter Prissie, in London now, probably saying to a lot of her young friends, who would be sitting around her flat on the floor, drinking red wine. 'Well, I got Grannie bedded down in the country today. Whew! Don't you think she's out of her ever-loving mind? An old thing like that all alone in the country?' Because Prissie secretly approved of what her Grannie had decided to do, and wanted her friends to approve of it, too, or maybe to defend her Grannie in case her friends disapproved. 'Mrs Hawkins is coming over every afternoon, Prissie, even Sunday for a cup of tea. And after I'm gone, the cottage is yours, you know,' Mrs Lilybanks had said that afternoon. Mrs Lilybanks smiled now in the darkness. She wasn't worried about loneliness. Friendly people were never lonely, she thought, and she had been in many strange places in the world, so she felt she knew. Mrs Hawkins said she wanted to introduce her to a couple of her former employers in the neighbourhood. Mrs Lilybanks had been quite touched by that. The couple next door was young, Mr Spark had told her, and hadn't been here very long. Mrs Lilybanks thought that in a few days she'd ask them over for tea. She'd have to go to Framlingham this week to buy odds and ends like potholders and curtain rods. That meant a taxi to Blycom Heath and a bus from there. Frannegan, they had called Framlingham in the old days in Suffolk, and perhaps the farm people still did ...

Mrs Lilybanks had had her tea-break and a short rest on the living-room sofa and was up again putting away things in the kitchen, when Alicia Bartleby came over the next morning at 11. Alicia was carrying a plate that held a quarter of an orange-iced cake under a paper napkin.

After she had introduced herself, Alicia said, 'I wish I could say I made the cake, but I didn't. But it's from a nice place in Ipswich.'

Mrs Lilybanks asked her to sit down and said she couldn't be more pleased to meet her new neighbour so soon, because she had been wondering when she would.

Alicia didn't want to sit down. 'I'd love to see around the house, if you don't mind my seeing it before you've settled in. I've never been here before.'

'No? Why of course I don't mind.' Mrs Lilybanks moved towards the stairs. 'I'd have thought you looked at this house when you bought yours.'

Alicia's face spread in a wide smile. 'They told us there was more to do here – plumbing and things – so we thought we'd take a house where there wasn't so much outlay. My husband and I have to watch our pennies. Turn them.'

The house had three rooms downstairs and three up, plus a new bathroom. The furniture was Mrs Lilybanks's from her London flat, she said, and from the look of it, plus its abundance, Alicia drew the conclusion that Mrs Lilybanks was quite well off.

'You're going to be here by yourself?' Alicia asked.

'Oh, yes. I don't mind being alone. In fact, I like it,' Mrs Lilybanks said cheerfully. 'It's been fifteen years since I last had a house in the country – in Surrey – with my husband, so I thought I'd like a taste of it again.'

'Have you got a car?' Alicia hadn't seen one around.

'No, but I think I'll manage with buses. Then there're the mobile butcher and greengrocer, I hear.'

They were standing in Mrs Lilybanks's bedroom. The morning sunlight showed the crêpe-like wrinkles below Mrs Lilybanks's blue eyes very plainly, and the wrinkles somehow fascinated Alicia. How was it possible to be so old one's skin got like that, and still to have such bright, young-looking eyes? Mrs Lilybanks's hands were smallish but very active and flexible, not gnarled like some old people's hands. Her nails had a pale pink polish, and on her left hand were the engagement ring and wedding ring one saw on most women's hands, and on the other an emerald ring set in silver.

Mrs Lilybanks was appraising Alicia at the same time, though without appearing to stare at her. She liked what she saw – a very natural-looking young woman of around twenty-five, she thought, with frankly curious eyes like a child or a painter, perhaps, and Mrs Lilybanks had noticed also the streak of blue paint on the paler blue slacks.

Alicia pivoted on restless feet and faced the painting over the mantel. 'That's an interesting landscape. Where is that?'

'Cannes,' said Mrs Lilybanks. 'I hung it just ten minutes ago. It's one of my early efforts.'

'Oh, you paint.' Alicia's eyes widened with interest. 'So do I. Some. Nothing as organized as that. Mine are sort of a mess.'

'Mine are getting worse,' Mrs Lilybanks said firmly and with a twinkle. 'But I've brought my kit and I hope the new scene here will inspire me. Can't I get you a cup of tea?'

They went downstairs again, but Alicia did not care for tea.

'If you ever need a lift – need a car for anywhere, please don't hesitate to ring us,' Alicia said. 'It's four six six. I'm there all the time, practically, and my husband's there most of the time.'

'That's very kind of you. Is your husband a painter, too?'

'No, he's a writer. Fiction. He's working on a novel. But lately he goes in to London about once a week to have a conference with another writer. Not a writer, but a friend who does some writing. They're trying to sell a serial to television. Not having any luck yet.' Alicia smiled as widely as if she had been reporting a triumph. 'My husband's an American.'

'Oh, how interesting. How does he like England?'

Alicia laughed. 'I suppose he likes most things. He's been here two years. Not quite. His name is Sydney. Sydney Smith Bartleby, isn't that funny? His father was crazy about Sydney Smith for some reason. I tell Syd it's the only English thing about him, that name.'

'What kind of fiction does he write?'

'Oh – not things with plots. At least not just now. His first two novels had more of a plot, but the thing he's working on now hasn't. It's called *The Planners*, and it's about a group of people who decide to plan the experiences they want in life and live accordingly. It sounds as if it'd have a plot, but it hasn't.' Alicia smiled. 'He can't sell it yet, either, though it's been finished for a year. His television ideas have plots, of course, absolutely crammed, but so far no luck with them.'

'Ah, well. The arts take time. Don't let him get discouraged.'

Alicia left, promising to call Mrs Lilybanks – her telephone was already in and her number was 275 – very soon and ask her for a meal.

Then Alicia skipped home, pausing only to pick a daisy at the edge of the road and pull its stem through a buttonhole of her shirt, went into her house and up the stairs to report to Sydney on their new neighbour.

Sydney was standing at the window of his study, smoking a cigarette. The door was ajar, so Alicia didn't knock, as she usually did when it was closed.

'Well, she's very nice. Not stuffy and she's even got a sense of humour, I think. She paints. One wasn't bad. But I only saw one. She's all alone there, really. I was quite surprised.' Alicia wasn't quite surprised, because they had not heard anything about anybody else with Mrs Lilybanks, but her remarks on the visit were petering out in the face of Sydney's lack of interest and his air of annoyance at having his thinking interrupted. 'I really liked her very much.'

'Good,' Sydney said. 'So she paints.' He tossed a pencil down on his cluttered, ink-stained worktable, where a blank sheet of paper gleamed expectantly in the typewriter.

'Um-um. Just an old lady's pastime, I suppose. Looks as if she's got plenty of money.'

Alicia went to Framlingham that afternoon to shop, and did not get back until five, because she ran into Elspeth Cragge in Carley and Webb (the grocery store where the Bartlebys often had a formidable bill that the store was very nice about), and they sat talking in a coffee shop for more than an hour. Elspeth was an Australian married to an Englishman, and she was expecting a child in three months. The sight of her growing body reawakened in Alicia her own vague yearning for a baby, but economics were against it at the moment and, more important, she wasn't sure how good a father Syd would be, wasn't even sure their marriage would last for ever. Alicia wanted a child, but now and then an awful thought crossed her mind: I want a child, but do I really want a child with Sydney? It was odd to have this ghastly thought and at the same time be rather in love with Sydney and to enjoy sleeping with him. And being in love, of course, meant his faults didn't really bother her, or shouldn't. It was a muddled state indeed, which was why she didn't often ponder it. Time would effect changes, time always did, so she waited for that to happen, for better or for worse.

Sydney came downstairs as Alicia was finishing putting away the groceries. 'I'm going to pop that stuff off to Alex in tomorrow morning's post, and ask him to come up Saturday, if it's all right with you. That means both of them, of course, and staying overnight, but I'm damned if I'm going to do this Ipswich–London shuttle again on the same story.'

'Of course it's all right with me, Syd.' Alicia's mind was going over the sheet situation, the fact that Friday would have to be spent cleaning (Hittie was not neat, but the Polk-Faradays' house was always cleaner than theirs), and what big meat dish could she serve, because Alex and Hittie were hearty eaters.

'If we don't wind the thing up this weekend, then the hell with it, and I'll start doping out another idea, I suppose.' He flung the yellow pencil down on the draining-board as if it were his desk, as if he were through with pencils for ever.

Alicia was used to the gesture, an outward turn of the wrist, the couple of bounces the pencil made, the pencil's stillness. She never remembered seeing him pick a pencil up, yet he always seemed to have one to throw down. 'Of course, darling, I'd rather like seeing them,' Alicia said with a sudden smile.

3

Alicia took the opportunity to invite Mrs Lilybanks for dinner on Saturday evening. If she was cooking so much, one more was no trouble, and she felt Mrs Lilybanks might enjoy meeting some people after nearly a week's solitude.

The Polk-Faradays arrived on Saturday at 3 o'clock, an hour later than they had anticipated, but they had had lunch on the road, and they had had difficulties leaving their children in the charge of their half-time daily, Lucy.

'No telephone in her house,' Alex said, 'so we had to get a series of people to deliver a message, then Lucy had to pack and trundle over.'

'She didn't come Friday,' Hittie explained further. 'Somebody sick in her family or something.' Hittie was a round-faced girl with straight blonde hair which she wore with bangs. The bangs made her look like a blonde Chinese.

'Well, you're here,' Alicia said. 'A drink? Anything?'

'Ah, nothing, my sweet,' said Alex, opening his arms and wrapping Alicia briefly in one. He was tall, dark and pale-skinned, a trifle overweight. 'It's so great to be in the country and smell the air! Oh, to be in England now that April's here. Except it's May. Do you mind if I remove this jacket?'

Sydney padded rapidly down the stairs, having deposited the Polk-Faradays' bag in the guest-room. 'What do you mean you don't want a drink?' he asked cheerily. 'Are you on the wagon?'

'No, it's because—' Alex winked a large brown eye at Alicia. 'Because we're exerting our great intellects this afternoon, and we're going to get that story in shape before sundown.'

'Or shoot ourselves at sunrise,' Sydney said.

'Yes. I'll shoot you and you shoot me, simultaneously,' Alex said.

Sydney and Alex hadn't got far by 5 p.m., though Sydney felt, as he inevitably felt when he hammered out ideas with Alex, that something tangible and important had been added to the story, simply because another mind had been at work on it. He also knew this feeling was unfounded.

A huge blackbird pecked in the grass in front of Sydney. Somewhere else, the bird that attempted to sing 'Blow, the Man Down' was trying again. Sydney wondered what kind of bird it was. The sailorbird, perhaps. He shivered under his sweater as the sun went behind a cloud. He was bored to the point of sleepiness. They needed a miracle, nothing short of a miracle would create a plot, an idea that would take only a second to enter the mind, but would be the spark of life. He thought this even as he listened to Alex's U drawl ('No, wait a mi-nute, wait a mi-nute. Nicky doesn't know the girl's *met* the jeweller, does he? Why should we assume or he assume she'd recognize him?'), and even as Sydney came up with an answer, he was blushing with professional shame, because a phrase like 'spark of life' had crossed his mind. He was also afraid one would never again come to him, therefore the phrase seemed presumptuous, one that only a writer to whom sparks of life did occasionally come was still privileged to think of. He was sick of Nicky Campbell, and wondered how Alex would show such enthusiasm for still another try. Well, Alex had a job, and he wasn't at this kind of thing half his time, only a tenth of his time. And Alex also was dying to make some extra money. He didn't get any from his wealthy family because, for some reason Sydney had forgotten, they disapproved of his marriage, and they disapproved of Alex's trying to be a writer. The family did something in Cornwall which they had wanted Alex to devote his life to. At the same time, they goaded Alex to earn more money, if he was going to produce a big family. Alex had told Sydney about them, laughing, yet obviously affected by what they said. Sydney continued his quiet exchanges with Alex while he daydreamt in the sun, until he was neither with his daydream nor with Alex, but somewhere in between, which was a place, or a state, of emptiness and nothingness.

He thought of his father, whom he hardly remembered, because he had died when Sydney was nine, and Sydney shook his head quickly, like a shudder. Sydney's mother had separated from his father when Sydney was six, he had seen his father only on five or six occasions after that, but his father had tried to be a playwright, plus being a full-time theatre manager in various theatres in Chicago. He had never made any money as a manager, and he had written only one play, *The Snowman*, that had ever got printed, and his father had printed that at his own expense. Often it occurred to Sydney that he was cursed with his father's mediocrity, doomed to failure, cursed too with his drive to write something that the world would love and respect and that would ensure his name's being remembered for a hundred years at least, and hopefully for longer. These were sterile and frightening moments, when Sydney thought these things. Then his present life in England, his being married to an English girl who seemed to have no cares in the world even when things went badly, the very house they lived in with its tricky plumbing, its very real slanting and charming wooden rafters on which he bumped his head nearly every day, the English soil that got under his nails when he gardened, Alicia's very snores that troubled his sleep about one night out of seven, seemed all unreal like a play he himself had cooked up, a not very good play. Above all, he wondered why he was here, if another girl would not have done as well (even though he believed he loved Alicia and was at least half in love with her), or if he needed a woman in his life at all. Sydney felt he was not realizing his potentials, and he was often baffled as to how he should start realizing them. Mainly he tried the usual method of plain hard work.

I don't like trying to think in the open air, Sydney thought suddenly with a rise of annoyance that woke him up from his semi-trance, and he almost said it to Alex.

'Let's try to go through it again,' Sydney said, 'episode by episode.'

This sometimes helped to give a sense of direction and movement to the thing, but by the time Sydney was narrating Episode Six from his notes, he felt merely tired, though Alex said it was shaping up.

'Definitely shaping up,' Alex repeated.

By then, they were ready for a Scotch and soda.

A little before seven, Sydney changed his clothes and even put on a tie, thinking it would please Alicia because of Mrs Lilybanks. Alex always wore a tie at dinner, of course, and one could not imagine him not wearing a tie at dinner unless he were ill to the brink of dying, in which case he would not have been eating. Sydney remembered a hot day last summer when Alex had worn a tie on a picnic.

'Why don't I go over and get her?' Sydney said to Alicia, when they were all for some reason congregated in the kitchen.

Alicia had just slid the roast beef into the oven.

'Lovely, darling. Go now. She's due.'

Sydney set his drink down and went. He trotted, still in his

19

tennis shoes. Mrs Lilybanks's front gate screeched. He hesitated, then went to the front door instead of the side kitchen door, which had the look of being more used and therefore more likely to open. He knocked with a heavy brass loop of a knocker. The knocker had just been polished.

Mrs Lilybanks opened the door.

'Good evening. I'm Sydney Bartleby,' Sydney said with a smile. 'I thought I'd walk with you over to the house.'

'Why, how nice of you! Won't you come in?'

Mrs Lilybanks was obviously ready, wearing a wide-brimmed hat and a dark blue shawl with a fringe draped in an interesting way around her shoulders and over one arm. Sydney said he wouldn't come in, if she was ready, so Mrs Lilybanks came out and closed the door, not locking it.

Sydney opened the creaky gate for her.

'Must put some oil on that,' Mrs Lilybanks murmured. 'It's enough to frighten all the birds away. Do you like birds?'

'I like them. I don't know much about them.'

'You're a writer, your wife told me.'

'Yes. And you paint.'

'I'm a Sunday painter. It's one of my pleasures,' she said, as if she had many.

Alicia introduced Mrs Lilybanks to Alex and Hittie in the living-room, then Sydney went off to make Mrs Lilybanks a light Scotch and soda, which she had chosen when offered a choice of gin, Scotch or sherry. Alicia was glad, because her present sherry was a rotten brand, and she had thought Mrs Lilybanks would opt for that.

'Where do you live in London?' Mrs Lilybanks asked Hittie, and Hittie told her, and the conversation rolled along easily about Mrs Lilybanks's old London neighbourhood, Kensington, and then branched off to Hittie's children.

Alicia went to check the roast and the Yorkshire pudding.

Sydney made the salad, opened the wine, and transferred mustard into their silver-topped mustard pot, one of the few valuable items they possessed in the way of table equipment. Sydney was feeling very merry now, singing in quite good voice, though not loudly, one of his parodies on popular songs.

'Sh-h!' Alicia warned him, pointing with a frown in the direction of the living-room and Mrs Lilybanks, because some of Sydney's words were rather dirty.

'Pickled peppers then?' he asked:

> 'I picked a peck of peppers in the briny – *dew*!
> I picked a peck of peppers in the coalbin – *too*!'

'Syd, she'll think you've lost your mind! She'll know it.'
More softly, Sydney wound it up, gazed at Alicia:

> 'I picked a peck, I picked a peck, I picked a peck,
> I picked a peck of peppers
> And they turned out to be *you* – hoo-*hoo*!

'So much for my splended *pizzicato*,' he said, shrugging. 'With my words, that song would have been a thousand times better known than it is, and would have taken its rightful place in light opera along with some of the better arias of Gilbert and Sullivan – ousting them, of course'

Alicia smiled tolerantly, wishing he could show that much self-confidence at 10 a.m.

Sydney was thinking at that moment that Alicia's decorum had no great intellect behind it; there were subjects he might have discussed with her, great themes he thought of writing about, that he couldn't discuss with her, because she wasn't interested. He'd thought when he met her, just because she was English and had a good accent—

'I'm worried the meat isn't done,' Alicia whispered. 'I forgot what time it was when I put it in – seven or a quarter past.'

Sydney leaned on the door jamb in the dining-room, and asked, 'Mrs Lilybanks, excuse me, how do you like your roast beef? Rare?'

Mrs Lilybanks raised her face and smiled. 'I do, rather.'

'Good. That's the way it'll be.' Then to Alicia, 'Stop engines, please. We all like it rare – Mrs Lilybanks, may I replenish your glass?' Sydney came forward and reached for it, but Mrs Lilybanks drew her glass back.

'Oh, no, thank you very much. One's quite enough for me.'

They assembled round the table, the Polk-Faradays with their unfinished drinks. Sydney carved, while Alicia as usual checked the table after she had sat down, and discovered two items missing, a butter knife and a fifth bread plate (which had to be taken from under a plant on the kitchen windowsill and washed), for which she made two trips. But the plates were hot enough to stay hot, everyone had second helpings, and the Polk-Faradays said Sydney had outdone himself on the salad.

'The rosemary happens to be out of a fresh box,' Sydney said modestly, though it had come from the garden.

Alex and Hittie asked Mrs Lilybanks about her new house, why she had decided to live in the country, and she told them it was strictly 'for pleasure and for a change'. She said she had a daughter Martha in Australia, and a grand-daughter Prissie who wanted to be an actress and who lived in London with five other young people in an enormous flat in Chelsea. Mrs Lilybanks had a couple of funny stories to tell about their Bohemian life – one about Prissie and her friends raising a young man by rope from the pavement to a window of his second-storey flat, from which he had locked himself out – and after the stories everyone was smiling and feeling more at ease and thinking Mrs Lilybanks was unusually with it for her years.

Sydney was thinking it with more envy than *bonhomie*. He was twenty-nine, and along with a lot of other things, he had let his youth slip by, he felt. He might have explored many, many more things besides Archangel on a merchant ship and the places in Europe that everyone else had explored, and now, being married, he couldn't. Married, one automatically became poor, it seemed, even though one married a rather well-to-do girl. Single, poorness didn't matter, one could do things, anyway. But a married man was a broke man, broken in spirit and pocket.

Alicia tried to carry too many dishes out from the table, and a wine glass slid off a stack of plates and broke on the brick floor of the kitchen. Sydney whirled around in sudden anger from the coffee-pot he was filling on the stove, and glared at her.

'Christ, is that the sixth or the tenth?' and a vision of bare feet shuffling over sharp crumbs of glass came painfully to him, though neither he nor Alicia had ever walked on the bricks barefoot, and every fragment could be got up with the Hoover.

Alicia was stifling a small giggle, the kind of giggle that came whenever she had a minor accident or did something wrong. 'Sorry I scared you, darling. They're two for one and six at the ironmonger's in Fram. Hardly heirlooms.'

Sydney glanced into the dining-room and saw that Mrs Lilybanks, who was just getting up from the table with the Polk-Faradays, had seen and heard it. Mrs Lilybanks smiled a little at him. Sydney took pains to be sociable and cheerful the rest of the evening. At Mrs Lilybanks's questions he gave her a synopsis of the serial he and Alex were struggling with, a recital that helped him more than the two-and-a-half hour session that he and Alex had had with it that afternoon.

'Perhaps you need a surprise,' Mrs Lilybanks said, after Sydney told her he was far from satisfied with it. 'Like the first tattoo not being real. On the dead man. A tattoo that's just oil-paint. Of course, I don't know where we go from there.'

'You're right. We need something unexpected. I'll think about it. A tattoo that's just oil-paint.'

Alicia had put the gramophone on with a Sinatra record, and the Polk-Faradays were dancing. 'I hope you don't mind this much noise, Mrs Lilybanks,' Alicia said, bending over her with concern. 'We would go out on the lawn – we have an extension – but it just started to rain.'

Mrs Lilybanks said she didn't mind at all.

'Maybe you'd even like to dance, Mrs Lilybanks,' Sydney said, springing to his feet from the floor by Mrs Lilybanks's chair. 'This is a nice song.' It was a slow torch song.

'No, thank you. Heart condition, alas,' Mrs Lilybanks said. 'That's why I move at the snail's pace I do. It'll keep me living longer than anyone I know, probably.' Half her words were drowned out by the volume of the music, she was sure.

Sydney took Alicia in his arms, and off they went, slowly shuffling over the floor that was bare now since Alicia had rolled back the carpet. It was a very worn oriental, Mrs Lilybanks noticed, bought probably because it fitted the square living-room. She studied the quartet of young people casually, not staring at any of them more than a few seconds, as she lit and smoked the last of the four cigarettes a day she permitted herself. Sydney was a nervous type, perhaps better fitted to be an actor than a writer. His face could show great changes of feeling, and when he laughed, it was a real laugh, as if he enjoyed it to his toes. He had black hair and blue eyes, like some Irish. But he was not a happy man, that she could see. Financial worries, perhaps. Alicia was far more easy-going, a bit of a spoilt child, but probably just the kind of wife he needed in the long run. But the Polk-Faradays were still better matched, looked as if they sang each other's praises constantly, and now were gazing into each other's eyes as if they had just met and were falling in love. And the Polk-Faradays were raising three small

24

children; children raising children, Mrs Lilybanks felt, and yet she and Clive had been no older when their two had been born.

Without being noticed, Mrs Lilybanks arose and found her way to the facilities upstairs. She passed Sydney's workroom, a bleak, pictureless room with a home-made bookshelf along one wall and a worktable for a desk, a green typewriter on it, dictionary, pencils, a stack of paper, a curtainless window beyond. A crumpled page had missed the basket and lay on the floor. The bedroom was gayer, to the left, and, since the door was open, Mrs Lilybanks paused a moment and looked in. She saw a rather sagged double bed with a blue counterpane, a banjo or mandolin fixed aslant on the wall above the bedstead, a striped wallpaper of raspberry vine pattern, more abstract pictures by Alicia, a chest of drawers and a straight chair with a pair of cotton trousers tossed across it. On the chest of drawers was a large rabbit doll of the kind Prissie still kept from her childhood days, and a silver-framed mirror of good quality. Mrs Lilybanks went on into the bathroom, which was between Sydney's study and the bedroom. Here the purple towels with one big yellow flower on them attracted her eyes, and following this the pinned-up newspaper photograph which she thought she remembered from an *Observer* front page about a year ago. It was of a group of public schoolboys in boaters and carrying umbrellas, and one was making a remark, inserted in a balloon, that made Mrs Lilybanks start, blush, and then smile. It *was* rather funny. Mrs Lilybanks washed her hands at the basin, while her eyes swam over the confusion of bottles on the glass tray below the medicine cabinet. Perfume, aspirin, iodine, deodorant, nail polish, shaving brush, talcum, shampoo, toothache solution, Enterovioform – looking like an aerial view of Manhattan skyscrapers, Mrs Lilybanks thought, and no doubt this was only the overflow from the sizeable cabinet above. She went downstairs again, was noticed and pressed to have a Drambuie or another cup of coffee, but she declined.

'I'll just stay ten minutes, then I must go, thank you,' Mrs Lilybanks said.

'It just came to me tonight that I'd love to do a portrait of you,' Alicia said to her. 'Would you mind? It's been so long since I've tried anything realistic. I mean, recognizable.'

'I'd be delighted,' said Mrs Lilybanks.

'You really wouldn't mind sitting? I mean, not reading. I like people to look at me or into space. Some people don't like to waste the time.'

'I've got time,' Mrs Lilybanks assured her.

Sydney insisted on seeing Mrs Lilybanks home, and with his own torch, though she had brought one in her handbag.

The Polk-Faradays went to bed shortly afterwards, as they were tired from the drive, and Alicia told Hittie she didn't need to help her with the dishes. Alicia and Sydney did the dishes.

'Was it a decent dinner, darling?' Alicia asked sleepily, her hands in the sink.

'It was great. Too bad the conversation didn't quite match it.'

Alicia smiled slyly, anticipating a small row, but not a big one, because the Polk-Faradays were in the house. Once Sydney had tripped her deliberately and sat her down in a carton full of orange skins and potato peelings. Now she said, 'That's because we're not all Sydney Smiths, I suppose. We just have to do the best we can conversation-wise.'

'That's not what I mean,' Sydney said with even more vicious sweetness. 'I mean the charming, the wifely crack about my writing being my first love, but she died several years ago, or something like that'

'What?' asked Alicia, who really didn't remember.

Sydney took a breath. 'Died years ago, or my muse isn't living here any more. You ought to remember, because you said it.

26

Everyone else heard it.' Sydney remembered the brief silence, the smiles at the table, and he recalled it not so much with pain as with pleasure in his resentment of Alicia, his continued resentment for her saying it.

'What?' on a higher note, and a chuckle. 'I think you're making it up. Or it's your inner voice. Really, Sydney, anyway it's true, isn't it? Otherwise it wouldn't bother you. Did you ever think of—'

He gave her a backhanded slap across the face with the damp dishcloth – which she called, in the English manner, a drying-up cloth.

Alicia started, straightened a little then hurled at him the cup she had been about to put in the drying rack. The cup missed him, but smashed against the refrigerator.

'Number two today,' Sydney said, bending to pick up the pieces. His heart raced. As he stood up with the glass fragments, he noticed with pleasure the pink streak on Alicia's cheek.

'You're barbaric,' she said.

'Yes.' Yes, and one day he'd go just a little too far and kill her. He had thought of it many times. One evening when they were here alone. He'd strike her in anger once, and instead of stopping, he'd just keep on until she was dead. Then as he looked again at Alicia, she smiled at him, and turned again to the sink. She smiled because she had had the last word, Sydney supposed, the thrown cup.

'Perhaps it's time I took another little trip. Let you cool off and get some work done,' Alicia said.

'Why not?'

She had several times taken trips to Brighton and stayed two or three days, and once she had gone to London and stayed with the Polk-Faradays, each time in sort of a huff and not saying clearly where she was going.

'Excuse me—' Alex stood at the kitchen door in an old

Sherlock Holmesian dressing-gown, oversized pyjamas, and soft felt shoes, which were why they hadn't heard him. 'Could you spare a glass of milk? One of Hittie's bedtime habits.'

'Oh, certainly, Alex. Syd, get a glass, would you?'

4

About ten days later, in the first week of June, Alicia finished her portrait of Grace Lilybanks. It was three-quarter length, a three-quarter view of Mrs Lilybanks just under life size. Mrs Lilybanks was holding some black and yellow pansies. Alicia had done it in her old style – starting with background first, closing in to the face, doing the face in quick strokes once she got there, the last touch of all the light that showed across the irises of Mrs Lilybanks's strongly blue eyes. Alicia was quite proud of the portrait – realistic to be sure, and realism was something to be looked down on, to apologize for, among people she knew, people who painted and people who didn't, but it was hardly more realistic than Picasso's famous portrait of Gertrude Stein, which Alicia and lots of her friends, too, considered a masterpiece.

'It's better than the one over the fireplace,' Sydney said, 'So why not put it there?' Alicia had not let him see it until it was completely finished. She had worked in her studio upstairs, where Mrs Lilybanks had come every morning at ten to sit for an hour or so.

But Alicia's pride in it did not go that far; it was still realistic, and therefore less of a work of art, somehow, than her most inferior abstract. She hung it on a side wall in the living-room, removing the abstract that had been there.

'Yes, I do like it,' Alicia said pensively, gazing at it. 'I'll pick up a frame at Abbott's or somewhere.' Abbott's was the large, barn-like, second-hand furniture place in Debenham, where the Bartlebys had acquired Sydney's worktable, their living-room sofa, chest of drawers, and many odds and ends around the house. 'It's funny not to know somebody for very long and succeed in getting a likeness, isn't it? But I've heard of writers who say that to write about a place they've known all their lives is harder than to write about a place they've known just three weeks, because they can't choose the right details about a place they've known so long.'

True, and Sydney knew exactly what she meant, but the words touched him like a personal, directly aimed criticism: he had been stewing too long over *The Planners*, he knew, and so did Alicia know. He couldn't really see any more details about it, or the whole of it, either, couldn't *see* it. And yet it was the best bet he had for making money in the near future, so he was sticking with it.

They went to Ipswich that evening for a Chinese dinner, then to the cinema. And when they came out, their Hillman had a flat tyre. Sydney took off his jacket so as not to soil it, and went to work with the jack and a wrench. Meanwhile, Alicia found a soft-drink machine and came back with containers of sick-making orange pop. Sydney would have liked a bottle of lager after his exertions, but he couldn't have got one, because it was 11, and the pubs closed at 10.30 p.m.

'Isn't it good Mrs Lilybanks didn't come,' Alicia said, 'with this flat. I wouldn't have known what to do with her.'

'Um-m.'

They were taking off again, after Sydney had left half his container of pop standing up on the kerb, because he could not see

30

a rubbish can anywhere. Alicia was still sipping hers. They had rung Mrs Lilybanks around six and asked her if she would like to go with them tonight, but she declined, saying she had had a hard day in the garden.

'She's got a gardener,' Sydney said. 'She must be pretty delicate.'

'Just a part-time gardener. Twice a week. Mr Cocksedge from Brandeston.'

'Cocksedge?' Sydney smiled. 'What a name. Cock sedge or cock's edge?'

'Oh, Sydney, I don't know.'

And Alicia's maiden name was Sneezum. Her whole name sounded like a sneeze, the inhaled suspense of Alicia, the confirmation of *Sneezum*! Sydney had used to tease her about her name and make them both laugh, using her name to sneeze by when he had to sneeze.

'She told me she had a bad heart. She may not live another two years,' Alicia said in a tone of quiet respect, as if she spoke about a relative. Alicia had become very close to Mrs Lilybanks during the painting sessions. They had both talked now and then in a quiet, absent way that had been curiously revealing, Alicia thought, and very good for her, at least. She had told Mrs Lilybanks about Sydney's difficulties with his work, his discouragement just now, and even hinted at her fears their marriage would not last. Mrs Lilybanks had talked about habit, daily life leading to lasting love, and of the crucial second to fourth year in marriage. Mrs Lilybanks said she had had something of the same feeling in her marriage, though her husband had been very successful as a naval engineer.

'Not so nice for the daily. Coming in one afternoon and finding Mrs Lilybanks dead in her chair,' Sydney said.

'Oh, Sydney! How awful! What a thing to think about!'

'It could happen. Couldn't it? She's alone most of the time.

Why should you think she'd be so obliging as to kick off when the daily or somebody else is there? – She'll probably die in bed, like my grandfather. Died in an afternoon nap. Certainly must've been peaceful, because no one in the house knew it until they tried to wake him up.'

Alicia felt uncomfortable and vaguely annoyed, also. 'Do we have to keep talking about dying?'

'Sorry. I'm a plotter,' Sydney said, slowing down to avoid hitting a rabbit that was zigzagging all over the road. The rabbit ran off to the left, up a grassy bank. 'I think of a lot of things.'

Alicia said nothing, not wanting to prolong the conversation. It would happen, of course, probably while she and Sydney were still living in their house. Alicia's eyes filled with tears – sentimental and dramatic tears, she thought reproachfully. She'd never be able to look at Mrs Lilybanks again without thinking she might die any minute, and it was thanks to Sydney's unnecessary remarks. 'I wish you could put some of your plotting into your work where it belongs,' she said. 'Some in your novel, for instance.'

'I'm working on the damned novel. What do you think I'm doing?'

'You're working on the back part. Maybe it needs a plot all the way through. If you're going to work on it for a while, why not try putting some plot in all the way through?'

'And why not stick to your painting and let me do the writing?'

'All right, but something's the matter with *The Planners*, or it'd sell. Isn't there?' she asked, unable to stop herself now.

'Oh, for God's sake,' Sydney said, speeding up a little.

'Not too fast, Syd.'

'First it's a pep talk about the best of novels getting kicked around for years, then it's "something's the matter with it or it'd sell". What'm I supposed to believe? Or are you just trying to be nasty tonight?'

32

'Nasty? I'm throwing out a suggestion about plotting. You say you're so full of plotting – off paper.'

It hit home, and Sydney smiled with a grim appreciation. 'Yes,' he said emphatically. Yes, and sometimes he plotted the murders, the robbery, the blackmail of people he and Alicia knew, though the people themselves knew nothing about it. Alex had died five times at least in Sydney's imagination. Alicia twenty times. She had died in a burning car, in a wrecked car, in the woods throttled by person or persons unknown, died falling down the stairs at home, drowned in her bath, died falling out the upstairs window while trying to rescue a bird in the eaves drain, died from poisoning that would leave no trace. But the best way, for him, was her dying by a blow in the house, and he removed her somewhere in the car, buried her somewhere, then told everyone that she had gone away for a few days, maybe to Brighton, maybe to London. Then Alicia wouldn't come back. The police wouldn't be able to find her. Sydney would admit to the police, to everyone, that their marriage hadn't been perfect lately, and that perhaps Alicia had wanted to run away from him and change her name, maybe even go to France on a false passport – but the last was sort of wild, France involving complications not in character with Alicia.

'Sydney!'

'What?'

'You went right past the house!'

'U'm.' Sydney braked and turned round.

Mrs Lilybanks's house was a dark lump in the milky light of the half-moon, but to Sydney it did not seem blind. It seemed to be staring intently at their car as he drove it up the short driveway and into the shelter of their wooden garage. He'd have to plan his murder of Alicia more carefully and be far more cautious about removing the body because of Mrs Lilybanks's nearness, Sydney thought automatically and as impersonally as if he were thinking about the actions of a character in a story. Then in due time, he would get Alicia's income, which would be nice. He would silence her voice permanently, that voice for ever sabotaging him. Sydney thought of his rewards in a detached manner, too – freedom and a little more money – as if they were coming to someone else.

Sydney's and Alex's joint Nicky Campbell effort, *Mark of the Killer*, the tattoo story, was turned down by the third and last possible buyer with a note saying, 'It isn't bad, but it's been done before.' The tired, terse rejection churned in Sydney's brain for days. He took aimless walks along roads, always wanting to find some woods, to walk into the fields; yet he found no woods, and the fields, deserted as they were, looked to him as if they belonged to some watchful farmer who would ask his business if he set foot in them. Well, what was his business? Nothing. That would sound more suspicious than anything, Sydney supposed. Better to have an answer like, 'I'm interested in rabbits and I thought I saw one disappear down a hole here.' He finally did venture into a few fields, but was never challenged. He would walk for miles, slowly, not thinking of food until he became hungry, which was always after 2.30 p.m., when the pubs were closed and he could get nothing. Then sometimes he would find a small grocery store and buy a package of Kraft's sliced Cheddar and an apple. It was out of anger and a sense of irony that his idea for The Whip came. When it came, Sydney turned and began to walk quickly towards home, thinking as he went.

The Whip would be a criminal character who did something ghastly in every episode, and this wouldn't be a serial, but something that could go on and on, a complete story in every programme. The audience saw everything through The Whip's eyes, did everything with him, finally plugged for him through thick and thin and hoped the police would fail, which they

34

always did. He wouldn't carry a whip or anything like that, but the nickname would be suggestive of depraved and secret habits. Might have a cigarette lighter with a whip design on it. Whip cufflinks, S-shaped. His first exploit might be a robbery, the robbery of a plush house belonging to some moneybags with whom the audience wouldn't be in sympathy, anyway. The police don't know his real name, but they suspect he is one of three known criminals whose dossiers they have. The Whip is none of them. He has no police record, because he has *always* been too clever for the police. And he started young, of course. No, that couldn't be conveyed, because The Whip had no intimates with whom he talked. That would be part of the fascination: the audience wouldn't know what was on The Whip's mind until he started doing things. Satisfy the public's appetite for corn, take-off and violence beyond control of the law, all in one.

Sydney's thoughts collapsed and vanished suddenly, he smiled and looked up at the blue but sunless sky. He had decided that the disposal of Alicia's body required a rug, which he would be carrying over his shoulder with the apparent intention of taking it to the cleaners, for instance; which meant he'd have to get one, because he couldn't leave the floor of the living-room or one bedroom naked. But his sensibilities balked at asking Alicia to come with him to choose one, and he thought of going to Abbott's by himself and bringing one home on his own. He'd say he was tired of looking at the threadbare thing on the living-room floor, which he was. Alicia had bought it very cheaply for its size and colours, red and blue, which went with the dark blue curtains her mother had given her. Sydney's mind went back to The Whip again. Near the house, he began trotting, and once in the house, he went straight to his typewriter.

He put a carbon in the machine, because he wanted to send a copy to Alex. Then he wrote:

The Whip: No one knows his real name. Even his bills come to his London flat addressed to six different people. He is thirty-five, suave, slender, brown-haired, brown-moustached, no distinguishing marks except those of a gentleman. Belongs to an exclusive club in Albemarle Street. Speaks French, German, Italian. He detests police and his gorge rises at the sight of any Bobby, though The Whip has never killed one; he simply outwits and defies them. He has no partner, no confidant, though many in the underworld (and upper-world) are willing to co-operate with him because, (a) he has helped them in the past or, (b) he pays well for favours. These will be hour-long shows, each complete in itself. As our first story opens, The Whip is getting low in funds, as we see from his scanning of bills in his chic mews flat in St John's Wood. An amused smile plays over his face. His face is eloquent, but not hammy, and The Whip never stoops to soliloquies by way of making his intentions clear. The Whip acts. He goes out and hails a taxi, asks the driver to drive him through certain moneyed neighbourhoods. His manner is relaxed as he cases these spots, making a note now and then in a small Moroccan notebook. Driver chats with him. He has no destination, but says he is looking at places where he used to live, tells driver he has been in India for the past fifteen years. It dawns slowly on the audience that he is putting on an act of being an elderly man. He has aged thirty years since getting into the taxi. The Whip dismisses the driver, and we have the feeling the driver would not be able to identify him, if his life depended on it. The Whip walks two streets, gazes at house he intends to burgle. He has the man's name in his little book: Rt Hon. Dingleby Haight, Q.C. Fade-out.

Fade-in on a mid-morning scene at tradesmen's entrance of the Haight mansion. The Whip is now nearly unrecognizable in the guise of a plumber, and is quite amusing to look at. The butler at the Haight house insists that they didn't send for a plumber, and The Whip insists just as firmly that they did. His workman's accent is impeccable. The Whip is admitted, and is shown to the bathroom on first floor. Whip observes maid in milady's boudoir. No matter, his kit contains chloroform, and his first victim is the butler, whom he conks with a spanner as the butler leaves bathroom. Maid comes to investigate reason for butler's (slight) outcry, and The Whip steps from behind bathroom door with ready handkerchief full of chloroform which he claps over maid's face. Maid swoons to ground. The Whip then takes his large kit, empty except for chloroform and . . .

'My, you're going great guns this afternoon. A brainstorm?' Alicia stood in the doorway with a large bowl of strawberries.

'Yep,' Sydney said over his shoulder, annoyed at being interrupted, but not as annoyed as usual.

'Sorry I crashed in, but your door wasn't shut, and Mrs Lilybanks just brought these over. Isn't that sweet of her? She got them in Fram. Want some now or wait till dinner?'

Sydney stood up and smiled politely. He looked straight at Alicia, though he really didn't see her. Even his eyes were still focused for the distance of the typewriter page. 'Save them for after dinner. For me, anyway.'

'Okay, darling. Sorry I bothered you.'

Sydney worked until dinner time, read his synopsis over, then took it to the post office in Blycom Heath, whence it wouldn't get off till early tomorrow morning, but he wanted it in the post tonight. This was Tuesday, and Alex would get it in the early post on Thursday. Sydney was pleased. The Whip had been taken by surprise by a man delivering wine, but had knocked him out on the way to the wine cellar. Then, amused by three prostrate forms in the house, The Whip had decided to make the robbery look like the work of a gang, and had soiled several glasses with beer and Scotch, though without leaving fingerprints, and wadded a few linen napkins up on the kitchen table. Coolly he had walked out of the front door with his bulging kit, entered a tube station, finally arrived at his own flat. He had telephoned his fence, who came that evening, finding The Whip in dinner clothes, displaying his loot which presumably had come from someone else, and driving a good bargain. The Whip received a sizeable sum, and the stolen jewellery and silver left the house via the fence.

'Another Nicky Campbell?' Alicia asked.

'No, something else,' Sydney answered. He was making the salad, rather hurriedly, as dinner was almost ready and it was soufflé tonight. Eggs were only one and six a dozen now in the country.

'A new character? What kind?'

'Well, just for luck – or superstition – maybe I shouldn't talk about it. It's so new. Born this afternoon at three o'clock.'

'A serial?'

'No, thank God. Complete episodes.' A crook this time, he started to say, but maybe it was bad luck to say even that much. 'Anyway, Alex ought to be able to write the first story from what I sent him.'

Then back again to *The Planners*, Sydney thought, which was going to have a plot now. He had never had much respect for plot, mainly because he thought in real life people were more separate than connected, and the connection of three or more people in a novel was an artifice of the author, who ruled out the rest of the world because it did not contribute. His first two books, however, had a bit of plot, he had to admit. *Monkey's Choice*, his first, had gone into paperback, and he still occasionally got a royalty, like $4.19, from hard-cover sales, as the book was only four years old. It was about his experiences in the Merchant Marine and involved some of the men he had met in the crew, but that was the kind of book one couldn't repeat. His second, *Shell Game*, had to do with three married couples in Manhattan, all young, all jockeying for position in the discount house where they worked, and for one another's wife or husband.

When Sydney was in the middle of writing *Shell Game*, he had been invited to a party in Sutton Place. There had been six or seven people at the party who might have been called celebrities – a television actor, an actress, a best-seller writer, a Broadway producer – and Alicia Sneezum, whom Sydney had liked from the moment he saw her. He had asked her if she were free for dinner and the theatre in the following week, but she wasn't, she was here for such a short time, etc. It had been a brush-off, and also a snub. Sydney had retreated to a corner for a few minutes, trying to think what to do, and had come up with something that he thought would both impress her and secure her company for at least one more evening: a party of celebrities. He would go up to each of the important people at the party and say, 'Excuse me, are you free for cocktails at my house next Wednesday at seven? So-and-so (naming someone like Mary Martin or Leonard Bernstein or Greta Garbo) will be coming, and she (or he) would like very much to see you, I know, because he (or she) told me so. So-and-so is coming, too.' The last named would be a celebrity at the party. Then by telephone or letter he would actually invite Mary Martin, Leonard Bernstein and Greta Garbo, and hope. Then he would invite Alicia, and drop a few names of the people who were also invited. He almost dared carry out his plan, but not quite. He used the idea later as an incident in *The Planners*, a young man with one bold stroke building a circle of important acquaintances, none of whom ever got on to his scheme, because his social life

39

rolled merrily on from there. However, that evening, he did pluck up his courage and approach Alicia again, this time with the tritest of ideas, a boat ride around Manhattan Island. This proposal might have reassured her as to his honourable intentions, since it had to take place in daylight among hundreds of people, or the tourism may have had some appeal to her, or his persistence might have tipped the scales – anyway, she accepted. Sydney feigned illness and took an afternoon off from his job in a discount house. From then on, Alicia was his, Sydney felt, though he took nothing for granted about her, and played everything very coolly for fear of losing her through a mis-step. They were simply in love with each other. He did not try to start an affair with her. He proposed, just before Alicia was to go back to England. Alicia accepted, but said they had to wait much longer – maybe three months – and that her parents would have to find out all about him, and perhaps her father in England would want to meet him. Sydney had confessed that he hadn't much money and that his ambition was to be a writer. He felt sure enough of himself to say that, and he was correct, because Alicia wanted to be a painter, 'or at least try to be'. She said she had an income of fifty pounds a month. Sydney met her mother, Mrs Clarissa Sneezum, and her American-based aunt, Mrs Pembroke of East 80th Street, where Alicia and her mother were staying. Alicia arranged to stay on another month while her mother went back to Kent, and this period was taken up with planning where they would live (in England) and how, and with Alicia's answering her father's questions by letter about Sydney. Finally came the parental consent, though Alicia had said she would marry him no matter what attitude her parents took. Her parents were not enthusiastic, Sydney knew. He felt he had just scraped by. Sydney and Alicia had decided to look for a house in the country rather than live in London. Both liked the country, and thought it would be better for writing and painting. On the honeymoon,

Sydney continued to work on *Shell Game*, and when it was bought in America (but not in England) Sydney had felt rather established. Alicia praised him and so did her friends. But the advance had been only $1,500 less agent's commission, and there had been only about $300 in royalties after that, and no paperback edition.

Sydney had started on *The Planners* in the glow of *Shell Game's* acceptance. He felt that *The Planners* declined in spirit as his own spirits declined when *Shell Game* didn't go into a second edition or sell to paperbacks. It was a kind of *Human Comedy*, with the planning of desirable experiences taking the place of Balzacian money-grubbing and social climbing. The six characters made bets with one another, and the ones who threw in the sponge (abandoned their plans) had to pay a forfeit to the others. Some were total failures, some succeeded. One man wanted to become a doctor, and did, at fifty. An unpromising but determined woman shed her husband and nearly grown family and married the man she really loved. Another man, attaining what he had wanted, died of melancholia.

On an afternoon when he went to Framlingham for white enamel paint, Sydney drove by Abbott's in Debenham and bought a carpet. It cost eight pounds, four times as much as they paid for the threadbare red and blue one, but it was in much better condition. And its colours were dark red and dark brown, still just as good with the curtains. Sydney carried the rolled carpet in and laid it at one side of the living-room. Alicia was evidently in her room painting, or perhaps visiting Mrs Lilybanks.

An hour later, when he was working, Sydney heard Alicia's voice downstairs:

'What's this?'

Sydney slid his chair back and stood up. 'Bought a new rug for us,' he yelled into the hall.

'Let's see it. Where? Debenham?'

'Yep.' Sydney came downstairs. 'Only three pounds.' He helped her to unroll it.

'Why, it's very nice. I didn't know you took an interest in carpets, darling, whether they're falling apart or not.'

Sydney smiled but made no comment. They pushed back and lifted the furniture, until the rug was in place. It touched the front and back walls, but they agreed it would be that much cosier in winter, and winter draughts were certainly something to contend with. Sydney rolled the old rug up, and started outdoors with it.

'It'll get damp in the toolhouse, Syd,' Alicia said. 'Or were you thinking of the garage?'

'I'll park it in the guest-room.' The guest-room had a rug, but he could leave the old one rolled somewhere out of the way.

'We might sell it. Trade it in or something,' Alicia said.

'You think they'd give us ten bob for it? Abbott's?' Sydney said as he climbed the stairs.

In the next week, Sydney received Alex's first draft of 'The Whip Strikes'. He went into his room and read it eagerly. From the first page, he felt it was incomparably better than anything he and Alex had done before. But Alex had written on his cover note merely:

Syd, dear boy,
    See what you think of this. Not so sure we need the exchange with stranger in Act Two, fourth scene, p. 71.
    Alex

Sydney thought the exchange with the stranger was great, adding a little humour to the suspense. He had no suggestions for Alex except to cut some of the conversation of The Whip and the cab driver at the beginning. As usual, Alex had done a good job on his side characters, people Sydney had not even written into the synopsis. Alex had a Dickensian gift for minor characters.

Sydney had an impulse to ring Alex and tell him how much he liked it. No, no use being gushy, just send it back ordinary post and say he liked it very much, and go ahead with the final typing after the cutting. After all, the script was no better than scripts ought to be, it was just that he and Alex weren't in the habit of writing them so good.

5

Sydney's euphoria over The Whip script enabled him to lose a day in Ipswich more or less cheerfully, getting the car serviced. He spent a couple of hours in the library, browsing in the stacks downstairs, and then upstairs in the reference department. He took out some books on his thirty-shilling-a-year card, then walked through the business and shopping part of town, gazing into windows with the indiscriminate curiosity of a sailor ashore after a long voyage. A pair of brass-rimmed binoculars in a junk-shop window caught his eye. They looked as if they had seen service with Montgomery in Africa, or maybe with Rommel. Their black leather was worn, and showed brown scuff marks between the brass-framed lenses. The strap was worn also, but looked still trustworthy. Sydney was tempted. The price was less than that for a bottle of gin. But did he need binoculars? Not really.

The car was waiting when he arrived at the garage at 3.30, the time they had told him to arrive, and Sydney as usual had the feeling the car had been ready long before. He felt in a good mood as he drove home. Tonight after dinner, he would polish another few pages of *The Planners* for typing up, then watch a suspense play at 9.10 on television.

'Letter for you in the living-room,' Alicia said when he came in. 'From Alex, I think.'

Sydney left the groceries in the kitchen for Alicia to unpack, and went to get his letter. It was in one of Alex's little buff envelopes. There was a letter from Barlock in it besides Alex's letter. The Barlock letter was a rejection of 'The Whip Strikes', which had been sent back to Alex:

Dear Mr Polk-Faraday,

I have read THE WHIP STRIKES with interest – more at the beginning than at the end, alas, because I am afraid it declines to what we already have too much of – crime, plain crime unrelieved by any hero-sleuth with whom the audience can identify . . .

Sydney muttered a curse at Barlock, then read Alex's letter. Alex's reactions were violently derogatory of Mr Barlock's brain and other things, and he went on:

. . . Too much crime? The TV men are turning out miles of film of good-looking heroes dabbling at catching crooks with one hand and fondling their girls with the other. We hardly see any crooks any more. I suggest we tell Barlock to boil his balls and I send this off to Plummer at Granada. Unless I get a ring from you tomorrow (Thursday) I'll do this in late Thursday post.

Alex

'Well?' Alicia said from the doorway.

'It's another rejection.' He tossed the two letters down on the telephone table. 'The hell with them all,' he said quietly.

'Well, it's only one person. Barlock, isn't it? What did he say?'

'Stuff that doesn't make any sense.' Sydney was talking calmly, but he twisted up the brown envelope until it was a tight, stiff length like a twig.

'Can I see it?'

'If you want to.' Sydney left the room, went upstairs, but near his study door he found he couldn't go in to his typewriter, didn't want to see his table or his chair. He turned around in the hallway, wishing he were anywhere but where he was. He wandered downstairs again and out into the garden, caught a snail – a hobneydod, Rutledge the handyman called it – on the lettuce and hurled it far across the road. He wandered about in slow strides, not doing anything constructive, though he noticed half a dozen things he might have done, pull a weed, put the hoe back in the toolhouse before the next rain, straighten a tomato stake. He paused and looked straight at Mrs Lilybanks's house with an air of defiance, but he didn't see her outside or in. He'd had the feeling she was looking at him.

At dinner, Alicia said, 'I read that rejection. Maybe he's right and it is old hat. I sometimes think Alex has a cramping effect on you. On your imagination.'

'It's I who think up the plots, dear,' Sydney replied, on guard against a coming dig from her. 'But he knows how to write a television play once he's got the plot.'

'But the fact the synopsis is going to him may be cramping you. I think you should go more on your own imagination. You act as if you're afraid of it.'

He felt as if she were poking at a raw wound deep within him. She wanted him to try something on his own and fall flat on his face, Sydney thought. It would hurt worse than a joint failure.

'You take it all much too seriously, anyway. You're—'

'You're not in my shoes,' he interrupted. 'You're not trying to make a go of anything, because you don't give a damn. You just go on painting with your little finger like Mrs Lilybanks.'

46

Alicia's eyes widened – with anger, not surprise. 'All that bitterness. My, my. How could you create anything – anything saleable? It's impossible.'

'It's certainly impossible with your heckling.'

'Heckling? Would you really like to see me heckle?' She laughed.

'I'd like to see you dare.'

She said more softly, 'This isn't the night to have a meal with you, is it? You might keep your temper while we're eating, anyway.'

But neither of them was eating now.

'Just like Mrs Lilybanks, sweetness and light,' Sydney said. 'But I'm at the beginning of my life, not the end.'

'You're at the end of your creative life, if you keep this up.'

'Who're you to tell me?'

Alicia got up. 'Whatever you say about Mrs Lilybanks, she's better company than you, and if you don't mind, I'll spend the rest of the evening with her.'

'Go ahead.'

She took a jacket from the clothes hook by the door, glanced into the mirror there to see if her face looked all right. Then the front door closed.

Sydney had no heart for any work on *The Planners* that evening, which made him feel more depressed, as he knew the work would have to be done at some time. He watched television, then went to bed with one of the books he had taken from the Ipswich Library. Alicia came in just after 10.

'I think I'm going to Brighton tomorrow,' she said, not looking at him.

'Um-m. For how long?'

'Several days.' She began to undress, taking her pyjamas out of the room to the bathroom, though she usually undressed in the bedroom.

There was nothing else to ask her about Brighton, so Sydney asked nothing more. It meant driving her to Ipswich tomorrow morning, unless she preferred to take the train at Campsey Ash, a bit closer home.

'I'm sorry, Syd, but when you get in these moods, they go on for days, and I find them unproductive and not at all fun.'

'I don't blame you, and I hope you have a nice time. Brighton is it?'

'Brighton or London.'

She didn't want him to know which it was, so he wasn't going to pin her down.

The next morning, he did the breakfast dishes, so he did not see what kind of clothes she packed into her navy-blue zippered suitcase. By 11.15, he was back at the house, alone. She had left from Campsey Ash, just outside Wickham Market. The day was rainy and miserable, and Sydney plunged back to work on *The Planners*. At 2 p.m. the drizzling rain became heavier, with thunderclaps.

Mrs Lilybanks telephoned. 'Hello, Sydney.' She now first-named them both, though Sydney could not get out of the habit of calling her Mrs Lilybanks. 'I wonder if Alicia's forgotten her clothes on the line?'

'Oh! I'll get them in. Thanks.' Sydney hung up and ran out for the clothes – half a dozen dishtowels and two of Alicia's cotton blouses on the square revolving tree. He dashed in the back door with them, and had just removed his raincoat, when the telephone rang again.

It was again Mrs Lilybanks. 'I wanted to say a word to Alicia, if I may, Sydney.'

'I'm sorry, she's not here. She's – I'm not quite sure where she is.'

'What do you mean?'

'I drove her to Campsey Ash this morning. For the train. I

48

think she's going to Brighton. I thought she might've mentioned it to you last night.'

'No.'

'Occasionally, she – you know, likes to get away for a while by herself.'

'Yes. Well, it's not important, I only wanted to tell her she didn't need to bring over that wild-flower book this afternoon, since it's raining so hard.'

Sydney knew which book she meant, an old Victorian flower album with coloured drawings made by some Victorian miss, which Alicia had picked up in a London bookshop. 'I'll tell her you called.'

'When will she be back?'

'I think in three or four days.'

'Well, if you get lonely, do come over,' Mrs Lilybanks said. 'Any time.'

Sydney thanked her and said he would.

That evening a little after 6, when the rates became cheaper for trunk calls, Sydney rang Inez and Carpie in London. They were two girls who shared a house together, and each had a baby about a year old. Inez was a Negro girl from New York, Carpie a Jamaican of nearly white skin, and they both were dancers, though since the babies they had retired from their London dance group. Their husbands were always away, in New York or the West Indies, or had been since Sydney and Alicia had known them, which was more than a year, and at last it had dawned on Sydney that the girls had no husbands. Alicia thought Sydney was probably right, so they had stopped asking the girls anything about their husbands. Certainly the babies looked no more than half what the girls were, the rest of them white. Inez and Carpie were hospitable, bright, and good fun. On one of her runaway trips, Alicia had stayed with them, as they had a three-storey house in a

49

mews. But Alicia was not with them now. Sydney spoke to Inez.

'Gosh. Well, you're not really worried, are you?' Inez asked.

'Oh, no. If she's not in London, she's in Brighton. It's happened before. Or she could be with the Polk-Faradays, I suppose.'

'If you want me to, I'll call a couple of places here and call you back. Save you some dough.' Inez was always mindful of economy.

'No, thanks, Inez. I'll ring Alex, because I want to talk to him about something, anyway.'

'But she's okay is she? Not mad or anything?'

'Oh, no. She just gets housebound out here now and then.' Then Sydney called the Polk-Faradays.

Hittie answered. 'Oh, hello, Syd! Alex is having a drink with someone tonight. He's not home yet.'

'I hope he's buttering up Plummer. That wouldn't be it, would it?'

"No, it's some new author for Verge Press. I'm sorry about the reject, Syd. I thought that script was super.'

'Well, it's down but not out. Yet. What I called up about is – I don't suppose Alicia is there, is she?'

'Here?'

'At your place.'

'No. You mean you don't know where she is?'

'She went off this morning, I thought maybe to London, but it looks like Brighton, because you're the second place I've called in London. Sometimes she likes to get away, and I can't blame her. I'm not the picture of cheer with one rejection after another.'

'Goodness. Did she take the car?'

'No, I put her on the train. For London. I'm not worried, because she's done it a couple of times before, you know.' He knew Hittie knew she'd done it a couple of times before. But he could almost hear Hittie's brain clicking over, thinking Alicia

50

wasn't a good wife to desert her husband just when he was dis-couraged.

'If you don't hear from her by tomorrow, do let us know, would you, Syd?'

'Thanks, Hittie. I will.'

6

Mrs Lilybanks rang the next day and asked if Sydney would come for dinner. 'The mobile butcher had a special treat today, fresh Dover sole, so I bought two, hoping you could join me.'

'Thanks, I'd like to. What can I contribute, and what time would you like me?'

'Is seven-thirty too early? If you're working hard, we'll make it later.'

'Seven-thirty's fine.'

'And don't bring anything, just yourself.'

But Sydney took the car to Framlingham and bought a bottle of white wine. He had worked well that day, and was in a good mood. So was Mrs Lilybanks for the same reason, she was pleased with her painting, and she said so (her work-in-progress was upstairs, so Sydney did not see it or ask to), but Sydney kept his good spirits to himself, pretending a slight loneliness and anxiety because his wife was not at home.

They ate in Mrs Lilybanks's half-sunken dining-room. Two corners of the room were filled with tall, polished sideboards, and along the waist-high shelf on one wall stood Delft plates and bric-à-brac. In her unhurried way, Mrs Lilybanks served a superb dinner, ending with home-made sponge cake and strawberry sauce. She asked Sydney questions about his writing, not prying questions, but the kind that kept him doing most of the talking and enjoying the sound of his own voice.

'You sound more pleased about The Whip than your other things,' she said as they were having coffee.

'Maybe because it's the latest,' Sydney said. 'Some more wine?'

Mrs Lilybanks had not finished her glass. 'No, thank you, but do have some. It's delicious. Just made the sole.'

Sydney took only an inch more, which left a glass or two for a meal for Mrs Lilybanks. 'I expect Alicia'll be back by Monday or Tuesday.'

'Oh, good. She's probably enjoying some exhibitions in London and just being by herself for a while.'

'I now don't think she's in London,' Sydney said somewhat awkwardly. 'I've called a few of our friends there. I think she went to Brighton. She's fond of Brighton.'

'Has she friends there?'

'No. At least not that I know of. No, she'd have mentioned them.' Sydney frowned slightly and looked at his coffee cup. He would be saying the same things, he thought, if Alicia were dead now, if he had killed her Friday morning instead of putting her on the train at Campsey Ash. Mrs Lilybanks would be saying the same things, too. The words were coming from both of them like lines in a play they were performing.

'Artists need to be by themselves now and then,' Mrs Lilybanks said kindly.

'Yes.' He glanced at her, grateful. 'I suppose I'll have a postcard Monday. Or a telephone call.' It sounded gloomy. It was only Saturday evening. And Alicia never wrote a postcard on these excursions, at least not to him. 'I'll use these days to get some work done, too – I mean, assuming Alicia's making sketches for new paintings in Brighton,' he added, feeling a blush come in his

53

face. He shifted back in his chair. 'More work on *The Planners*, you know.'

'Well, suppose we leave all this and listen to some music There's a concert on the BBC tonight that starts in five minutes.'

'If we've got five minutes,' Sydney said cheerfully, bouncing up, too, 'I'll help you clear away.'

He insisted over Mrs Lilybanks's brief protest, and in a trice, they had the table clear and the dishes ready for washing in the kitchen. Then they listened to a concert of Bach and Hindemith, while Mrs Lilybanks embroidered a pillowcase for her daughter.

As he was leaving, Sydney said, 'I'm going to Ipswich Monday, if you'd like to go. Just a little shopping trip.'

'No, thank you, not this time. I seem to be pretty well supplied at the moment,' Mrs Lilybanks said.

And Sydney was secretly relieved, because he wasn't really going to Ipswich – not unless Alicia called and asked him to meet her there – but he hadn't been able to think of any other kindness he might do Mrs Lilybanks.

When he had gone, Mrs Lilybanks put on an apron and did the dishes, then left the pots and pans in the sink to soak overnight. The dishes, she felt, were enough exertion for the evening, and she would be up tomorrow before Mrs Hawkins arrived and would have all the pans washed and put away. She never left dishes for Mrs Hawkins, because she felt there was so much else to do. She had enjoyed her evening with Sydney, and she thought he had, too, but her pleasant train of thought kept hitting the snag of his anxiety over Alicia. All wasn't well there, Mrs Lilybanks could see easily. She remembered what Alicia had said, that she wasn't sure she wanted to have a child with Sydney, though maybe she ought to go ahead and have one. That wasn't the right way to have a child, Mrs Lilybanks thought, yet who was she to prophesy? Alicia must have gone away a little piqued, or she'd have told Sydney where she was and when to expect her back. Mrs

Lilybanks recalled Sydney's sudden bitter anger the evening she had gone for dinner and met the Polk-Faradays. 'Christ, is that the sixth or the tenth?' Sydney had said when Alicia dropped a glass, and his tone had been shockingly fierce. And then Alicia at the table, talking about Sydney's muse not living with them any more, or some such thing. That hadn't been nice, either, and Mrs Lilybanks had seen Sydney's resentment growing in his embarrassed face.

Best to be neighbourly to both and not meddle, she warned herself.

Later, in her nightdress and her red woollen dressing-gown, Mrs Lilybanks took a last look at her new painting before she went to bed. It was a yellow vase of white roses and pale lavender clematis, and though it had dash, it did not look as good now as it had at 5 o'clock when she stopped work. Or as good, Mrs Lilybanks thought with resignation, as it would have looked had she spent her life painting instead of her Sundays. Art, as they said, was long, and the life so short.

7

Alicia sat tensely in a tea-room in Brighton called The Eclair, having a pot of tea and a Sally Lunn. It was 11 a.m. on Sunday. She was waiting for Edward Tilbury, who was due at any moment. On Friday, after reaching Liverpool Street station, Alicia had taken a taxi to Victoria and bought her ticket to Brighton, but she had decided to take a later train (there were trains every hour) and enjoy a little shopping in the West End. She had checked her suitcase, and caught a bus to Piccadilly, and had browsed for a while in Fortnum & Mason's – her mother's favourite store. Ah, the good old days, Alicia thought, when she and her mother had gone on shopping trips to Fortnum's, never thinking of money, buying what pleased them, finally having tea and divine pastry in the busy tea-room of the store, her mother feeling exhausted yet virtuous with her afternoon, which had been two or three hours of the most wanton self-indulgence. Now Alicia bought herself only a box of half a dozen handkerchiefs, with a four-leaf clover embroidered in green at their corners, for sixteen and six. Then coming out of Fortnum's, she had run into a man she had met at Inez and Carpie's last party. She hadn't been sure of his name, but he had said, lifting his hat:

'Oh, hello! It's Alicia! – Edward Tilbury.'

He was about thirty, slender and brown-haired with brown eyes. He was wearing a beautiful suit, and she remembered that he had been wearing another beautiful suit the night she met him. She also remembered that he had said he was a lawyer. He had flirted with her very boldly at the party, and had asked her if she were free for dinner the next evening, and when Alicia had answered with a smile that she was going to be back in Suffolk with her husband, Edward had showed the most charming embarrassment, and had apologized. Of course, Alicia had led him on a little, too. It had been after one of her and Sydney's more ghastly quarrels, and Sydney had stayed across the room all evening.

'Shopping?' Alicia had asked.

'Yes. I don't have to. Something for my kitchen. I'd gladly put it off, if you're free for lunch.'

It was 1.10. They lunched at Overton's, because Alicia said she had an errand to do near Victoria. Over lunch, which went extremely well, because they found so many things in common like a love of the seaside, Braque, and Antonioni, Alicia confessed that she was off to Brighton for a few days just to get away from domestic routine.

'If you're going to be there on Sunday – I'd love to come down and join you for the afternoon,' Edward said. 'If you're free.'

Alicia had been just a little startled, but after all it was only for the afternoon. 'Yes, that sounds lovely. But I don't know where I'm going to be. I'd better meet you at the station.'

'But I'd drive down.'

So Alicia proposed their meeting at The Eclair, the first place that came to her mind except the lobbies of a few large hotels where she would not be stopping.

Her heart took a somersault as Edward walked through the pink-curtained door. He looked nervous before he saw her, then he started towards her with a smile.

They spent a glorious day, lunching at the Angus Steak House, strolling along the Downs, driving to the Plough Inn in Pycombe for a cosy tea, then lolling in chairs in the late sun on the beach. Edward was sweet and good-natured, such a relief after Sydney. He didn't mention Sydney, and neither did Alicia. She had been afraid Edward would, that he'd naturally suspect a bad quarrel. It gave Edward full marks in Alicia's book that he didn't try to pump a thing out of her.

'Have you seen Inez and Carpie lately?' Alicia asked.

'No. Not since the party.' Edward turned his eyes to her for an instant, smiling. He was driving then. 'I don't know them very well.'

Alicia felt relieved at that. She didn't want their mutual friends in London to know Edward had come down to Brighton to see her. No doubt Edward realized that, too. She sensed that he could be most discreet, if he had to be. As far as Alicia knew, she and Edward had no friends in common except Inez and Carpie, and they seemed to be only acquaintances. They were always having people they scarcely knew to their parties. Edward was certainly more and better mannered than most of their guests. Edward's fast driving was the only thing about him that made her uneasy, though she could tell he was a good driver. A fear of speed was one of her neuroses. Speed and aeroplanes. She simply couldn't fly without getting into a state of terror, so she hadn't attempted to take a plane since her last nightmarish flight to Paris when she was twenty.

They had a dinner even more delicious than their lunch. It was wonderful to eat anything, anywhere, and not worry about the bill. Edward started off a little before 10 p.m. for London, and Alicia was genuinely sorry to see him go.

8

At 10 o'clock the following Monday evening, Sydney was typing the last sentence of the second Whip synopsis, in which The Whip murdered, for a woman friend with whom he had no emotional involvement, the woman's husband. The husband was an almost unmitigated cad – almost, because his sadism, selfishness, philandering and alcoholism had to be relieved by some minor good qualities, or he could hardly be believed. At any rate, no one could possibly like the husband, and Sydney could foresee The Whip's strangle-murder of him being cheered by man, woman and child of the television audience. Of course, The Whip got off scot-free and the wife, too, as The Whip had made her spend the weekend in a town sixty miles away. Sydney wrote:

Monday 10.10 p.m.

Alex, old pal,

Here is another synopsis, packed with Whiplike action that should make Robin Hood look like a sitting duck. Don't be downcast about that one rejection. We'll lash them with Whip stories till they open their glassy eyes and see how good they are. Next year we should be writing these from our own island in Greece.

Yours for ever,
Syd.

Then singing his own words to 'After the Ball Is Over', he went down to the kitchen with his empty cup and saucer, and treated himself to a Scotch and soda. He was glad Alicia was out of the house for a while, because he felt her absence would give The Whip a chance.

In fact Alicia was dead. He had pushed her down the stairs the morning she had intended to leave. Her suitcase had fallen down the stairs with her, burst open, and there had been a mess on the living-room floor of scattered clothing, contents of handbag, Alicia sprawled with one shoe off, but no blood. Only a broken neck. Then Sydney had wrapped her in the red and blue carpet, the old one, and installed her against the front door on the floor. He had gathered up her things, put the handbag into the suitcase, the suitcase into the car, and driven to – to where? Towards Parham, about five miles away, where there was a small forest. Hard enough to find forests in Suffolk where a man wouldn't be disturbed digging, but Sydney had found a place to bury the suit-case, and then he had driven on about a quarter of a mile and started digging another larger hole for the body tomorrow. Because of summer foliage, he hadn't been visible from the road while digging. That had been Friday afternoon.

Then on Saturday morning, very early, when it was just light enough to see things and the birds were starting to chirp, Sydney had carried the rug with Alicia in it out the back door to the car. Mrs Lilybanks had been peering out her window – God knew what she was looking at at that hour, or maybe she always got up that early – but all she had seen was him carrying a heavy carpet over his shoulder, and if she asked him about it, he'd say it was their old living-room rug he had taken out to dump somewhere. Anyway, she hadn't asked him (Saturday evening), because the light was so dim, she probably hadn't seen him at all. Or if she had, she hadn't considered it worth asking a question about. And Saturday afternoon, he had made the telephone calls to the Polk-Faradays and to Inez and Carpie, preparing the ground. As the days passed, hotels in Brighton would be checked, then London hotels, finally overseas aircraft (though Alicia hated flying, and he would say so) and boats and trains. Because Alicia hadn't written and hadn't come home.

Alicia's parents would be notified, and would come bustling up from Kent. Sydney would tell them – this would probably be next Thursday or Friday – that he had put Alicia on the train at Ipswich Friday morning. Ipswich was better than Campsey Ash, because it was much bigger and there was less chance of anyone having noticed them. He would be firm in refusing Alicia's fifty-pound-a-month income, because he didn't want it, in fact. Not for him the Smith-brides-in-a-bath murders for peanuts, for petty gains that were incredibly part of what had betrayed Smith, the other part being his stupidity in repeating his method.

On Tuesday, Sydney was back at *The Planners* again. He had only twenty more pages of typing to do, but since he was rewriting as he went, it was more than a day's work. At a little past noon, a car drew up at the house. Sydney heard the motor through his back window, but went on typing, thinking if it were the cleaners or someone dropping in, he would wait for a knock. The car drove off, and then Sydney heard the front door opening.

'Syd?' Alicia's voice called.

'Hi,' he said without enthusiasm; but automatically he walked into the hall to the stairway, stood leaning against the top post with one foot dangling over the first step. Alicia was below with her suitcase, in high heels and in her best suit. 'Have a nice time?'

'Very nice, thanks. Did you get some work done?' She was removing her left glove.

'Yes, quite a bit,' Sydney said, descending the stairs. 'I suppose you want this – mounted?' He gripped the handle of her suitcase.

'Oh, leave it, if you like. It's not heavy.'

But he took it up to their bedroom.

Alicia followed. 'Sorry I didn't write you a postcard, Syd, but I really didn't feel like it. I hope you weren't worried.'

She had never apologized before for not sending a postcard. 'Nope. Neither was anybody else.'

'Why should they be? – Who?'

'Oh – Mrs Lilybanks. Or Alex and Hittie.'

'I suppose you told them I just went off for a few days by myself.'

Sydney's eyes narrowed. For the first time, he suspected she had had a date with a man. Alicia seemed unusually tense about something. Who, Sydney wondered? And he found himself unable to begin guessing, unable to think of a single man. 'Meet anybody interesting?'

'No,' Alicia said casually, and her expression, if any, was hidden by the sweater she was pulling over her head.

He heard Alicia go out around 2, heard the back door close, and absently he got up and looked out the window. She was going by way of the back gardens to Mrs Lilybanks's. Sydney realized he was hungry, and went down to the kitchen. Alicia had found her post, he saw as he crossed the living-room. She had had three or four letters, among them one from her mother. Sydney made some coffee while he ate a hot dog. Alicia had put out the pork roast, the potatoes, the veg – courgettes – on the kitchen table in her usual line-up. He did not look forward to her company tonight. And he felt her presence put a jinx on the synopsis he had posted to Alex from Ipswich that morning. She was a far cry from Hittie, who gave Alex encouragement at every turn.

He worked until nearly 6, then went out to do some weeding in the garden. He cut some of the wild roses that grew by the garage, and took them in to put on the table. Alicia was cooking, and Sydney went in to make the salad.

'You're awfully quiet,' Alicia said.

'I haven't been doing anything exciting. You have.'

'You had dinner with Mrs Lilybanks, I heard.'

'Yes. A very good dinner, too. Saturday night.'

'We should have her over for a meal soon.'

Sydney said nothing, grinding parsley with the Mouli into his sauce.

'What're you working on? *The Planners?*'

Sydney took a breath and said, 'I did another synopsis for The Whip and sent it off to Alex this morning.' There it was, out, a vulnerable, helpless target, like a yellow duckling waddling over a green lawn, an ugly duckling. 'And now I'm back on *The Planners*, yes.'

'What does Alex think about documentary one-hours? Not documentary, but things with a theme. Like bad housing, or birth control versus the church.'

Sydney looked at her rather blankly.

'The last few television reviews I've read in *The Times* are about plays with a theme. Management versus labour. You know.' She was pouring hot water off the potatoes.

'You're suggesting I drop The Whip and try something like that? What do I know about the inside of an English workshop?'

'I'm not suggesting anything. I wouldn't dream of it,' she said with sudden nervous hostility. 'I'm making a remark about the market now. The public seems to be tired of silly entertainment, and they want something controversial. Or they seem to.'

'I'd rather give The Whip a chance first.'

'You might do both.'

'And *The Planners*, too? I'd be pretty busy.'

It didn't seem to Alicia that it should make a person overly busy to be doing three things at once. 'I meant irons in the fire. That's all. You once said they were important. It takes a month or more for a synopsis to make the rounds, doesn't it?'

'At least. And I might do five, six, seven Whip synopses. I think they're good. Good entertainment and not silly entertainment.'

'I didn't say The Whip was silly.' Alicia sighed.

Sydney fixed them both a drink, and handed Alicia's to her. 'The Whip is not silly,' he said, and since the remark came two minutes after Alicia had last spoken, it hung heavily.

Alicia looked at him and felt curiously detached. It seemed absurd to her to take an idea like The Whip with as much seriousness as Shakespeare had taken *King Lear*, and maybe more. It was selling something, even something as lightweight as a jingle for a commercial, that Sydney took seriously, and until he did, life was going to be hell. Alicia suddenly wished she were back in Brighton with Edward, spending this evening and all of tonight with him. 'Let's hope you sell it,' she said crisply, and turned to the sink.

The clipped, English-accented words plucked at Sydney's nerves with every syllable. She'd be there saying, 'I told you so,' with the next rejection, with the rejection of the second synopsis, and possibly the third. 'I intend to keep trying,' he said, trying to be just as crisp, but with his accent, it was impossible.

On Thursday at breakfast, Sydney proposed going to Ipswich. They could always think of a reason to go – the library, a piece of hardware Framlingham didn't have, a Chinese lunch or dinner to vary their menu – but Sydney proposed it on Thursday just for a change of scene. Alicia agreed, though without much enthusiasm. She detested and despised him, Sydney felt. She considered him 'inferior'. But she was too cowardly or too unenterprising to make a move to get away from him. A divorce was too much trouble, perhaps, or her family would be too upset. Sydney felt that both he and Alicia were waiting for a sign, a sign of anything – of hostility or love – and that either one could tip the balance. If Alicia, for instance, would only put her arms around his neck and say, 'Sydney, darling, I love you whether you've sold anything or not,' then things might have been different. Or if he had been able to go to her and say, 'Alicia, I know I've been crabby for weeks. I promise I won't be like that any more, ever.' But as it was, they drifted like a pair of old people in their accustomed ruts, getting up, making breakfast, making the bed, sweeping the kitchen, hardly talking to each other, not hostile but barely tolerating the other's presence.

As they were leaving the house on Thursday morning, the telephone rang, and since Sydney was nearer, he answered. But he noticed as he picked the telephone up Alicia's brief expression of alarm, then her pretended unconcern as she stared out the open front door, within hearing. Was she fearing a call from a boy friend?

'Hello,' Sydney said.

'Syd. Alex here. Got your synopsis this morning before I left the house, and I thought I'd ring you on office money. I like it.'

'Good. Any suggestions?'

'I think we might play up the suspect a little more. The wife's friend. Make him really look guilty from the point of view of the police. I'll drop you a note. I really rang to ask if Alicia got back.'

'Yes, she did. Tuesday.'

'Ah, good. And you sound positively depressed about it,' Alex said with a chuckle, as if for a husband to be depressed by a wife's return was an impossibility.

'Well, maybe I am.'

'Better luck next time, chum. Maybe she'll stay away for ever, like.' Alex's voice became sinister. 'Like in the drink, like, in

Brighton. Oh, her hubby's ever so down in the mouth, but he's got her—' Alex laughed in his merry, yelping way.

Her income. Alex would think of that. 'I appreciate your good wishes. I'll keep my fingers crossed for next time.'

'There go the pips. I'll be writing you. Love to Alicia.'

They hung up.

Alicia, still facing the door, walked out.

Sydney changed his books at the library, offered to get something for Alicia, but she said she had a couple of paperbacks at home she was reading. Things she had picked up in Brighton, perhaps, and hadn't had time for, Sydney thought. They agreed to meet in half an hour at the car in Cox Lane car park. Sydney set out on a ramble that would take him eventually to the junk shop where he had seen the binoculars.

The junk-shop window was full of interesting articles as usual, brass post horns, old military kit-bags, brass-cornered Wellington chests, but the binoculars were gone. Sydney looked over the cluttered window again, then peered into the darkish interior of the shop to see if they had been put back into one of the cases, but he couldn't see them. He might have bought them, if they'd been in the window. He was too shy to go in and ask about them, because he wasn't sure he would buy them, if he really could. Sydney turned and began the walk back to the shopping district and the car park.

The sky darkened, and it began to sprinkle. Umbrellas of the provident were lifted, many people took shelter, and then as the drops began to pelt, people on the street ran. Alicia was standing by the car, holding her bundles next to her underneath her rain-coat, looking like a pregnant woman holding her belly. The straw shopping basket at her feet was full.

'Of all days when I didn't bring my keys!' she said, laughing.

'Sorry.' Sydney licked rain off his upper lip and opened the car door as quickly as he could.

It rained all the way back home, and they were silent. They were silent as they unpacked the groceries, except for Alicia saying, 'I got liver for tonight. Liver and bacon. All right?'

'That's fine.'

Then the telephone rang.

'That's probably Mrs Lilybanks,' Sydney said. 'Don't you want to take it?'

Alicia went to get it, and Sydney unpacked the rest of the groceries.

Then Alicia came to the kitchen door, smiling, and said, 'It's Alex again. He forgot to ask us if we want to come to a party Saturday night. They'll be glad to put us up, he said.'

They had stayed at the Polk-Faradays' before. The living-room couch opened into a double bed.

'I don't care to go. You go, if you like.'

'Oh, Syd. Hotchkiss is going to be there, Alex said. He wants you to meet him.'

Hotchkiss was a new young writer Alex's publishing house had discovered. Aged twenty-six, Sydney remembered Alex saying. Like Keats. 'I just don't care to go, but take the car and go. Or take the car to Ipswich and take the train.'

"Please, Syd. – He's on the line still.' Alicia gestured helplessly towards the telephone.

'I don't want to go,' Sydney said stubbornly. 'Go yourself.' The repetition of it made him want to scream. 'Tell him I've got to work.'

Alicia went back to the telephone. She talked a minute more, then came back to the kitchen. He avoided her eyes, though he had to walk towards her to go out of the door.

Somehow lunch was forgotten by both of them, and Sydney could tell from Alicia's manner in the house – though he did not even see her after he went to his study – that she was not going to the party on Saturday night.

Alicia, that morning around 8, had been putting out some empty milk bottles on the front doorstep, when the postman arrived and handed her the post, a bill from Eastern Electric and a letter addressed to her which she had sensed at once was from Edward Tilbury. She had stuck the letter folded into the pocket of her dressing-gown, and read it later in her studio, after breakfast. The letter made her giggle with its exaggerated formality and thanks for the delightful and salubrious day at the sea in Brighton, and he trusted that by now she was home again, refreshed by her brief excursion.

... I find you a refreshing companion and would be most pleased to accompany you or join you if you are planning another outing down Brighton way ...

Edward gave his address and telephone number in Sloane Street. His statement that he would like to see her again made Alicia feel pleasantly excited and happy all that morning, even when she was getting soaked in the rain in Ipswich. Then Sydney's refusal to go to the Polk-Faradays' party had soured everything. There was no reason for Sydney to refuse, he wasn't working all that hard, he simply wanted to be grim, nasty – and like himself. She went over to see Mrs Lilybanks at 4 for a much needed change of atmosphere. She had told Mrs Lilybanks that she had had a very good time in Brighton, and she showed her a few sketches she had made, but she had not mentioned Edward Tilbury.

But she thought about Edward a great deal, and that evening she wished she were cooking dinner for him instead of for Sydney. There were times when Alicia felt that Sydney absolutely loathed her, that he hated her enough to kill her, if he dared. She felt that he considered himself trapped by their lack of money, and that he felt she was some kind of jinx on his work. His silly, trite Whip thing was going to fall through, she was sure, and she dreaded being around Sydney when it would, in a month or six weeks.

Sydney came down to the kitchen around 7.30 for a drink – Alicia had just made herself a Scotch and soda – and his face was like dark, unexploded thunder as he stared at the liver and bacon and the marrow (squash to Sydney) that she had lined up on the kitchen table. He carried a lettuce and a tomato in his hands from the garden.

'Anything the matter?' Alicia asked.

'That liver. A bit sick-making.' Once in a while, Sydney felt disturbed by the sight of raw meat.

'I agree. Pity it's so good for us,' she said with an irrepressible edge in her tone. 'You must've had a sick-making afternoon.'

'Not particularly.' He started on the salad dressing. 'If I weren't here, I suppose you'd go to the Polk-Faradays' party, wouldn't you?' she asked.

He lifted his head and looked at her. 'No. Why do you say that?'

Because without her, he wouldn't play games of trying to hurt her, Alicia thought. He'd have liked to go to the party, but he liked more to keep her from going. For an instant, she had an impulse to go by herself, then it left her, because she wouldn't really have enjoyed it by herself, plus the long trip up to London and back alone. 'You'd really like to kill me sometimes, wouldn't you, Syd?'

He stared at her, looking tongue-tied.

She could tell she had touched the truth. 'You'd like me out of the way sometimes – maybe all the time – just as if I were some character in your plots that you could eliminate.'

He looked at the half-peeled potato in her left hand, the paring knife in her right. 'Oh, stop being dramatic'

'So why don't we pretend that for a while? I can be gone for weeks. Work as hard as you like—' Her voice shook a little, to her annoyance. 'And we'll see what happens, all right?'

Sydney pressed his lips together, then said, 'All right.'

'You'll – stay on here, I suppose?'

He nodded. 'Yes. I suppose you'll go to your mother's? It's cheaper for any length of time.'

'I suppose. I do think, Syd, we've had such awful times – such real *crises* – that it'll take something pretty drastic to get us really over them. Or not. As the French say, *pour les grands mats, les grands remèdes.*'

'I agree.'

'We won't communicate. Let's make a promise.'

'I promise.'

'No matter how long I'm gone. I'll get in touch with you – when I want to. And when I do, you may not want to see me again, anyway.' Now her voice really shook, and Sydney turned away, embarrassed.

'All right, Alicia. I agree. It's a promise. Stay away as long as you – as you think you want to,' he said gently, more gently than he had said anything to her in a long while.

9

'Oh, say I'm at mother's,' Alicia had said that morning, in answer to the only question Sydney had put to her, where should he say she was.

It hung in the silence of the living-room and repeated itself like an echo. Sydney walked about slowly. Now he was alone, and for the next several weeks, probably. They had talked a little more since Thursday night. It was not to be a break-up, not to be a trial period, or a separation, or anything one could label, to any of their friends. If anything, said Alicia, he should say they both wanted to try working apart for a while. Sydney looked at a brass-rubbing he had made of Sir Robert de Bures' mailed feet crossed upon a small worried lion. It was from the church in Acton. He and Alicia had been together that day, very much together, pic-nicking in the car because it had started to rain, coming home, making love, trimming and matting the brass-rubbing on purple velvet ready for the framer. They had also visited Lavenham and Long Melford churches, Alicia making sketches, Sydney scrib-bling notes that he thought he might use some time. He had even scribbled a poem.

He trudged upstairs towards his study, remembering he was on page 262 of his manuscript, and had only five more pages to type. Then a reading through, and off to new publishers, the original to America, the carbon to London, and one copy for safety here. He paused in the hall, and stared through the open door of the spare bedroom. The rolled end of the old red and blue carpet just showed against the far wall. All right, go through with it, he thought. See how it feels. He might use it some time in a book. And also, he might purge himself of his rather petulant hostility against Alicia, as the psychiatrists would say. He made a move-ment towards the stairs, to go off now and start the hole he meant to dig, but that was absurd. He was supposed to do it in the morn-ing, early tomorrow morning, because it was the only logical time to do it. If he overslept, bad luck. Or rather, he just wouldn't do it.

Though he had a perfectly good day from a working point of view, and a quiet evening of reading, he lay a long time awake. There was an occasional *bump-bump* from downstairs, and at last he got up to investigate, and found that the little window which opened like a door in the larger window of the living-room had come unlatched and was swinging in the summer breeze. He went foggily back to bed and slept. A couple of hours later, he woke up, alert as he seldom was on waking. The dawn was grey at the window, and it was still so dark he could barely see the time on his wristwatch. Ten past 4. Now or never, he thought, though there was nothing urgent in his thinking, only a quiet compul-sion. He went downstairs, put on coffee, then went up again to dress in old chinos, tennis shoes and a woollen shirt. Sydney drank some coffee in the kitchen, then went to the toolhouse and got the fork, which he put on the floor of the car. He backed the car out of the garage into the driveway and stopped near the back corner of the house.

In the guest-room, he carefully lifted the rolled carpet to his shoulder, as if it were heavier than it was and contained the body of Alicia, walked out the back door, and laid the carpet on the back seat of the car. It was no light weight even empty, and with a body in it, it would have been a staggering matter, Sydney thought. Remember that for a future book. Sydney glanced around him. Nobody in sight. Nothing but a few twittering birds. No light at Mrs Lilybanks's windows. Sydney drove off. It was five miles or so to the forest he had in mind. At last he turned off the Framlingham road on to the straight level road with its border of tall trees that suggested the Route Napoleon. On either side lay woods. Nothing passed him as he drove along except a lorry going in the opposite direction. Sydney pulled up on a green verge at the left side of the road.

He got out the fork, and walked perhaps fifty yards into the woods before he found an area of fifteen square feet without trees on it, where only grass and bare, moist earth showed. He began to dig at the far edge of this. It was slow, hard work, despite the softness of the ground, and he wished he had brought a shovel as well. He would have liked to fold the rolled carpet in half and barely cover it with earth, but he forced himself to make a long trough as if he had to bury a real body that wouldn't fold so easily, and he made himself dig deep, nearly four feet. When a car passed – three did – Sydney could not even see them through the foliage, only heard their motors. Therefore, he thought, no one could see him. When the grave was nearly deep enough, he went back to the car for the carpet. By now, it was much brighter, and the sun was touching the tops of the trees. He lifted the carpet on to his shoulder again, and pushed the car door to with his knee. A big green truck thundered down the road just then and sped past, ruffling his hair a little. Sydney trudged into the woods. He put the roll of carpet down, then doggedly made the trench six inches deeper its whole length, hacking vainly at the tough roots that crossed it, finally jumping in and stamping on the roots to slacken them. He rolled the carpet in, by now so tired in the arms, the carpet seemed really to contain a great weight. But if there had been a body in it, he thought, his fear would have given him more strength, and the task would have been easier. Sydney shovelled and pushed the dirt in with his fork. And like a real criminal, he began to feel more sure of himself with the body underground and out of sight. He walked about on the loose dirt to pack it down, and dragged the fork across the grave to obliterate the tracks of his tennis shoes.

Then he walked back towards the car, turned once to look behind him in the direction of the grave, and saw nothing unusual. He realized he had torn open the butt of the one cigarette he had smoked, and scattered the bits in the breeze. And what other signs of himself might he have left? Flattened grassblades where he walked? Well, it would take a super-Sherlock Holmes to find those after a rain, and a genius at extra-sensory perception to attach the bent grass-blades to him. Of course, there was the carpet itself, which Abbott's might have a record of selling to Alicia, and there were their friends who could identify it, but after all, there wasn't any corpse in it. Sydney started the car. Ahead, the sunlight lay bright on the road, speckled with blurry shadows from the leaves of the trees. It promised to be a lovely day.

The Sunday passed quietly. Sydney began the reading through of *The Planners*, and with some optimism. Now the front part seemed to be tending towards the back part – which at last showed some plot and a winding up of events.

On Monday at 6 p.m. Mrs Lilybanks knocked on the back door with a pound of gooseberries for him. Sydney invited her in.

'They were two pounds for three and six, and I can't possibly use more than one pound,' she said. 'Do you like making gooseberry fool, or do you think it's too much trouble?'

'I like it. I've never made it,' Sydney said. 'Alicia sometimes makes it.'

'If you'd like, I can make your fool with mine. Two won't be

74

any more trouble than one. It's just topping and tailing and strain-ing them, you know.' She looked up at him with a smile. 'Then you can stop by for it around seven-thirty this evening, and I'll just poke it at you, and you won't have to lose any time with me delivering it.'

Sydney was touched by all the kindness. 'I'm not losing time. I've lots of time.'

'Alicia said you wanted to work very hard these days, so I didn't want to interrupt you. Otherwise I'd have asked you to dinner yesterday.'

'Thank you,' Sydney said awkwardly. He was still in a daze of *The Planners*.

Mrs Lilybanks tugged her green cardigan down, and picked up the bowl of gooseberries. 'How're you finding bachelor life?' She moved towards the door.

'Won't you sit down for a minute?' He realized with embar-rassment he had not yet asked her.

'No, I'll be off, thanks. Alicia's at her mother's house in Kent, she told me.'

'Yes.'

'I wonder if you'd give me the address? I'd like to drop her a note.'

'Of course. Just a minute.' Sydney went into the living-room to get a pencil from the telephone table.

'It's silly of me not to have asked her for the address,' Mrs Lilybanks said, following him slowly. 'Oh, I see you've got a new carpet. This is very pretty.'

'Yes,' Sydney said as he wrote. He felt a rise and fall of his heart at her words. Like real guilt, he thought. 'Here we are. Mrs Hardey Sneezum, Poke's Corner, Rayburn, Kent.'

'Sneezum,' said Mrs Lilybanks, reading.

'Yes.' Sydney smiled. 'I used to kid her about that. Until I heard several funnier names.'

75

'One of my favourites is Bultitude,' said Mrs Lilybanks. 'Covers a Bultitude of sins and all that. Then Smelly I like, and Giddy and Snook. These are all local names, you know.'

'And Oxborrow,' Sydney contributed feebly, grinning. He couldn't come out with Cocksedge.

Mrs Lilybanks laughed, her small, substantial figure rocking back a little. 'Lilybanks isn't far behind, I hope. Lovely name for a tombstone, I always think. My husband used to be ragged unmercifully as a boy, he told me. In school, they called him "the Undertaker".'

Sydney saw her smile diminish as she looked at him, because he hadn't smiled. For a second, he had seen a vision of Alicia's grave in the woods banked with white lilies. He felt he actually went pale. 'It is funny. A funny name.'

'I'll be off so you can work, and don't forget to collect your fool before eight.' She started back through the kitchen to the door.

That week, Inez rang from London to ask if she and Carpie and a couple of friends could drive by on Saturday and bring a picnic lunch.

'You're very welcome,' Sydney said, 'but Alicia won't be here.'

'Oh. That's too bad. I ran into Alex and Hittie at the Gondola the other day. They said she was back.'

'Yes, but she went off again. Wants to stay down at her mother's for a while, I think.'

'Oh. Well, you sure it's okay if we come by? We'll bring the eats, never fear, and you and I can hol' the American fort!'

'Okay,' Sydney said. 'And I'll provide the liquid refreshment.'

'Oh, some wine'll do for us. This drink stuff runs into dough.'

Inez and Carpie gave only wine parties, Sydney remembered. 'Leave it to me.'

'Say, you got Alicia's address handy before this call runs out? I mean her phone number.'

Sydney gave it to her.

IO

Sydney debated asking Mrs Lilybanks to join them in the picnic, then decided to. Mrs Lilybanks accepted.

Inez and Carpie, with babies, arrived in a blue Volkswagen station wagon driven by a curly-haired, skinny young man dressed in old clothes whose name was Reggie Mulligan. He did something in the theatre, Sydney was told. The other man was older and better dressed, and owned the Volkswagen, though he hadn't cared to drive. Fortunately, it was a sunny day, and they spread blankets – two from the car, one contributed by Sydney – on the grass behind the house. Sydney had brought out one of the two deckchairs for Mrs Lilybanks. Inez and Carpie spent more time pulling their babies back from the plates of sandwiches and out of the cake than they did eating. Sydney had taken them all on a tour of the house, which ordinarily he found boring but today he rather enjoyed, as if he were showing them his castle. What if the bedsteads were second hand (the mattresses were not, however), the bookshelves and chests of drawers a little banged up, the living-room sofa not exacdy spruce? What kind of undersized dumps did Mulligan and the other man live in in London? Here Sydney had privacy, space and fresh air. The house also looked quite tidy, considering there was no woman in it. He was pleased that his study, with its stacks of paper, his obviously busy type-writer, and his sharpened pencils, gave an impression of diligence and productivity.

'Working on an old novel at the moment,' Sydney had said in answer to Vassily's, the older man's, question, 'but Alex and I have a couple of television synopses in the works now, too.'

The girls had been to the house before, of course.

It was in the middle of the al fresco lunch, just when Sydney thought everything was rolling along beautifully after their second martinis and the first plunge into sandwiches, that Inez said:

'Hey, Syd, I tried to call Alicia last night, and her mother said she isn't there and she doesn't know where she is. You better check up on your wife.' Inez's thick lips spread in a smile that showed most of her white teeth, and a ripple of amusement went around the blanket's edge.

'That's funny,' Sydney said. 'Well, maybe she's in Brighton again, but she said she was going to her mother's. I didn't try to pin her down.'

'Didn't try to pin her *down*?' from Carpie, and there was more laughter.

'No, if she wants to paint for a while by herself—' Sydney tried to make a casual gesture and spilt some *vin rosé* on his trouser cuff.

Mrs Lilybanks had stopped talking to Vassily, though they had been going great guns before. Sydney started to say something else, but decided not to. He reached for a devilled ham sandwich. Then he looked at Inez and asked, 'Her mother didn't sound worried, did she?' By now Reggie and Carpie were talking together.

'Oh, no. Well, I don't *know*, because I don't know her that well,' said Inez, who always recited the obvious very carefully. 'I think she certainly wanted to know where she was. She even asked me if I had any ideas. Her mother didn't call you?'

'No,' Sydney said, and concentrated on his sandwich. It would certainly sound like a marital tiff, he supposed, to Inez and her crowd. Well, let it. He was vaguely ashamed of that, but how much better it was they thought that than suspected the hideous truth, that Alicia was six feet under. Well, four feet. Sydney smiled slightly to himself. He noticed that Mrs Lilybanks was watching him. Sydney looked away from her.

Inez and Carpie and the two men stayed until about 4.30, then took off in the station wagon for London. Mrs Lilybanks insisted on helping him wash up and put away things. Sydney had thought she meant to pump him about Alicia, her whereabouts and whether a quarrel had caused her to go, but Mrs Lilybanks didn't mention Alicia. She talked about starting an apple and pear orchard behind her house, the quality of Suffolk light in painting and how it had influenced Constable, and how pleased she was that every bit of her lemon cake (which she contributed to the picnic) had been finished. When the last cup was put away, she thanked Sydney for a delightful afternoon.

'You must meet my granddaughter Prissie next time she comes. She was here once, but on such a flying visit, I didn't ask you to come over. I think she might be up next Saturday.'

'I'd like to meet her,' Sydney said.

'She's only twenty-two, but I think she may get somewhere in the theatre, if she keeps at it. Good-bye, Sydney, and thanks again.'

'Good-bye, Mrs Lilybanks.'

Mrs Lilybanks made her way slowly along the side of the road towards her house.

When she entered her living-room, her eyes were drawn to the unframed watercolour Alicia had made of a vase of flowers one afternoon when she had been here. The paper was propped up on the mantel, braced by the edge of a framed photograph of Martha with Prissie as a baby. Mrs Lilybanks wondered what Alicia was

79

doing at this moment and if she were happy or unhappy. Alicia would drop her a line soon, wherever she was, Mrs Lilybanks felt sure. Maybe Sydney knew by now where she was and wasn't saying, because Alicia wanted to be quite alone, not even in communication with her friends. At any rate, Mrs Lilybanks thought the best thing to do was not to mention Alicia any more to Sydney, not to speak of her unless he did, because obviously the situation caused him some embarrassment. But why had he smiled to himself just after he had been embarrassed? Well, he was a writer, and probably all sorts of things flitted through his mind, imaginary things. And tangents.

11

That same evening, Saturday, Sydney felt he ought to write a note to Alicia's mother, so he did. It went:

> July 9th, 19—

Dear Mrs Sneezum,

I am sorry to have told several people to write to Alicia at your house in Kent, but I had thought that she was going there, at least at first. She wanted to get away from this rather deadly quiet house and the equally dull countryside for a while to paint some and just be alone for a bit. She did not seem to want to tell me exactly where she was going, perhaps wasn't sure herself, but I'm writing this to assure you she was in a calm frame of mind when she left. When you hear from her, I'd appreciate it if you told me where she is, but only if she is agreeable to letting me know. I know she does not want to be disturbed for a while, so I have no intention of disturbing her.

Life goes on here quietly. I am working, though with no notable success as yet. I hope you and Mr Sneezum are well.

Affectionately yours,
Sydney.

His letter, which he forgot to post until after the 3 p.m. collection on Sunday, brought a telephone call from Mrs Sneezum on Tuesday morning.

'I wondered if you'd heard anything from Alicia?' she asked.

'No, I haven't, but I wasn't—'

'When did she leave?'

'She left Saturday before last. July second.'

'Good heavens. I've rung a couple of her friends in London, but she's not there and nobody has any idea where she is, which I think is most unusual.'

'I think there's a strong chance she's in Brighton, Mrs Sneezum. She went to Brighton for a few days about three weeks ago, as you probably know.' Sydney was sure Mrs Sneezum knew, because Alicia had said she had dropped her mother a postcard.

'Oh,' Mrs Sneezum said thoughtfully. She excused herself to speak to her husband, then said, 'How long did she say she might be gone?'

'She didn't say. A few weeks – I don't know. I hope you won't be worried about her.'

'But it's not like Alicia not to tell *anybody* where she's going. Being alone is one thing but being so secretive isn't like her at all. Was she upset about anything?'

'No. It was Alicia's idea.'

Mrs Sneezum was silent, but Sydney heard her impatient sigh.

'Also Alicia's not very good about writing, as you know.' But Alicia was fairly good about writing to her mother. Sydney thought of Smith, saying one of his brides-in-the-bath had injured her right hand.

'Didn't she say where to forward her post?'

'No, she didn't. There're only three letters here. They don't look important.'

'Well, Sydney, would you let us know as soon as you hear anything from her? Ring us and reverse the charges, that doesn't matter. You're all by yourself down there?'

'Oh, yes,' Sydney said. Did she think he had a girl with him? 'I'll say good-bye. Do ring us.'

Sydney said he would, then hung up. The sun was boiling through the living-room window. It was a rare day, rather warm, hot for England. The conversation would have been the same, Sydney thought, if he had killed Alicia and he were trying to make her mother and everyone else believe that she had taken herself off to Brighton. Alicia was probably lolling in a beach chair at Brighton, wriggling her toes in the pebbles, with her long, pretty face turned up to the sun and her eyes closed. It should be lovely in Brighton with a sea breeze thrown in. Meanwhile, the Sneezums – ka-choo! – were getting worried down in Kent, mainly because they had nothing else to occupy themselves with. Mr Sneezum had retired before Alicia's marriage, with plenty of money and a heart condition that kept him from eating meat, Sydney remembered. He had a passion for gardening, and the Chelsea Flower show was the high spot of his year. Mrs Sneezum was active in county politics and various do-gooder kind of things. She was smaller than Alicia and thinner. Alicia was their only child. Naturally, they'd be a little worried.

He started to re-read the next page of his manuscript, then reached for a brown notebook at the back of his desk. The notebook was blank except for two poems, hastily written, which Sydney had intended to polish at some time and never had. He wrote, five blank pages beyond the last poem:

July 11. The first of many conversations, no doubt, with Mrs Sneezum. This in response to my letter of Saturday explaining Alicia's absence and silence. I carried it off calmly, in fact felt no anxiety whatsoever. I wonder if things would have been different had I been face to face with her? She asked me about

Alicia's post. Well, it is strange: Alicia left no address to which she wanted her post sent. Can I help that? The worst is yet to come, when A.'s monthly cheque will not be claimed on August 22nd. I'll then have to manufacture a man she is staying with. And best to start now.

This gave Sydney a pleasant feeling of both creating something and of being a murderer. He would fill in the preceding pages, he thought, with an actual account of the murder some time when he felt in the mood, pushing her down the stairs, keeping the body overnight, carrying it out the next morning – and perhaps being seen by Mrs Lilybanks, or only fearing that he had been.

Just before 5 p.m., the telephone rang, and Sydney thought it was probably Mrs Sneezum again.

'Polk-Faraday speaking,' said Alex.

'Bartleby the Scrivener scrivening,' Sydney replied.

'Syd, my friend, guess what?' Alex said.

Sydney guessed what, but he could hardly believe it. Hittie had just rung Alex at his office to say that Plummer of Granada would buy 'The Whip Strikes', if they could show one or two other finished scripts plus some synopses of equal calibre. Hittie had opened the letter and rung Alex immediately.

'I haven't buzzed him back,' Alex said. 'I'll tell him an unqualified yes, no? We'll deliver the goods.'

'Tell him we'll produce an indefinite number of super Whips. Meanwhile, I hope that second story's coming along?' It was the one about the murdered husband.

'It is, it is,' Alex assured him. 'First draft nearly done.'

'I'll get to work right away on a new synopsis.'

'Good. Want to come up tonight, old pal, and we'll kick an idea around? Provided you've got an idea to kick around.'

Sydney was tempted, but he knew they'd roar around congratulating themselves and not get any work done. 'Thanks, but

84

it might be better if I stayed here and kept my nose to the tomb-stone. The grindstone,' he corrected, laughing.

Alex laughed, too. 'Okay, but don't be too much of a recluse. How's Alicia? Sorry you two didn't come up for the party that night. Alicia wanted to come, you spoilsport.'

'Yes. Sorry. I was working that weekend. She could have gone by herself. When I get this novel done—'

'Give Alicia our love.'

Sydney took a breath and said, 'Alicia's not here. She went off to Brighton again, I think.'

'Again? When's she coming back?'

There went the pips.

'She might stay longer this time. A few weeks.'

'She's getting fed up with your grindstone. I'll sign off, old pal.'

Sydney stood by the telephone, dazzled with hope, turned slowly around, then looked at the telephone again. He wished he could pick it up and ring Alicia to tell her the news. But she'd hear about The Whip through their friends, if they sold it. Nonsense, she was dead and underground, he reminded himself, and smiling, he ran up the stairs back to his study.

12

Mrs Edward Ponsonby – otherwise Alicia – had installed herself in Brighton at a larger and more comfortable hostelry than the bed-and-breakfast place she had been in before, where the curfew, or the landlady's retiring time, had been 10 p.m., according to a sign inside the front door. She was in a real hotel now, the Sinclair, though it was a modest one and she had no private bath. Her monthly cheque of fifty pounds had come in 2 July, the day she had left home, so she had cashed it in Ipswich. She and Sydney had a joint account at the Ipswich bank with about a hundred pounds in it, but she didn't want to write cheques on that and deprive Sydney, and a cheque would also betray where she was. She intended to live on her fifty pounds as long as it lasted, then perhaps take a job as a clerk somewhere, not in London but in a small town with a restful atmosphere. Her bill at the end of a week at the Hotel Sinclair had diminished her resources by nine pounds nine, but her meals out cost very little, and she thought she might last until her next cheque, and from cheque to cheque, but she foresaw that life might become boring without a job. And how to get the next cheque was a slight problem, because it would come to Blycom Heath and Sydney wouldn't know where to forward it, and she did not want to tell her bank, and consequently Sydney, where she was. Her personal post was not important, she could let that go. Also, it would look as if she really had disappeared off the face of the earth, if she took no interest in her post, and therefore Sydney could play his games. She supposed he would act as guilty as possible, as if he had really murdered her, and irritate everyone. Just how far he went, Alicia thought, would be a good indication of his sanity and maturity. She had some misgivings about both.

She thought of ringing Edward Tilbury one evening, or some Sunday afternoon. She might ask him, really not caring whether he came or not (he might have an all-absorbing interest in London by now), if he would like to come down on a weekend. Alicia played with several fantasies: Edward would come down some Saturday and they would register at an hotel under another name, maybe Ponsonby, and they'd have a wicked weekend; or Edward would spend another Saturday with her and a real love would develop between them, causing her to do something drastic, like divorce Sydney; or a passionate love affair would start, Edward would wangle a month's leave from his firm, and they'd take a cottage somewhere. Or Edward might commute to London to his job, and spend the nights and weekends in Brighton. In case of a long affair, it was wiser if they took a cottage outside of Brighton, because some of their London friends might realize they were both 'missing', and draw a conclusion and think of Brighton because people knew she liked it.

Alicia was obsessed with the colour blue now, and she had bought sheets of heavy blue paper which she cut into six-by-eight inch rectangles. With these in a drawing pad, her fountain-pen that drew in Indian ink, and a single colour pencil – a red one – she sat for hours on the beach and promenade benches making abstract drawings of the scene around her. She was inspired to send a few of them to Mrs Lilybanks, but she didn't. She did not want even Mrs Lilybanks to know where she was. Mrs Lilybanks would naturally tell Sydney. Sydney might think she was in Brighton, but Alicia didn't want him to be sure of it.

Two weeks passed, and Alicia felt much calmer and happier. She imagined her parents being a little worried about her, but she thought Sydney could smooth that over. Her parents should realize that, if anything serious happened to her, it would be in the newspapers. But in the third week, Alicia grew tired of the speckled strawberry sundaes in tall glasses at The Eclair, of the *scaloppine* at the Italian restaurant, of the rotten pastry in the tea shop that she could afford and she even grew tired of her four walls in the Hotel Sinclair (papered with a tiny boat design, pink on cream) which had looked so delightful at first because the room was new to her, and her own. One evening she indulged in two double gins in a pub in Steine Street, and at the end of the second, she rang Edward in London.

Edward was in, rather to her surprise, and she took it as a favourable omen.

It was all arranged in an incredibly short time, even before the first three minutes had run out Edward would come down the following Saturday morning, on the 10 a.m. train which arrived at 11, and he would stay over Saturday night and Sunday. He sounded extremely pleased that she had rung him.

She met him at the railway station and nearly missed him among the people getting off, because he seemed to be ducking his head, and he also seemed shorter than she remembered. But his happy, open smile was the same when he saw her; he swept his hat off, and kissed her on one cheek. They had a drink in the buffet of the station.

'I suppose you think I'm mad,' Alicia said, 'but I'm taking another vacation, a longer one this time, and doing quite a bit of drawing. I brought my oil-paints, too.'

'My dear, I think you're delightful,' Edward said. 'What's mad about it?'

From that, and his tone, she knew he would not tell any of his London friends he had seen her, and would not ask anything about Sydney.

'Where're you stopping?'

'At the Hotel Sinclair,' Alicia answered. 'Nothing grand, but it's quite adequate.'

'Would you object if I took a room there? Or would you prefer me to go to another hotel?' He smiled his boyish, shy smile. 'It's so much easier for us to meet, if we're under the same roof.'

'Of course, I don't mind. I should think the Sinclair's big enough for both of us.'

Edward had a hold-all with him, which contained a shirt, swimming trunks and pyjamas, he said. So they went to the hotel from the station, and Alicia explained that, because she didn't want Sydney or her parents to know where she was, she had registered under another name, Mrs Edward Ponsonby.

'I hope you don't mind the Edward,' she said.

'I'm pleased,' said Edward Tilbury.

Alicia had no intention of starting an affair with Edward really, so she didn't. Edward was obviously willing. She felt guilty about having asked him down to Brighton without sleeping with him, but curiously he seemed to be content with the situation. They spent a Saturday afternoon and evening and Sunday as pleasant as their first Sunday, and Alicia gave him an antique tie pin which she had bought in a spare moment on Saturday afternoon. She did not say anything about when they might see each other next, but Edward asked if she would be in Brighton next weekend. Alicia said she thought she would be, and Edward asked if he might come down again.

'Yes, I'd love it. If you've nothing better to do,' she added automatically, but she loved Edward at that moment, and he had never come nearer to possessing her.

13

At the end of July, when Alicia had been gone nearly four weeks, the Polk-Faradays came up to Suffolk for a weekend with Sydney. Sydney was working out the plot of his third Whip story, 'The Second Sir Quentin', which concerned The Whip's impersonation of an English diplomat. It was Sydney's first entertaining, apart from the Inez and Carpie picnic, since Alicia had left, and with unwonted enthusiasm he bought a chicken, a roast, a bottle of Haig, several bottles of wine, and all kinds of delicatessen from a shop in Ipswich.

The Polk-Faradays arrived at 8.30 p.m. on Friday, and Sydney greeted them at the back door. They contributed ale, wine, and a couple of custard pies made by Hittie.

'This is going to be a great weekend,' Sydney said, fixing the first drinks in the kitchen.

'Yes, it's raining already,' Alex said, though not gloomily.

Hittie said, 'May I? It smells super!' and opened the oven door. 'Umm-m. Want me to mash some potatoes?'

Sydney was cooking the roast beef. 'The potatoes are done, if you want to mash them.'

Hittie did.

'You're looking well,' Alex said. 'Bachelor life agrees with you.'

'Oh, I dunno.' Sydney recalled that Mrs Lilybanks had said the same thing a few days ago. The prospect of the sale of The Whip had picked him up tremendously, but he didn't want to say that to Alex for fear it would bring bad luck.

Hittie came in with her drink, looked around the living-room, and bent to admire the yellow roses Sydney had put into the cracked white vase in front of the fireplace. 'Oh – isn't this a different carpet?' Hittie asked.

Sydney started a little, as he had when Mrs Lilybanks mentioned the carpet. 'Yes, I – we thought the other was getting pretty cruddy.' He glanced at Alex, causing Alex to look at him. 'We picked this up very cheaply at a second-hand place.'

'It's nice.' Hittie looked from the carpet up at Sydney. 'Any news from Alicia?'

'No. I'm not expecting to hear from her, you know. She really does want to be alone for a while. It's annoying in a way, because her mother keeps expecting me to hear from her, and apparently Alicia isn't writing to her mother either.' Sydney shrugged, aware he was talking at too great a length, simply because it had been three or four days – since the last time he had seen Mrs Lilybanks – since he had said twenty consecutive words to anyone, even shopkeepers.

'Where do you think she is?' Hittie asked.

'Brighton,' Sydney said.

'He's done away with her,' said Alex, getting up with his empty glass, going towards the kitchen. He winked one eye and kept it shut, peering with the other into Sydney's face. 'He's done her in, he's going to live off her income, and he's going to stick the story of the murder in the Whip series and make a mint on it.'

Sydney laughed politely.

'You're not worried about Alicia?' Hittie said rather than asked, but her blonde-Chinese face looked worried, her brown-pencilled brows moved in straight, slanting lines and nearly met over her nose.

'No. I don't see any reason to be,' Sydney said.

'And how long will she be gone?'

Sydney had a feeling Hittie was pumping him for information she intended to pass on to interested parties in London. 'I suppose,' he said, 'it could be six months. Alicia said she wasn't sure how long she wanted to be away. I don't want to say that to her mother, because the Sneezums – ah-*choo*! – might really get worried. They don't understand the younger generation.' Sydney took Hittie's glass and went off to the kitchen with it. It wasn't empty, but he wanted to be a good host.

Sydney spent the last part of the dinner telling them about 'The Second Sir Quentin'.

'When the story opens,' Sydney said, 'Sir Quentin Ogilvie, K.C.M.G., G.C.B. – which stands for Grand Crashing Bore – is assassinated by a bomb thrown at him in a dark street in Ankara. We'll show the bomb sequence first, before we know anything about anybody. Bang. Sir Quentin is just leaving the house of one of his mistresses. It's crucial that Sir Quentin make an appearance in London at a diplomatic conference, therefore crucial that neither the Turkish nor the English officials know he's been killed. This is where The Whip –'

'Why?' asked Alex, sitting sideways in his chair, legs crossed.

'Because of diplomatic conditions in Turkey – versus England – at the moment. The valet of Sir Quentin, who is no fool, hears about the death through a street urchin, who comes to Sir Quentin's house. The valet and the urchin get the body off the street in the darkness and hide it in Sir Quentin's garage under some tarpaulins. Then the valet makes a call to London to the C.I.D. The C.I.D. contact one of their middlemen – that is, with whom they have no further connection, a blind alley—'

'Um-m,' Alex said, looking down sleepily and dubiously at his plate, mopping the last sauce with a last bite of roast beef.

Hittie at least seemed to be following him, so Sydney continued. 'We see The Whip in his London flat, talking to the middleman who's just rung up. The Whip smiles and says he'll do the job, though we don't know what the job is. Then, back in Ankara, we see the Turkish assassins looking sore and puzzled, because their assassination plan has apparently failed. There's Sir Quentin walking around town hale as ever except for a bandage over part of his head and one eye, presumably from the bomb. It's The Whip, assuming a perfect disguise as the old G.C.B., Sir Quentin.'

Hittie was taking away the dishes on tiptoe, listening, bringing in the pie. Sydney heard the coffee perking behind him in the kitchen. He went on:

'Plenty of opportunity for comedy in this, Alex. We can have one of Sir Quentin's luscious mistresses turning up on his threshold, missing him, you know, and not taking no for an answer, but if The Whip sleeps with her, he's afraid it might reveal the fact he's not the Grand Crashing Bore, as indeed it might.' Sydney gave a clap of laughter, and was pleased by Hittie's giggle.

'Umm-hm,' said Alex, smiling but close-mouthed. His eyes looked a trifle drunk, or perhaps were merely bloodshot from driving.

'Every now and then, we flash to the tarpaulins in Sir Quentin's garage. The garageman comes to correct a faulty tail-light on the Rolls, for instance. The valet hovers around, stopping the garageman from taking one of the tarpaulins to lie on when he's crawling under the car, something like that.'

'I'm lost,' Alex complained.

'Oh, it'll be better on paper. You won't be lost then. It's a simple story – like all good stories,' Sydney said.

'I'm not lost. Go on,' Hittie said, sitting down at her place. She had distributed the pie on plates with fresh forks.

'Well – Ogilvie, alias The Whip—'

'You mean, The Whip alias Ogilvie,' said Alex.

'Any way you like,' said Sydney. 'He comes to London with pomp and protocol for the conference, does his part brilliantly, saves the conference, averts war and so forth . . .' Sydney trailed off, for in fact he hadn't got beyond this. 'It needs a good wind-up at the end. And the tarpaulins in the garage—' Sydney stared at the centre of the table for a moment, thought of the red and blue rug he had buried, the inside-out-rolled rug with Alicia's body in it. What did one do with a body besides bury it? 'I suppose it'll have to be buried somewhere finally.'

'M-m. By whom?' asked Alex, starting on his pie.

'By the valet and a couple of chums like the street urchins. They all know an international crisis has been averted. They'll play along with a little thing like getting rid of the body.'

'Of course, later, Ogilvie'll be missed. I presume The Whip stays on in London?' Alex asked.

'Oh, sure. Ready for our next story,' Sydney said. 'Ogilvie'll finally be missed, but we don't have to show that. By then the crisis is over.'

'What crisis?'

'Alex!' Hittie said reproachfully. 'You might give Sydney the courtesy of listening.'

'I am listening. I didn't get the crisis,' Alex said, lifting his long pale face, one black brow frowning as he looked at his wife. 'I haven't the foggiest what the crisis is about, and I don't think Sydney has.'

Hittie sighed deploringly, with a glance at Sydney.

They were all tired, even with the second pot of coffee which Sydney made to help Hittie and him get through the dishes. Alex was plainly too exhausted to help. In the kitchen, Hittie said:

'I hope you'll forgive Alex for being grumpy tonight. He's had a hard week, working late three nights, and then the drive.'

94

'Oh, think nothing of it,' Sydney said cheerfully. 'He was kidding me, I know.' His hands were deep in soap suds.

'The big bowls go here?' Hittie asked. She was drying and putting away at the same time.

'Dear girl, I don't give a damn where you put them. I'd like them in a different place for a change.'

When Hittie returned for the next dish in the rack, she said, 'It must be awfully lonely for you here without Alicia. I think you're bearing up wonderfully.'

Sydney turned his slightly smiling face towards her. He was bearing up superbly, but he realized that with extroverts and togetherness people like the Polk-Faradays, one wasn't supposed to be superbly happy alone. 'No, I like it. I'm not lonely. Don't forget, I was an only child. I'm used to being alone.' And it was hard for Sydney to understand why people chose to live in groups sometimes, like big Italian families, for example, unless out of economic necessity. Crowds troubled him, a mass of people standing in a cinema lobby waiting to go inside troubled him emotionally. Their assemblage seemed to have some hostile intent, like the assemblage of men for an army. Assembly did not seem to Sydney a condition normal people should desire. He was an ochlophobe.

But Hittie's face still registered sympathetic concern. 'Alex was saying – Alicia gets a monthly income, doesn't she?'

She was about to say, Sydney thought, 'If Alicia's dead, it'll go to you, won't it?' He smiled a little. 'Yes. It's due the first of August. Monday.'

'It comes through the post to her?'

'Yes. Comes in the second.'

Hittie stood on one foot and scratched the bottom of her other foot. She had removed her new sandals after dinner because they pinched, and now she was barelegged and barefooted. 'If it doesn't come, Alex was saying, you could write the bank or ring them and ask where Alicia told them to forward it. I suppose she's told them.'

'I'm sure she has, but I don't think Alicia wants me to know where she is. It was an agreement between us. She wanted absolute privacy. You see?' Sydney hoped that was the end of it.

'But aren't *you* curious?'

'No,' Sydney said, and pulled the plug out of the sink. He remembered the dirty coffee-pot and quickly put the plug in again. He banged the grounds out in the box destined for the compost heap, washed the pot, scoured the sink with Ajax, dried his hands, then lifted one of Hittie's hands to his lips and said, 'Thank you, my sweet. How about a night-cap?'

'Oh, no, I couldn't. Thanks.'

Sydney didn't have one either. Fifteen minutes later, he was asleep in the double bed in the bedroom.

He woke up at the sound of an amorous pigeon – 'Oo-oo-ooo-oo-oo' – so loud that it might have been in the room with him. He went downstairs and put on coffee. Then he went up to his study, put a sheet of paper into the typewriter, and wrote: 'The Second Sir Quentin, Act One', and began to bang away. After twenty minutes and two cups of coffee, he had three-and-a-half pages of synopsis with a crystal-clear government crisis. Around 9, he woke the Polk-Faradays up with cups of coffee on a tray, then got his synopsis from his study.

'Take a look at this, if you like. I think it's clearer.'

Sydney had perceived, by the dawn's early light, that his story lacked a middle part, so he provided it by having the assassins make further attempts on The Whip, who they of course thought to be the real Sir Quentin. The Whip outwitted and at last captured the little band of assassins before flying off for the London conference. Sydney went down to see about breakfast.

Alex came down a few minutes later, and said he thought the story was quite interesting. 'I didn't really get it last night. Sorry, old boy. I was bushed. It might be the best of the three so far.'

After breakfast, Sydney and Alex drove off to Framlingham,

and Sydney bought charcoal and a thick steak. He was inspired to make a charcoal pit. Hittie put their grocery purchases away when they got home, and Sydney went out to the toolhouse for the fork. Alex followed him, curious to see how a pit was made.

Sydney plunged the fork into the tough, grassy soil, and prized up the first clump. The fork, Sydney noticed, had darker coloured and now dry lumps of earth stuck high up between its tines – soil from the place where he had buried Alicia – and it seemed to him Alex was looking at the fork with a speculative frown, and that he was going to make some comment about it in the next moment.

'How deep do they have to be?' Alex asked.

'About a foot. They can be very deep, but then they're big, for roasting whole animals. I'm just making this for steaks.'

Alex was just as amiable all day as he had been grouchy the previous evening. They spent a productive couple of hours in the sun after lunch, talking over the story and arranging it in three acts and about twenty scenes. Meanwhile, Alex was ready to start typing up the second Whip script. Sydney knew he'd be a good two weeks in the typing.

'If you'd post it to me,' Sydney said, 'I'll type it.'

'Oh, there's always little last-minute changes I have to make. You know how it is.'

Sydney sighed, impatient for the acceptance. 'We really won't know anything before the end of August, will we?'

'You mean from Plummer. Probably not. I don't think I can get this third one done before the end of August, and he wanted three finished.'

Sydney swatted a gnat that had just stung his forearm. 'How about me trying to write "Sir Quentin"? We've got it so well laid out.'

'Um-m. Better not, Syd. We're doing so well like this. Let's not take a chance.'

97

Sydney said nothing. He was a little annoyed by Alex's proprietary attitude. The ideas, after all, came from him. And why should Alex have a monopoly on playwriting? Sydney got up and said, 'Let's have a drink. Sun's way over the yardarm and practically in the sea.'

They were all on second drinks by the time Sydney struck a match to his charcoal, on which he had poured some fuel to make it light instantly. It did light instantly, and the flaming bowl in the earth pleased him tremendously. Hittie wrapped the potatoes in foil and baked them on the coals. They were all very merry, and Sydney sang for them:

'Under the britches of Paris with you
I'll make your screams come true . . .'

Hittie screamed with laughter, and Sydney did, too, because he was making up the words as he went along. He hoped they didn't carry to Mrs Lilybanks.

'You see, bachelor life suits him,' Alex said to Hittie. 'I never saw him this cheerful when Alicia was around.'

'Oh, Alex,' Hittie said, ready to defend the sacred bliss of matrimony.

'Aren't you more cheerful, Syd?' Alex asked.

'That's right. No more hidden bananas and stuff like that. And just wait till her income starts pouring in. Boy! That plus The Whip, I'll be rolling!' Sydney was on one knee, testing the heat of the coals with his palm.

'Hidden bananas?' Hittie asked. Her accent broadened every 'a'.

'Alicia liked them – likes them,' he corrected, 'less ripe than I do, so to get any ripe before she eats them, I had to hide them behind books and things. Then every six months or so when Alicia would dust the books, she'd say, "*Eeeeeeek!* Good God! Another banana and what a *state* it's in!"'

Hittie and Alex roared.

'Hidden bananas!' Hittie kept saying, leaning on Alex to keep her balance.

'Hittie was saying, you can tell where Alicia is from where she told her bank to send her income, can't you?' Alex asked.

'Yes, but as I was saying to Hittie, I don't think Alicia wants me to know.' Hittie must have told him that, Sydney thought, and he didn't want to go into it again. He didn't want to talk about Alicia at all.

'You will let us know if she collects her cheque, won't you, Syd?' Alex asked.

'Sure. If she collects it? I'm sure she'll collect it. She'll need it.' Unless she were staying with some friend, Sydney thought, but he couldn't imagine who it might be. He didn't think it was anyone in London, and she didn't know any people well enough anywhere outside London to stay with. A couple of married school friends, yes, but Alicia wouldn't want to stay with them, he was certain. He got to his feet. 'While there's some light, I want to look for a grill,' he said, and went off to the toolhouse.

When he came back with a square of criss-crossed wire, just the thing, Hittie and Alex were having a murmured conversation.

'You have a joint bank account, haven't you, Syd?' Alex asked. 'You could tell from—'

'Yes, but – she wouldn't take everything out of that and leave me flat.'

They ate indoors, but the glowing orange coals in the pit drew them out again later, and they sat long around it, Hittie sipping coffee, Sydney and Alex finishing the wine. Sydney was trying to think of a fourth story for The Whip.

14

The Polk-Faradays had been right to attach such importance to Alicia's collecting her income, Sydney discovered. Alicia's cheque arrived from the Westminster Bank on 2 August, Tuesday, and only half an hour after its delivery, before 9 o'clock, Mrs Sneezum rang up to ask if the cheque had come. Sydney said it had, but that he didn't know where to send it.

'It must mean Alicia intends to come home soon,' Mrs Sneezum said. 'I was hoping she might be back now – because I rang the Westminster Bank a couple of days ago and was told she hadn't given any forwarding address. Have you heard from her?'

'No.'

'Neither have we. What about your bank in Ipswich? Has she been drawing money out of that?'

Sydney didn't know, and Mrs Sneezum seemed surprised and annoyed that he hadn't bothered to find out. She asked if he would ring the bank and ask, and then ring her back reverse charges, and Sydney said that he would.

Then he waited, feeling somehow like a reproached child and resenting it, until 9.30, which he thought was the earliest possible hour to call a bank. It was a boring, embarrassing chore. Never mind, he told himself, if you'd killed her, you'd have to be going through the same motions. People in your stories have to do it all the time, and this is what it feels like. He called the Ipswich bank. It took several minutes to get the right clerk to find this information, and the news was that no cheques signed by Mrs Bartleby had come in since 26 June, and that was a cheque dated 24 June. Alicia had left on 2 July. Sydney called Mrs Sneezum back and reported.

'Really? I wonder what she's doing for money – or if something's actually happened to her?'

'Well, she went off with fifty pounds from her July cheque. It had just come in and she cashed it in Ipswich.'

'Yes, I supposed she did. But it's not like Alicia not to want her money as soon as she can get it. Not to run out of money, either.'

Three days later, on a shopping expedition in Ipswich, he called at the bank and asked again. No cheque signed by Mrs Bartleby had come in. That was on a Friday. Who was keeping her, Sydney wondered. A man? What man? The telephone was ringing as Sydney got back home. It was Mrs Sneezum. Sydney told her his lack of news.

'My husband thinks it's time we asked the police to look for her, and so do I. I think you'll agree, too, Sydney,' she said in a matter-of-fact and somewhat impatient tone. 'I'm sure when the police hear the story, they'll wonder why we haven't spoken to them weeks before.'

Sydney felt this was a direct slap at him, but only agreed politely that they should ask for police help.

'I think the police should start with Brighton and go on from there, if they have to,' Mrs Sneezum said. 'We might need a couple of photographs, if she's doing something silly like staying somewhere under another name, you know. Perhaps you can post me some, Sydney? A couple of clear ones. You probably have some that are more up-to-date than the ones we've got here.'

It took him half an hour to find two snapshots that showed Alicia's face clearly, one of her in jeans in a deckchair behind the house, the other in a summer dress, from last year, standing by the apple tree between their house and Mrs Lilybanks's. 'SUFFOLK GIRL FOUND MURDERED,' Sydney imagined the headline over it. No. 'HAVE YOU SEEN HER? POLICE SUSPECT FOUL PLAY.' Oh, rot, he thought, and went into his workshop to get an envelope. Interesting that the Sneezums didn't trust him to call in the police and get things moving properly.

Sydney drove to the Blycom Heath post office with the enve-lope. He needed some jam, so after dropping the envelope into the box outside the door, he went into the store. It was a com-bined post office and general store, not very big.

'Some orange marmalade, please, Mr Fowler,' Sydney said, thinking that by tomorrow or the next day, Mr Fowler wouldn't go off for his purchase so quickly, but would stop and say, 'Oh, Mr Bartleby, I saw about your wife in the paper . . . ' Sydney had told Mr Fowler and also Edith, his daughter who helped out, and also Rutledge, the handyman, and the milkman who had asked about Alicia last week, and even Fred Hartung at the garage in Blycom Heath where he bought most of his petrol – he had said to all of them that Alicia was in Kent with her mother. Now it would come out in the papers that he had known for about three weeks that Alicia wasn't with her mother, yet he had kept on giving out that story. Mrs Lilybanks knew, and had known since the Inez and Carpie picnic, Sydney realized. She must not have told anybody in the neighbourhood, which was nice of her.

'Thick-cut, right?' Mr Fowler asked, thunking the jar down. He was a tallish, slender man with a bushy black moustache rather like Rudyard Kipling's.

'Right,' Sydney said, pleased that he remembered his preference.

'All right like that?' Mr Fowler asked, meaning should he wrap it.

'Oh, certainly. Nothing else to carry.' With a wave, Sydney walked towards the door.

'I hope Mrs Bartleby's keeping all right,' said Mr Fowler.

Sydney turned. 'I think she's all right. She's not much for writing,' he said, looking Mr Fowler in the eye, then he went on. Just what a killer would say, Sydney thought. Just like G. J. Smith.

August 2. Tuesday. Sydney looked at the date on the calendar – contributed by their Framlingham dairy, two Scottie pups in plaid collars in the picture – and he felt it would have profound significance for him. Nothing would happen today, but today was a turning point because of the entry of the police. It was also the day he intended to send off a carbon of *The Planners* to Potter and Desch in London. He had sent the original by surface mail to his agent in New York ten days ago, but because London was more immediate and personally important, he had kept his second copy and continued to look at it, though without changing anything. Just before 6 p.m., when the post office closed, Sydney wrote a covering letter to Potter and Desch, wrapped the manuscript, and sent it.

The next morning at 10, a young police constable knocked on Sydney's door. The young officer was blond, fresh-faced and very earnest behind his smile. He pulled out a notebook and fountain-pen, and Sydney offered him a chair. He sat down stiffly, and prepared to write on his knees. 'It's about your wife. Have you heard anything from her?'

'Not a thing,' Sydney said. He sat down on the sofa.

The first questions were of the kind Sydney anticipated. The date he had seen her last? July 2. Where? He had put her on the train to London at Ipswich that morning, Saturday, around 11.30 a.m. Where did she say she was going? She said to her mother's. What kind of mood had she been in? In quite a good mood. She was going to do some painting, and she wanted to be by herself for a while. Wasn't it unusual that she hadn't written a word to him or anyone since? No, not really, because she had said she wouldn't write to him until she wanted to come back, and she asked him not to try to communicate with her. But wasn't it unusual that she hadn't written to her mother? Perhaps it was.

Sydney rubbed his palms together slowly between his knees, and waited attentively for the next questions.

'The police are looking around Brighton now, but it's important that we get some information from you, too. Do you know any other places she might have gone?'

'I can't think of any.'

'Did she say how long she might be away?'

'Not specifically. She said, "No matter how long I'm gone" – that she didn't want me to try to find her. I gathered it could be months. Maybe six months.'

'Really?' He wrote it down. '*She* said that?'

'She said she didn't know.' Sydney shrugged a little, nervously. 'She took two suitcases with her and some of her winter clothes. She thought – some time apart might do us both good,' Sydney said, feeling himself sliding deeper into suspicious-sounding replies, perfectly truthful replies, yet he was doing what murderers always did, say their victims had said they would be absent for an indefinite length of time.

'In that case, maybe there's not so much reason for Mrs Bartleby's parents to be worried,' said the constable.

'No, and I suppose something's in the papers this morning. I only saw *The Times*. If my wife knows her family's so concerned, she'll communicate. Probably today.'

'It's in the papers this morning with a photograph. It's in the *Express*. Mrs Bartleby's parents don't know she might stay away as long as six months?' the young constable asked with a frown.

'I don't know. I didn't tell her mother that for fear she might be more worried. Also because I wasn't sure Alicia really would stay away that long. But now that her mother's already upset,

I—' Sydney stopped, floundering. Another gaffe, another boner, he thought. Why hadn't he told Mrs Sneezum? Because he was lying, because he had made up the whole story and hadn't planned carefully enough to tell everyone the same story.

The constable stood up. 'I think that's all we have to ask you at the moment, Mr Bartleby. Let's hope today, with the publicity, she'll answer from somewhere.'

Sydney went back upstairs to his study, then on an impulse, went into the bedroom and looked out of its front window. The young constable was on the road's edge, by his bicycle, looking at his notes. Then he turned his bicycle, mounted it, and pedalled off towards Mrs Lilybanks's house, where he dismounted, parked his bicycle, and approached her front door.

And had the neighbours seen anything suspicious lately around the Bartleby house?

Sydney did not stand at the window waiting to see when the officer came out, but when he looked again ten minutes later, the bicycle was still leaning against the front gatepost. Mrs Lilybanks might have seen him carrying out the carpet, of course. Sydney had thought of that before. But he hadn't really thought that the police would be called in. Not really. Alicia might have had enough consideration to write her parents, he thought. She could have told them not to tell him where she was, if she wanted to keep it a secret.

Sydney felt vaguely guilty and ashamed of himself. It was neither a pleasant nor an interesting sensation.

Mrs Lilybanks was glad to talk to someone about Alicia, but she hadn't known that anything was in the newspapers that day, that people were alarmed because Alicia was missing, and when she heard that, Mrs Lilybanks thought she should be careful about saying how surprised she was at not hearing anything from her. There was no use in adding to the alarm.

'Would you say you know the Bartlebys pretty well?' the young officer asked after he had finished with some preliminary questions.

'No, just as neighbours. I've been here only since the end of May. Alicia and I did a little painting together.'

The officer glanced at the green smock she wore over her dress. 'You've seen Mr Bartleby a few times since his wife's been gone?'

'Oh, yes. He's been here for dinner, and I went over to his house for a picnic one afternoon.' She could have said more about that afternoon, that it was the afternoon she learned that Alicia wasn't at her parents', about three weeks ago, and that her London friends had been surprised by that fact, but Mrs Lilybanks thought it best not to prattle.

'Did he seem worried about her?'

'Not a bit. She did want to stay away for a while, she said.'

'She said or Mr Bartleby said?'

'She said it. Alicia came by to see me the Thursday or Friday before the Saturday she left. I suppose it was Friday. She said she wanted to be by herself for a while and paint, and she thought a little solitude might do her husband good, too.'

The officer nodded. 'She was in good spirits?'

'Quite good, yes.'

'Have you heard from her?'

'Oh, no. I'd have told Mr Bartleby, if I had.'

'Did you expect to hear from her?

'I did – really,' said Mrs Lilybanks carefully. 'But – she may not be able to write easily, even a postcard, and she may really want to cut everything off for a while.'

'Do you think they were getting along all right? The Bartlebys? It might be a help as to what Mrs Bartleby decided to do with herself, take a job under another name or go to another country, like. I didn't ask Mr Bartleby that because I could see he meant to say they were getting along very well, just decided to separate for six months.'

'Six months?' Mrs Lilybanks asked.

'That's what Mr Bartleby said. He wouldn't be surprised if it was six months she was gone, he said. Mrs Bartleby didn't say that to you?'

'No, I'm sure she didn't or I'd have remembered. I got the idea she'd be away a few weeks, perhaps about a month.' Mrs Lilybanks was sitting up alertly on her sofa, with her hands crossed in her lap.

'Well—' He made a short note in his book. He was perched on a hassock with his long legs pressed together to make a writing place. 'Do you mind telling me how they were getting on, you think?'

Mrs Lilybanks chose her words. 'I think well enough. I saw them together with other people – as I said.' And she had seen Sydney's temper in the kitchen that evening, too, a shocking flare of temper, but was it logical to attach great importance to that?

'You noticed nothing unusual around the time Mrs Bartleby left?'

Mrs Lilybanks jumped slightly and resettled herself. She had a vision of Sydney carrying something heavy over his shoulder in the garden the morning after the day Alicia had left – or was supposed to have left. Very early it had been, still hardly daylight. She had been trying to bird-watch with her binoculars, but since it was still not light enough, though the birds were singing, she had gone downstairs to start her tea water. When she had looked out of the upstairs window again, Sydney's car had been moving off down the road. 'No,' she said, 'nothing unusual.'

'Mrs Bartleby didn't say anything unusual to you, like she was going to meet anybody?'

'No,' said Mrs Lilybanks.

15

For two days, 4 and 5 August, the *Daily Express* and the *Evening Standard* ran a photograph, a different one on different days, of Alicia Bartleby. The captions read: 'SEEN HER?' and 'STILL MISSING' and 'SEARCH CONTINUES' and 'WHERE IS SHE?' The short items below stated that Mrs Alicia Bartleby, 26, of Blycom Heath, Suffolk, had gone off, presumably to her parents' home in Kent on 2 July, but had not arrived there and had not been heard from since. Her husband now believed she was in Brighton, and the police were making a search of the Brighton area.

On Thursday, when the first photographs appeared, Edward Tilbury was to come down to Brighton by train and take the bus to Arundel, on whose outskirts he and Alicia had rented a small house. It was Edward's birthday, otherwise he would not have made the trip in mid-week. He usually came down Friday evening and stayed until Monday morning. Edward came down, though he was quite shaken by the photographs in the morning and evening newspapers, and his detraining at Brighton and boarding of the Arundel bus had been more furtive than usual. He was even more upset by the change in Alicia's appearance. She had taken the scooter to Littlehampton that afternoon, she said, and got her hair cut and tinted at a beauty parlour there. She had baked a cake with pink icing and candles, as yet unlit, which stood on the coffee-table.

'Happy birthday, darling! – Don't you like it?' she asked, running her fingers through her hair in a gay upward gesture.

'Yes, it's all right. I gather you saw the papers. What're you going to do, darling? – Why don't you sit down?'

'You're not sitting down. Of course I've seen the papers. I was going to make you a drink. I've got a surprise for dinner. I hope you can't tell what it is from the smell.' She went off to the kitchen.

Edward laid his brief-case down. He had brought a brief to study, and was glad he had got through most of it on the train. He had hoped to find Alicia sobered and a little frightened, in which case he would have comforted her and tried to persuade her to go to her parents. She had had a couple of drinks, he could tell.

Alicia came back with a Scotch and soda for him and for herself. 'Cheers, darling. And happy returns.'

He stared at her reddish hair. He supposed it was what they called auburn. It was certainly on the red side.

'You're not even going to kiss me?'

He kissed her, on the cheek, then the lips.

'How's your foot, darling?'

'Oh, it's all right,' Edward said, baring his teeth briefly in a grimace. He had trodden on a piece of glass on Sunday on the beach. His foot wasn't infected, he had made quite sure of that by frequent examinations and doctoring of it; but he had to limp a little to spare it, and at the office he had had to say he trod on a drawing-pin, barefoot, at home. 'I gather you have no intention of – telling anybody where you are?'

'No, dear, I haven't. But I would like to leave here. I was thinking of Angmering. It's also on the sea and – a little closer to Brighton for the bus.' Alicia smiled.

'It certainly will look odd, your changing your hair. Just today.'

Alicia sat down on the brown velour sofa, and pulled Edward down beside her. 'Don't be nervy, darling. By the time people start looking for me, what do you think they'll see? This.' She held a four-inch length of hair up from the top of her head.

'Alicia, I'm not so sure it's wise. As for myself, *I* can't afford to be dragged into some silly business of deceiving the police – for a love affair.'

'Is that all it is?'

'Oh, you know I want to marry you, but this isn't the way to begin. You don't want me to begin by losing my position, do you?' he asked with a nervous laugh. 'I admit I was damned uneasy coming down here this evening.'

'Oh, Edward. I'll give you courage. Now look, if we move from here tomorrow – I can move what little we've got here, never fear – we'll lose only five days of the fortnight's rent we've paid.'

'That's of no importance.'

'Money is always important. I'll ring you tomorrow in the office and tell you where I've –'

'Dearest, don't ever ring me in the office. I've told you that before.'

'All right, I'll meet you at the Brighton station tomorrow at seven. Or six-thirty, or whenever.'

Edward said nothing, and tried to remain calm, or become calm. He had the feeling Alicia didn't mean anything she was saying, or rather that she couldn't carry through anything she was saying, even if she meant to. She would give *him* courage? When she was so full of anxieties, even about his driving, that she had made him stop driving down to Brighton? Alicia was afraid to go more than twenty miles an hour on the scooter, too, and he'd had a hard time convincing her that they needed one down here, though Alicia had a licence to drive one that dated from when she was nineteen. The licence was under the name of Alicia

Sneezum. Edward took a deep pull on his drink, then said, 'And how long is it going to go on?'

'Oh – maybe a few more weeks. Darling, don't you think we have a happy life?' She caressed his right hand.

'It was happy.'

'Still is.' She leaned closer to him, put her arm around his neck, and kissed him.

It was a long, beautiful kiss. Edward relaxed. Yes, it still was a happy life, he supposed. Alicia was the most exciting woman he had ever been to bed with. Edward did not forget that. 'It's only the police that bother me,' he said when the kiss was over.

'But what do you want me to do about them?' Alicia asked helplessly.

'Can't you – for instance – instead of going to Angmering tomorrow, go home to Kent, tell your parents you've been in some little towns around Brighton, painting, apologize for not writing to them, tell them you want a divorce from Sydney and then tell Sydney? And leave me out of it till then.'

Alicia felt vaguely hurt. Edward wasn't in the spirit of the thing at all. 'You'd think there was something illegal about what we're doing.'

Edward gave a laugh. 'Darling, there is. And it's worse with the police in it.'

'If I do what you suggested, I won't be able to see you or be with you for months and months.'

That was true. Edward was silenced for a moment, torn.

Alicia went into the kitchen to attend to the dinner.

16

By Saturday, the police had come a second time to Sydney's house and also to Mrs Lilybanks's, the same young constable plus an older man in plain clothes from Ipswich, Inspector Brockway. He was a tall, rugged man of about fifty who spoke softly but coughed every few minutes very loudly. By Saturday, it had dawned on Sydney that Alicia was playing her part, too, and with determination, in a make-believe drama in which he had done away with her. She was not going to be heard from by him or anyone else, if she could help it.

And Saturday, Sydney felt suspicion emanating from Inspector Brockway. Curiously, Sydney felt a bit guilty and nervous. Yet he also felt quite sure of himself, because he hadn't done away with her. However, he quite genuinely dropped a cup in the kitchen as he was pouring a cup of coffee for himself (the Inspector and the constable had declined coffee), and both men had been watching from the dining-room at the time. He stammered. He said first that he had put his wife on the train at Campsey Ash, then as the young constable corrected him on the basis of his first statement, Sydney changed it to Ipswich.

'Did you see anyone you knew that day at Ipswich? Anyone at the station?' asked the Inspector.

'Unfortunately, no,' Sydney had answered quickly, and he saw the Inspector catch the word 'unfortunately'.

It was astonishing how naturally all the imaginary guilt came out.

The Inspector asked to see Alicia's room upstairs, which meant the bedroom and her studio, and Sydney remarked that she had taken her paint box, the size of a small suitcase, but not her easel. The Inspector slid out the top drawer, which was Alicia's, in the chest of drawers in the bedroom, perhaps looking for something no woman would have left behind, like a lipstick or a compact, but the drawer contained four lipsticks and two old compacts still, besides a stack of handkerchiefs and scarves, manicure scissors, a small sewing kit, and several belts. Inspector Brockway asked what kind of suitcase she had taken, and Sydney told him two, a navy-blue one with brown leather corners, and a larger brown leather one with a strap. She had taken some winter suits and a cloth coat with a fur collar. What had she been wearing? Sydney couldn't remember. But she had carried her tan raincoat over her arm.

Then Inspector Brockway and the young constable walked out of the back door without saying anything, and Sydney trailed after them, puzzled, until it occurred to him that the Inspector wanted to see if the back yard and garden showed any signs of digging. Sydney was somewhat interested, as it reminded him of Christie, and he did his best to imagine himself really guilty of having killed and buried his wife under a couple of square yards of grass, which he would have carefully replaced after cutting it up into six-inch-square divots, but he couldn't really imagine much internally, and as for externally, he supposed a guilty man would have done the same as he, looked up at the sky and the birds, and let the police be. A guilty man would of course have kept a lookout for what the police might be finding, and Sydney had done this, casting a glance now and then from his distance of some forty feet. The Inspector had looked at the garage also, and noted that it had a wooden floor. It certainly wasn't a thorough search, Sydney thought. A proper investigation would have meant going on hands and knees over every foot of the place, poking and even digging in spots, and tearing up the garage floorboards. But still, that was what the Inspector's look around was for, a buried corpse, and closer inspection might come later. The two or three rains in the last month would have obliterated any signs of freshly turned earth since Alicia had been gone, and no doubt the Inspector was thinking this, too.

The Inspector's good-bye, courteous but stiff, was without any cheery word about keeping his chin up, or any promise to ring him as soon as they found out anything.

Sydney lit a cigarette, and watched the two officers walking towards Mrs Lilybanks's house. The Inspector's car was at the edge of the road in front of Sydney's house. Mrs Lilybanks, he supposed, would put in a good word for him and counteract some of the suspicion he had raised in the Inspector's mind. On the other hand, the Inspector might hint at his suspicion and plant some in her mind. They'd be trying to get all they could out of Mrs Lilybanks, naturally. She might mention the carpet, if she had seen it. Sydney wished very much that he could listen in on the conversation.

Several hours later, around 5 p.m., Mrs Lilybanks telephoned and asked Sydney if it would be convenient if she came over for a minute, or perhaps he would like to come to her and have a cup of tea or a drink?'

'Either way. Why don't you come here?' Sydney said. 'I have both those things, too.'

Mrs Lilybanks said she would come over. But it took her nearly ten minutes to get out of the house. She glanced at herself two or three times in the mirror to be sure she hadn't any paint smudges on her face, as she had just been painting, or trying to. The visit from the Ipswich Inspector had shaken her terribly. She had taken a spoonful of the medicine that Dr Underwood had told her to take only when she really felt fluttery, and then she had lain down for an hour, though without sleeping. *We are obliged to consider the possibility that Mr Bartleby may have killed his wife, Mrs Lilybanks . . .* Then he went on qualifying it, minimizing it, but the words had made Mrs Lilybanks realize that she had a faint suspicion too. It was possible, that was the awful thing. Then she realized that she had only one way of finding out, if she had the courage. Courage it would take, but the doubt she felt now would be worse to live with, she thought. Doubt in a thing like this was like a horrible pain itself. And this was not something she could pass on to Inspector Brockway, because if she did, he'd attach perhaps too much importance to it. Sydney might be quite innocent.

At last Mrs Lilybanks set out, and knocked on the Bartlebys' front door at 5.15, and at the same moment she remembered, uncomfortably, Alex Polk-Faraday's telephone call of two days ago that had been essentially to find out what she thought about Alicia's being gone, and about Sydney. Yes, Mr Polk-Faraday's mind had been quite ready for any suggestion of guilt she might have offered, and since he was supposed to be a friend and a partner of Sydney, Mrs Lilybanks hadn't liked that in him at all.

Sydney swung the door open and greeted her with a smile.

'How are you, Sydney?'

'Oh – more police calls today. I saw they came to you, too. But no news, I'm afraid.'

'No. I'm sorry, Sydney.'

'I suppose she's lying low – willing to stand the publicity to keep her seclusion, wherever she is. Her parents are going to be sore when she gets back. They're very proper people. Sit down, Mrs Lilybanks. Can I get you a Scotch? Or would you prefer tea?'

'Neither, thanks.'

'Neither?' he said, disappointed.

'I really came over,' she said, turning a little from him, looking down at the rug under her feet, 'to ask you where you bought this carpet. I need a carpet in my house. I wondered if you know a good place –'

Sydney's face looked startled for an instant, then he said, 'I got it at Abbott's in Debenham. They had a few orientals like this, not many, but you might give it a try. This was only – eight pounds, I think.'

Mrs Lilybanks sat down slowly on the sofa, watching Sydney. 'I really quite liked the old one you had here. I'd buy that from you,' she said, forcing a chuckle.

'But we haven't got it. I took it—' he smiled. 'I took that old carpet out and dumped it. We didn't want to give it house-room, and I doubt if anyone would've given ten shillings for it.'

Mrs Lilybanks heard her heart pounding under her green cardigan. Sydney had turned a little pale, she thought. He looked guilty. He acted guilty. Yet her unwillingness to believe he was guilty was keeping her from labelling him guilty, definitely. Now he was watching *her* carefully. 'Well, it's no matter,' Mrs Lilybanks said. 'I'll try Abbott's. I know it's very popular with everyone in the neighbourhood. – Well, Sydney, I mustn't keep you,' she said, getting up. 'You're probably still working.'

'Oh, I work off and on all the time,' he said more cheerfully. 'No fixed schedule. Interruptions don't bother me. In fact, I get a little lonely sometimes and enjoy an interruption.'

Now was the time to ask him for dinner tonight and let him see the binoculars, Mrs Lilybanks thought, talk to him about birdwatching in the early hours and see his reaction to that, but she was simply not up to it, not tonight. 'You must come again for dinner soon,' she said. She went to the door and turned. 'I pray that Alicia's all right, Sydney, wherever she is. And do let me know, won't you, if—'

He was still watching her warily. 'Oh, of course, Mrs Lilybanks, if I hear from her. You bet I will.'

She went slowly back to her own house. It was strange, she thought, that he hadn't asked her what the police had talked to her about. Wouldn't anybody have wanted to know, anybody who wasn't guilty?

Sydney at that moment was daydreaming over Alex's final script of 'The Second Sir Quentin', which had come in the morning post, a very fast job on Alex's part. Mrs Lilybanks had seen him with the old carpet on his shoulder. His silly pantomime of a corpse removal that morning had actually had an audience of one. And how did he feel? A little guilty, to be sure. As if the playacting of other people had convinced him of the validity of their suspicions, not his own playacting.

The telephone rang. Sydney ran down to answer it, thinking it might be a London friend calling to report a police visit. Today Inspector Brockway had asked him for the names of Alicia's closest friends, and he had given Inez and Carpie, the Polk-Faradays, and a couple of the schoolfriends whose names he had looked up in the address book – the only address book they had between them, the Inspector had ascertained, and which Alicia had not taken.

'Hello, you scheming murderer,' a sinister voice said.

Sydney laughed. 'Hello, Alex. I'm a happy, scheming murderer, thank you.'

'I'm just looking over your synopsis. Came in the afternoon post. Very nice.'

Sydney waited. This was about The Whip's assassination of an incipient dictator.

'The police called on me a few minutes ago,' Alex said. 'Good God, man, what've you been telling them down there? Or acting like?'

'What do you mean?'

'They act as if they suspect you of doing away with Alicia. What've you been doing, kidding them? That can be dangerous, you know. They were asking me about your character. You don't want me to tell 'em duh *troot*, do you?'

'I hope you made it properly black, befitting the creator of The Whip?'

'I said you were a highly suspicious character, addicted to wife-beating, had a morbid imagination, were fond of making up sinister words to songs, and obviously you'd persuaded your young *rich* wife to take a house in the country in a lonely spot – Blycom Heath – so you could do her in and bury her in the woods somewhere.' Alex gave his falsetto laugh. 'Ah-hah-ah-hah-ah-*hah*!' which he gave only when he was genuinely amused, and which sounded like an American take-off of an Englishman's laugh.

Sydney smiled. 'What did they really ask you?'

'Well, dear Sydney, I'm not far off the mark. They asked me how I thought you and Alicia were getting along. I said I thought quite well. Asked me if I thought Alicia were possibly seeing another man. I said I certainly didn't think so. Do you?'

'No. No, I don't,' Sydney said, but he did think it was possible. Alicia would have been most discreet, of course, and never have given him a hint. 'You haven't heard anything, have you? About any man in London?'

'Not a word, no. Not a breath of scandal.'

'Of course, you know she's six feet under in the woods near here, so I don't know why I'm wasting my breath talking about boy friends.'

'How did you kill her, Bartleby? You know everything's up now. You may as well come clean.'

'Pushed her down the stairs. Broke her neck. Then I buried her the next morning before dawn. Never felt better in my life. I'm glad I did it. I'd do it again, if I could.'

'Thank you, Mr Bartleby, I know our audience has enjoyed

your first-hand – uh – straight-from-the-killer's mouth comments on a sport millions of us would like to take up. If we could afford it.' Pips sounded on his last words, and he said hastily, 'Back to The Whip for both of us. Let's clinch this thing.'

They hung up.

By 10 o'clock, Sydney had finished his fine-toothed-comb reading of 'The Second Sir Quentin', and put it into a Manila envelope, not yet sealed, for posting tomorrow. He wondered what Alicia was doing at this moment. And why hadn't he heard from the Sneezums in the last four days? He looked up Inez and Carpie's number in the address book, and called them.

Carpie answered. Inez was out, and Carpie was staying in with the kids. 'No news, Syd, I gather,' she said in her resonant West Indian voice, though with an English accent.

'No news, no.'

'The police came by today. Inez was here. They came by just before six.'

'I had to give them your names, Carpie. They were interested in knowing who Alicia's London friends are. I hope you didn't mind.'

'Oh, of course not, Syd. But they were asking some very funny questions about you, we thought. Were you and Alicia happily married and had we ever seen you quarrelling. Naturally, we said no. I said you were a couple of artists and liked to be alone now and then. Asked us if we thought Alicia was seeing some other man. We said we didn't think so. You don't think so, do you, Syd?'

'No,' Sydney said.

'I hope they're not going to nadder you – just because they haven't anyone else.'

'If they do, I can't blame them. They've got a job to do.'

'Very true, but it's a nasty way of doing it. Don't ever lose your temper with them, Syd, it'll make things that much worse.'

'I'm perfectly good-tempered with them.' Then Sydney made the usual promise to ring in case he heard any news.

Sydney thought, as he was getting ready for bed, that it was very strange to be friends with an accuser who could not prove (Alex), and someone who could prove but would not accuse (Mrs Lilybanks). It was like being punished and exonerated at the same time. He might make a story out of that. And he jotted the thought down in his notebook.

Mrs Lilybanks stood at her dining-room table, slowly putting flowers into an orange and white bowl that had sockets for stems at the bottom. It was a quarter past 4, and Mrs Hawkins was upstairs cleaning the bathroom, which she always did last. The house looked especially nice, as all the furniture had had a polishing today. Sydney was coming for dinner at 7.30. Mrs Lilybanks went into the kitchen to start the tea water for Mrs Hawkins and herself.

Mrs Hawkins was a middle-sized, lean woman of fifty with unruly grey hair that stuck out from her black braid and bun. She had alert grey eyes, a lumpy nose, and a vaguely anxious manner – not a soothing person to be around, but she was extremely dependable, and had never missed coming to Mrs Lilybanks's house when she said she would, though her cleaning days had to vary, because of her own family's demands. She did not come every day now, as she had when Mrs Lilybanks had moved in, because Mrs Lilybanks had said it wasn't necessary. The daily visit had been an idea of Dr Underwood in London, seconded by Mrs Lilybanks's granddaughter Prissie, who had spoken to Mrs Hawkins when Mrs Lilybanks had moved in. But Mrs Hawkins did ring up every day between 3 and 4 p.m. to see if she was all right. Every day since the news of Alicia's disappearance had been in the papers, Mrs Hawkins had asked if Mrs Lilybanks had heard anything. And she was one of many in the neighbourhood who suspected Sydney of foul play of some kind, possibly even of murder, because Mrs Hawkins, like everyone else, had found out through the newspapers that Sydney had known for weeks that his wife wasn't at her parents' house, and hadn't told even his and his wife's best friends. 'That shows he was up to something,' Mrs Hawkins said several times to Mrs Lilybanks, and Mrs Lilybanks let it go by as best she could, knowing the hopelessness of explaining to someone like Mrs Hawkins that Alicia and Sydney, being painter and writer, might enjoy a vacation from each other for a while, one not knowing where the other was. But after the carpet conversation with Sydney, Mrs Hawkins's 'That shows he was up to something' began to eat into Mrs Lilybanks's defences, and she felt exhausted with trying to protect Sydney, and felt moreover that the common sense of simple people like Mrs Hawkins and Mr Fowler and Mr Veery, the butcher, might be right and her rationalizations wrong. But Mrs Lilybanks gave no sign to Mrs Hawkins that she was beginning to agree with her.

They had tea in the dining-room at the table where the flower bowl stood.

'No news, well, well,' Mrs Hawkins said, shaking her head, stirring her tea.

She had found that out two hours before, when she had arrived.

Mrs Lilybanks felt irked and also tongue-tied by the subject. Mrs Hawkins would have a fit if she knew Sydney Bartleby was coming for dinner, and she hoped Mrs Hawkins would not find out. But all it would take would be Rutledge driving past in his banged-up hauler, and seeing Sydney enter her house at 7.30. Mr Fowler would know the next morning, and so would everyone else.

'He looks so pleased with himself,' Mrs Hawkins went on. 'Sort of a smile on his face whenever you see him. Not like a man who's worried about his wife, oh, no.'

'I don't think he is worried, Mrs Hawkins. I knew Alicia slightly, you know.' Mrs Lilybanks realized she had used the past tense. 'She likes to go off by herself now and then.'

'Americans are violent. Everyone knows that. *I say*, when are they going to prove anything? The police should be digging around his house. Like the Christie case. Not waiting till a grave grows so old they can't find it. Is that window too chilly on you, Mrs Lilybanks?' she asked, meaning the kitchen window.

'No, no, thank you.'

'I raised it because I was using a good bit of ammonia in there this afternoon. Never liked the smell of ammonia.' She smiled with sudden cheer.

A few moments later, she was gone, promising to come two days from now, on Saturday, and to telephone tomorrow as usual. 'I hope you're keeping your doors well locked at night, Mrs Lilybanks. I don't envy you living here and neither does anybody else.'

The words lingered unpleasantly in Mrs Lilybanks's ears. She went upstairs and solemnly, with a feeling of ceremoniousness, got the binoculars from the top drawer of her bureau, carried them downstairs, and put them on a corner of the sideboard in the dining-room. Her eyes were drawn to an innocent-looking sparrow that alighted on the window-sill, looked her in the eyes for an instant, then flew off again. Mrs Lilybanks went upstairs to rest for a while before she came down and started her dinner.

Rap-rap-rap – rap-rap sounded on Mrs Lilybanks's front door at 7.35. She went to open it.

'Greetings, Mrs Lilybanks,' Sydney said. 'I bring some coals to Newcastle. Ipswich's best.' He handed her a bunch of long-stemmed red gladioli wrapped in tissue paper.

'Why, thank you, Sydney. How nice.'

'And this. For tonight or for the future.' He presented a bottle of red wine wrapped in purple tissue paper from the off-licence.

'Well! What's the occasion? Have you—' She couldn't ask if he had heard from Alicia.

'Mr Plummer of ITV likes The Whip a little more today. Hasn't bought it yet, but he likes our first three stories and— I'm rather optimistic and so is Alex. Mrs Lilybanks, you'll have to get a television set to see my masterpieces of flumdubbery. I'll buy you one.' Sydney waved a hand airily.

'No, you won't. I have been thinking of getting one before the winter. Sydney, that's marvellous. I do hope it works out. I know how you've laboured over that.'

Sydney stood on tiptoe, sniffing. He was wearing his best shoes, and he had given them a shine. 'What's that celestial smell emanating from yon humble country kitchen?'

'Duck. I hope you like duck. Just let me put these in water, and I'll make you a drink. No, you come and make yourself a drink.'

'With pleasure.' He followed her through the dining-room and into the kitchen.

They stayed nearly five minutes in the kitchen while Mrs Lilybanks put the gladioli into a tall vase and Sydney made himself a Scotch and water with ice and a Scotch and water without ice for Mrs Lilybanks. They chatted, but Mrs Lilybanks found herself a bit strained, because she couldn't or didn't want to say things like, 'What a pity you can't ring Alicia up somewhere and tell her about The Whip.'

They carried their drinks across the dining-room towards the living-room. Mrs Lilybanks turned before she entered the living-room, turned deliberately, and her right hand tightened and trembled on her glass at what she saw. Sydney had stopped with one foot extended for a step, and he was staring at the binoculars, his lips slightly parted, as they had parted when she mentioned the old carpet.

He saw her looking at him. 'Oh – those binoculars—' He rubbed his forehead quickly with his fingertips.

'Yes?'

'You got them in Ipswich, didn't you?' He advanced slowly towards her, and she went on into the living-room. 'At that second-hand shop.'

'Yes,' Mrs Lilybanks said. 'I bought them for bird-watching.'

'I started to buy them myself. That's why I was looking at them. One day I went to the shop – I'd seen them once before – and they weren't in the window. I was disappointed. That's why they gave me such a turn just now. It's like seeing something I thought I own. Owned.'

Mrs Lilybanks sat down on the sofa. Sydney looked too restless to sit down. She did not ask him to. 'I watch birds sometimes in the early morning. Around dawn.'

Again he looked at her warily, waiting for what she might say.

He's pretending all of this, Mrs Lilybanks thought suddenly. He'll probably put it in one of his stories. But what had been in the carpet that made it so heavy, and why had he carried it out before dawn? Neither of the Bartlebys liked to get up very early, not that early. Alicia had once said so. Why had Sydney been up so early the very day after Alicia left?

'Did you see in the paper today that that Frenchman made it in his boat? A twelve-foot boat from Marseille to Tangier?' Sydney asked.

And they talked of other things throughout dinner.

Mrs Lilybanks knew exactly what she ought to say, if she pursued the matter. It was only a question of courage, she felt. And why shouldn't she show some? Suppose Sydney got suddenly angry and struck her dead? She did not know from one week to the next when she might die. If Sydney did her harm, it would at least serve the purpose of proving his guilt. If he had killed Alicia, it was horrible, and it must be brought out into the open. Mrs Lilybanks approached the task with a weary resignation and a curious gloom, as she had approached the matter of dying, some six months before, when her doctor told her she might have only two more years in which to live.

'I saw you one morning early,' Mrs Lilybanks began pleasantly as they were having their coffee, 'through the binoculars. I think it was the morning you were disposing of your old carpet. You had something heavy over your shoulder.'

'Yes? Oh, yes,' Sydney said, and his cup chattered as he replaced it in his saucer. 'That was the carpet.'

The trembling was real, Mrs Lilybanks saw. No one could pretend this well, and Sydney was obviously trying to control himself. A start of fear tingled along Mrs Lilybanks's spine, then disappeared, the kind of tingle that might come from seeing a ghost. 'I was surprised to see you up that early. I often am, though. It was the morning after Alicia left, because I remember looking around for Alicia, too, then remembering she'd left the day before.'

'Oh, that day,' Sydney said.

She saw his underlip come out – in stubbornness, or was it a sign of defeat, that the game was up? – and he stared at the centre of the table. She wished desperately that he would say something. 'What did you do with the carpet?' she asked, still in a pleasant tone.

'Oh, I got rid of it – completely,' Sydney said just as pleasantly.

'You buried it,' Mrs Lilybanks said with a try at a smile.

'Yes.' Now there was a glint in his eyes like madness, as if he meant to reach across the table and strike her. Then just as suddenly, it went away. 'Yes, I thought the thing had some moths in it – so it was just as well to bury it. Or burn it, but I didn't want people to think the forest was on fire.'

'You buried it in a forest?'

'No, just out in the country.' He waved a hand vaguely.

'Is that why you got up so early? So you wouldn't be seen?' Mrs Lilybanks sat stiffly now. Her heart had stepped up its beats. She put out her half-finished cigarette, and decided to have not a drop more coffee.

'I suppose so,' Sydney said, watching her.

'What was in the carpet?'

Sydney's right hand was clenched beside his cup and saucer, his thumb tucked into his fist. He was going to break out in a cold sweat in a moment, she thought. Or burst out in a fury and strike her.

'You seem to be accusing me. Like Alex and Mrs Hawkins and Mr Fowler and all the rest. Like the police.' His voice was not loud, but it shook.

'I'm not accusing you of anything. Really. I am asking.'

'You think I killed Alicia and carried her body out in the carpet and buried her. You're trying to prove it.'

'I'm not trying to prove anything.'

'Yes, you are. Testing me. Offering to buy the old carpet, when you'd seen me carrying it out of the house.'

She didn't need to test him, she thought. Here was proof enough. She felt anything but triumphant. She could have collapsed gratefully on the table, laid her head down, disappeared. 'If you tell me there was nothing in the carpet, then I'll believe you. And I do not intend to tell anyone that I saw you with the carpet – not the neighbours and not the police.'

He still looked at her in a frightened way. 'I'm not sure I believe that.'

'You should. I could have told the police this week – last week – that I saw you carrying a carpet to your car, driving away with it. But I didn't.'

'Why?'

Mrs Lilybanks didn't want to say, because she hadn't been sure it was important until now. 'If you are guilty of anything, it will come out. I leave it to you, Sydney, entirely.' Now she saw the perspiration on his forehead. He continued to stare at her. 'I have some brandy in the house. Would you like some?'

'Yes. Yes, please.'

She was relieved that he accepted it, that he had answered politely. It was the brandy she kept for herself, as medicine, but she had not taken any since she had moved into the cottage. She brought a large stemmed glass and gave Sydney a good measure. He began to sip it, leaning a little over the table.

'Some more coffee,' Mrs Lilybanks said, pouring some from the silver pot into Sydney's cup.

'This can't go on – like this,' Sydney said, as if to himself.

'What can't?'

'Your not saying – that you saw anything.'

She tried to look at him calmly. 'You don't know me well, perhaps. I can keep my promises. This is a promise to myself, not to you. It's not my business to bring suspicion against anyone, Sydney. Especially suspicion that may be false.'

He was calming down. Perhaps the brandy was helping. He even started talking about television sets, about Suffolk's being good for reception because it was flat. But he was ill at ease, and he looked at her with a different eye.

'Prissie's coming down this weekend,' Mrs Lilybanks said. 'You must meet her this time. I'm sorry you missed her the last time.' She had been waiting for an opportunity to say that, the most mitigating thing she could possibly say, she thought, for what person would introduce a young granddaughter to someone she thought was a murderer?

'I'd like to,' Sydney replied.

He smoked only part of a cigarette in the living-room, and then took his leave, without offering to help her with the dishes as he had on other occasions. Mrs Lilybanks sat on the sofa for several minutes, trying to collect herself. She had endangered herself, certainly, but perhaps the danger point was past now. Sydney knew now he was open to serious suspicion, and if he were guilty, Mrs Lilybanks thought, his nervousness would be the thing that would betray him. That and the pressure of guilt in which she strongly believed. Most murderers had a great compulsion to confess, to be caught. She had started the ball rolling, as Sydney might say, so all in all she did not think she had done badly that evening. Furthermore, she had discovered something: she really believed Sydney had done away with Alicia.

18

The following morning, Mrs Sneezum telephoned Sydney and said that she and her husband would like to come and see him in the afternoon. Just that, brief and crisp. Sydney of course said he would be very glad to see them. They would arrive around 3 p.m., said Mrs Sneezum.

After they had hung up, Sydney wandered about the house, straightening things, though the place looked quite presentable, he thought. Sydney did remove the newspaper photograph-with-balloon from the bathroom wall, which he realized Mrs Lilybanks must have seen on the one or two occasions she had visited the loo. He supposed the Sneezums, if they were doing a good job of casing the place, might call on Mrs Lilybanks, too. Alicia must have told her mother a great deal about her.

This was Saturday, Sydney realized, the day Mrs Lilybanks's granddaughter Prissie would arrive. A busy day. Reluctantly, he left a Whip synopsis he was stewing over, and took the car to Blycom Heath for some shopping. His synopsis was nearly done, and needed only one more twist to complete it. In this story, his fifth, The Whip assumed a feminine dress in order to impersonate a wealthy elderly woman who had been presumed dead. The

Whip managed to fool even the woman's husband, not to mention the lawyers, and got his hands on a great deal of cash and jewels before disappearing. It was a lively plot, full of laughs, and Sydney was ready to chalk up his fifth Whip winner. He needed a title. 'Skirting the Issue'? Ugh.

'Morning, Mr Veery,' Sydney said to the butcher.

'Morning.' Mr Veery gave a glum nod, then proceeded to look at Sydney's face, his hands, his clothes with a stunned expression as if he might not hear Sydney's order when it came.

'Any nice steaks today?' Sydney asked.

Sydney bought two steaks and a half pound of streaky bacon, and Mr Veery handed him the package, then his change, as if fearful his fingertips might come in contact with Sydney's palm. A customer edged away as Sydney went to the door, yet stared at him all the while, too. Sydney looked back through the window, and saw Mr Veery and the woman already in animated conversation.

Mrs Lilybanks rang and asked if he would come for strawberries and coffee with her and Prissie around 2.30 that afternoon. Sydney had noticed a red Viva, which had arrived while he was at the butcher's, in front of Mrs Lilybanks's house.

'Yes, thanks, I'd like to,' Sydney said. 'I can't stay long, because Mr and Mrs Sneezum are coming at three. Alicia's parents.' His voice was as open and cheerful as if Thursday night had never happened.

Mrs Lilybanks sounded just as usual also.

He supposed he had frightened Mrs Lilybanks that night, but she had also frightened him. His pretending, which he had meant to be comical or amusing, only to himself, had suddenly become real. No one could produce a cold sweat on the forehead just by trying to, Sydney thought, not the greatest actor. Well, he knew what it felt like, all right, to be suspected of murder by a nice old lady. It felt awful, unspeakably embarrassing, shameful, bizarre, even mad.

At 2.15, he finished his synopsis, then went over to Mrs Lilybanks's. Priscilla Holloway was what Sydney thought a knock-out, a smallish, slender but well-rounded girl with long straight brown hair, almond eyes, a smooth olive complexion, and a fantastic sex appeal that perhaps she, and probably Mrs Lilybanks, was unaware of. Prissie affected an extremely calm and poised manner, perhaps because she was trying to look older and more sophisticated than she was. And also perhaps because Mrs Lilybanks had told her something about him and about Alicia's disappearance, but Sydney did not think Mrs Lilybanks had told her of her suspicions. Prissie looked at him as if she thought he were a man of mystery, but not a criminal.

Alicia was not mentioned in the half hour he spent with them. They talked about London, a play Prissie had a bit part in now called *A Cup of Summer*, and she asked Sydney about his television series, which she had heard about from her grandmother.

'Grannie, you haven't shown me your paintings yet,' Prissie said.

'Oh, I will, but not now, because Sydney can't stay very long, and he's seen most of them anyway.'

'Yes, I must go,' said Sydney, getting up. 'You haven't met the Sneezums, have you, Mrs Lilybanks?'

'No. I'd like to. Would you like to ask them over for some tea?'

'Oh, thanks, I was going to give them tea myself. I'll give you a ring later and we'll see how things are.' He looked at Mrs Lilybanks in a frank, pleasant way. 'Thanks so much for the strawberries. Nice to have met you, Miss Holloway.' He left.

The Sneezums were ten minutes early. Looking at them as they got out of their grey Mercedes-Benz, Sydney thought they both looked older, that the strain of anxiety showed in both their faces. Mr Sneezum was a smallish, slight man with thin red hair and a pale complexion. His wife was as tall if not taller, blonde and a bit chinless, though with determined nose and eyes. Alicia was a luckily handsome combination of both of them.

'Hello, Sydney,' Mrs Sneezum said as she came through the gate, though without extending her hand. 'How are you?'

Sydney stood midway on the flagstones of the front walk. 'Well enough, thank you. How are you?'

They went into the house. Sydney offered them sherry, which they declined, then tea, which they also refused, saying it was a bit early. They both looked around the living-room as if for clues to the mystery of Alicia's departure. For the next five minutes or so, Mrs Sneezum went over the questions she had been asking Sydney for the past weeks on the telephone, but now Sydney realized that she was mainly interested in seeing his face as he gave his answers. Mr Sneezum sat quietly, concentrating upon Sydney also, and looking like a smaller and more wizened effigy of Sinclair Lewis.

'You're sure she didn't *change* trains at Ipswich,' said Mrs Sneezum, 'get off the one she was on and take another north-bound, for instance?'

'I saw the train move off,' Sydney replied. 'We – waved to each other.' They hadn't waved, but he had seen the train move off.

Mrs Sneezum rested her cool, calculating grey eyes on him. 'Um-hm. The police have tried to find a railway official who remembered seeing Alicia getting on that morning or—'

'Oh, that would be difficult, I suppose,' Sydney interrupted, with a smile.

'Yes. No one does remember.' Mrs Sneezum glanced at her husband, who only looked glum and rubbed a forefinger along his nose. She sat up on the sofa and recrossed her slender legs. She wore a black and blue printed silk dress, and gave off a scent of perfume Sydney could not identify, probably because its costliness was out of the range of his acquaintance. 'I must ask you, Sydney, if you'd had any serious quarrel with Alicia just before she left?'

'No. Honestly, Mrs Sneezum.' He moistened his lips and raised his hands from his knees and brought them gently down again. 'She wanted to be alone for a while and paint, and she said she'd get in touch with me when she wanted to see me again – or come home. That's why I'm staying here when I could go to a little town for a change of scene myself. I'd like to be here when she writes or telephones.' He was rattling on again, he realized, and he could feel the disbelief his over-explaining had generated. He wondered if they were thinking, 'Sydney is staying close to home, because he wants to guard the body in the garden. Look how long Christie lived at his place.' Sydney shrugged involuntarily, and saw Mrs Sneezum notice it.

'Writers and painters. They think they know it all.' Mrs Sneezum looked to her husband for support.

'Oh, so do all young people,' he said feebly and grumpily.

'They refuse to live the way the rest of society lives, quietly and calmly, taking the ups and the downs, and then they're thrown by the strains their bizarre lives put upon them. You know what I mean, Hartley.' She looked at him again.

But Hartley wasn't saying anything this time, only looking at the carpet with pursed lips and raised eyebrows.

'In my opinion, the Bohemian life has no place in ordinary, everyday society. The people who lead it know that they are not behaving the way society means them to behave, means and intends them to behave, and consequently they crack up under their own philosophy – because it's false and pretended.'

A false god, Sydney thought, as he listened with solemn respect, like someone at a church sermon. Society to Mrs Sneezum was like some abstract god – very abstract – to whom unquestioning devotion and dedication was due.

'Therefore Alicia is paying,' Mrs Sneezum said heavily, still sitting up straight, and looking at Sydney.

'Yes,' Sydney murmured automatically.

'She was unhappy – naturally.' Mrs Sneezum looked at Sydney with satisfaction, upholder of her way of life, of her daughter's natural way of life, which her daughter had gone against.

'Yes,' Sydney said.

They all pondered this in a moment of silent prayer.

Then Sydney said, 'My neighbour, Mrs Lilybanks, asked me to ask you both if you'd like to come over for tea around four. She got to know Alicia quite well. Probably Alicia's mentioned her.'

Mrs Sneezum lifted her head quizzically to her husband. 'I don't know, Hartley. What do you think? Of course we should let Mrs Lilybanks know. Yes, I have heard Alicia speak of her,' she added to Sydney.

'Might have to be getting back a little sooner than that,' Hartley Sneezum put in.

Sydney showed them Alicia's room upstairs, at Mrs Sneezum's request, and Mrs Sneezum commented indifferently and negatively on some of Alicia's latest abstracts.

'She did quite a good portrait of Mrs Lilybanks,' Sydney said. 'It's downstairs in the living-room. Maybe you didn't notice it.'

Mrs Sneezum hadn't but covered up the fact by saying, 'Oh, yes. I must look at that again.'

They left the house at ten to 4. On the front walk, Mrs Sneezum looked toward Mrs Lilybanks's house and said vaguely, 'We might drop in at Mrs Lilybanks's, Hartley, just to meet her, but we mustn't stay for tea.'

'No,' Hartley agreed.

They all said good-bye politely, promised to get in touch at once in case of news, and then Sydney went back into the house. He knew the Sneezums would stay at Mrs Lilybanks's for at least half an hour, and would certainly accept tea. They had simply eased him out of it so they could speak to Mrs Lilybanks alone. But since Prissie was there, Sydney thought, there would be a limit to what Mrs Lilybanks would tell them. He didn't think she would tell them about the carpet, however, whether Prissie was there or not.

Fifteen minutes later, a car motor started, and Sydney stood up to see out the window. Prissie's red Viva was moving off, in the direction of Ipswich and London.

19

Mrs Lilybanks had been a little surprised to see the Sneezums without Sydney, and she immediately grasped the import. The first few minutes, while Prissie had been with them, had gone easily enough, but the tension began when Prissie left. The Sneezums pumped her, slowly, gently and inexorably. What did she really think of Sydney's and Alicia's Bohemian life? Of that unkempt front lawn, so bad for the morale, really? Mrs Lilybanks managed to get a polite smile from the Sneezums with some of her tolerant replies, but the smiles were brief, and Mrs Sneezum returned to the attack.

'I never trusted Sydney to make her happy,' said Mrs Sneezum. 'The marriage was quite without our wholehearted approval, you know, but we didn't want to stand in the way like a pair of grim, old-fashioned parents. But we feared the worst, didn't we, Hartley?'

'Yes, we did,' Hartley Sneezum confirmed.

'Alicia's always thought she wanted her own way, and she's usually had it. She had her own way when she married Sydney. She can go along all right just so far and then –' Mrs Sneezum slapped the back of one hand into the palm of the other. 'She is *not* capable of strain, whatever she may think. She needs a stable life, the life she was brought up to lead. I didn't care much for Sydney Bartleby when she married him, and I don't like his manner now, quite frankly,' said Mrs Sneezum, looking quite frankly at Mrs Lilybanks.

'What do you mean by his manner now?' asked Mrs Lilybanks.

'He doesn't act like a man whose wife is missing,' Mrs Sneezum asserted. 'Not like my idea of the way a husband should react. He's so cool about it. It's as if he knows where she is and isn't saying. But I don't think he does. I don't think he *cares*, that's what I mean to say. I hope you'll forgive me for speaking so frankly, Mrs Lilybanks, but this is a serious matter and we've both been upset for a month. Do you think Alicia and Sydney have some secret agreement they're not letting anybody in on?'

Mrs Lilybanks lifted the teapot to pour more tea, but was met by a small shake of the head from Mrs Sneezum. 'Sydney told me – and so did Alicia – they wanted to be apart for a while.'

'Yes, I've heard that till I'm quite sick of it. So is Hartley. I meant a more serious agreement – like a divorce.'

'Oh, certainly not that I know of,' Mrs Lilybanks said. 'But then, Alicia wouldn't have told me of anything like that, I think.'

'She never mentioned any other man?' asked Mrs Sneezum.

'No, indeed.'

'We have to think of all sorts of unpleasant possibilities,' Mrs Sneezum said. Then, after a pause, 'Even that Sydney might have killed her.'

Mrs Lilybanks looked at Mrs Sneezum, who was watching her, plainly to see if the same idea had occurred to her. Mr Sneezum showed no reaction, so he and his wife must have talked about this before.

'Has that crossed your mind?' asked Mrs Sneezum.

'Clarissa,' said Mr Sneezum gently, 'don't let your imagination run away with you.'

'Look at the facts,' said his wife with grim calm. 'The police haven't found Alicia in Brighton or anywhere else. She hasn't come forth, though her pictures were in every newspaper in England more than a week ago. Sydney Bartleby never had a bean in his life, and he stands to gain a good deal if Alicia's dead.'

'Really, my dear, it's too much like a detective story.'

'That's what they all say until it's too late,' his wife replied. 'I think it's time for a good detective myself.' She waited for Mrs Lilybanks to say something.

Mrs Lilybanks could not speak, and several seconds passed.

'I hope you can feel free and will be honest enough to tell me if you suspect Sydney of any foul play, Mrs Lilybanks. If you've noticed anything – even a quarrel they had . . .'

Mrs Lilybanks could see the tears in Alicia's mother's eyes. She felt kindly towards her then, as she had not before. 'I'm sure they had their small quarrels, like any other married couple.'

'You sound as if you saw some. When?'

'Oh—' Mrs Lilybanks floundered. 'A raised voice in the kitchen one night when I was there for dinner. It was nothing, it lasted a second. I'm sure every couple does it.'

'Whose voice?'

'Sydney's. It was only for an instant.'

Mrs Sneezum did not appear satisfied with this. 'And a quarrel just before Alicia left?'

'No. I certainly didn't hear of any,' Mrs Lilybanks replied.

'Did you ever see him strike her?' asked Mrs Sneezum.

'Oh, dear, no.'

'So you – like Sydney?'

Mrs Lilybanks took a breath and said carefully, 'I find him interesting – and very amusing sometimes. He's full of ideas.'

'For stories that he can't sell.'

'Well – there's some hope about his Whip series. Didn't he mention it? They're television plays.'

'Oh.' Mrs Sneezum glanced at her husband, who showed no interest in this information. 'I suppose he's doing them with Alex Polk-Faraday.'

'Yes, I think he is,' said Mrs Lilybanks.

'There's a nice young man. Not too proud to take a job, even if he does want to be a writer.'

Mrs Lilybanks said nothing, and felt her liking for Mrs Sneezum ebb again. But shouldn't she, in all fairness, tell her about the carpet incident, she wondered. It would be breaking her promise to Sydney, but wasn't it cowardly to withhold information just for fear of being hated by a guilty man? Or called a troublemaker by an innocent one? If Mrs Sneezum hadn't been such an emotional type, Mrs Lilybanks might have told the Sneezums, cautioning them to speak quietly to the police about it, to present the facts – blurred as they were by the dawn light and her own failing eyes – and let the police do the rest, but Mrs Lilybanks knew she could not trust Mrs Sneezum to do it coolly.

'So you like Sydney,' Mrs Sneezum said.

'My dear, I don't think you should quiz our hostess so thoroughly,' said Mr Sneezum, coming down on the last word.

The Sneezums got up a few moments later and took their leave, thanking Mrs Lilybanks for her tea. Mrs Lilybanks was touched by the fact Mrs Sneezum had an impulse to kiss her on the cheek, and just restrained herself. Even Mr Sneezum held her hand warmly in both his for an instant.

'Alicia speaks so well of you,' Mr Sneezum said. 'She's very fond of you.'

'That's why I think it's strange she hasn't written to her, dear,' said Mrs Sneezum.

They went out to their car, which was near Sydney's front door.

Mrs Lilybanks put away the tea things, put the dishes in the sink ready for washing, then forced herself to the telephone. She had come to a decision while talking to the Sneezums, and didn't want to backslide about it. She called the police in Ipswich and asked to speak to Inspector Brockway. Inspector Brockway was not in.

'I have something to tell him that I think may be of importance,' she said. 'It's about Alicia Bartleby.'

'Yes? Well, can I take the message for you, Mrs Lilybanks?'

'No. Thank you. I don't want to give it over the telephone. I'd like to speak to the Inspector in person.'

They said they could get a message to him by 7 p.m., and if he were not able to come to her house then, they would ask him to ring her. Mrs Lilybanks told them she would be in all evening.

When she hung up, she realized that in order to tell the whole truth, she would have to tell Inspector Brockway about the sudden uproar from Sydney the evening Alicia dropped a glass. It may have ended there, but it certainly showed that Sydney had some violence in him. Alicia had told her of two occasions when Sydney had struck her. *Sydney can get into an absolute fury – just like that*, Alicia had said, and snapped her finger. It had crossed Mrs Lilybanks's mind that Alicia might be off on some spree of her own, perhaps even with a man friend, by way of bolstering her ego and getting back at Sydney. After the visit from the Sneezums, this somehow seemed less likely to Mrs Lilybanks, and it seemed more likely that Sydney had gone too far in one of his tempers. Inspector Brockway had asked her what she thought of Sydney's character, or rather his temperament. She could imagine Sydney angry enough to kill someone, and imagine him cool enough afterward to carry it off, at least as well as he was carrying it off now.

Inspector Brockway rang at 7.20, and came to Mrs Lilybanks's house at a quarter to 9.

From Mrs Lilybanks's house, he went next door to speak to Sydney Bartleby.

20

Sitting on the living-room sofa, with the gramophone playing *Sacre du Printemps*, Sydney wrote in his little brown notebook:

Aug. 13. I can't really imagine it to my satisfaction. Something always seems to be missing. I think the murderer is not within us all, as I feel too awful imagining even as far as I can get. Or does this mean I'm getting near the truth? A combination of mental, even physical discomfort, extreme malaise, sordidness, disconnection with the human race, a sense of showing a mask to the world, of shame at one's own cruelty, which cannot entirely be assuaged by thinking of or inventing childhood experiences that may have led to it. Some killers are cocky. Or do they just try not to think, or are they incapable? I am not satisfied with my imaginings, and I suppose the trouble is, I am not really a killer. I don't suppose a real killer would have the same thoughts and feelings as I. Why should he? My reactions are the result of conditioning, and I prefer to call conditioning sets of attitudes. I have more than I thought.

He was looking into space with his pen poised, when an

unexpected knock came at the door, a solid knock, not Mrs Lilybanks's. Sydney put his pen down, closed his notebook and went to the door. He was surprised to see Brockway's huge form.

'Professor Brockway! Inspector – excuse me,' Sydney said. Mrs Lilybanks had told the Sneezums about the carpet burial, Sydney thought, but the realization did not bring his usual seizure of guilt.

'Good evening,' said Inspector Brockway, bringing his fist up to his mouth and coughing explosively. 'Hope I'm not intruding.'

Sydney was so close, he jumped at the cough. 'Not at all. Come in. I'll turn this off.' He went to the gramophone and stopped it.

The Inspector unbuttoned the jacket of his blue and brown tweed suit, removed his hat and took a chair. 'I understand you saw the Sneezums today.'

'Yes, I did. They came by around three.'

'No news, I take it?'

'No.'

'And you've had none either?' Inspector Brockway's eyes looked somewhat troubledly about the room, at the coffee table, alighted for an instant on the brown notebook which was worn flabby from time more than use, then lifted to Sydney's face again.

'No.' Sydney wished the notebook were upstairs, out of sight. Now the Inspector was actually touching it with the fingertips of his right hand, pushing it a couple of inches away from him.

'Mrs Lilybanks told me this evening of seeing you with a carpet that you said you buried somewhere. Is that true?'

'Yes,' Sydney said, his voice dramatically and quite accidentally breaking. 'An old carpet with moth eggs in it. I didn't want to burn it, and the garbage gets taken away only once a fortnight, so I buried it.'

'When did you bury it?' the Inspector asked.

'Oh – weeks ago.'

'In July?'

'Yes.'

'Do you remember exactly when in July?'

'Yes, it was just after my wife left, I remember. I woke up early – the day after she left.'

'Almost before dawn?'

'Yes.' Go straight through, he told himself. The facts, damning though they might be.

'Where did you bury it?'

'Somewhere near Parham. On the Parham road from here, in the woods.'

The Inspector frowned and looked at him. 'Tell me how you did it.'

Sydney took a deep and genuinely painful breath. I pushed her down the stairs first, he thought. Kept her body overnight. He smoothed his hair with his hand, and stared blankly at the opposite side of the room, then looked at Brockway. 'I just dug a hole with a fork.'

Inspector Brockway produced a package of cigarettes, and extended it to Sydney, but Sydney shook his head. It was the first time the Inspector had smoked in his presence. Was he relaxing, now that the case was solved? 'I suppose you could find the spot again?'

'I think so. Have a go at it, anyway,' Sydney said with a weak smile. It was indeed all coming true.

'Good.' The Inspector exhaled his first draught, stood up and approached the window, then coughed in the explosive way that made Sydney jump again, and suddenly he knew what the cough reminded him of: a foot smashing down on an empty pine crate, splintering it. 'It's not dark yet. Shall we give it a try?' asked the Inspector.

'Certainly.'

The Inspector's car was in front of Mrs Lilybanks's house. He knew the road to Parham, and Sydney guided him only as they approached the straight section of road where the woods lay.

'It's on the left,' said Sydney. 'Slow down a bit.'

The Inspector did.

Sydney led him into the forest, looking all around him and trying to remember certain trees, clumps of bush, and failing. Well, if he failed, so what? Sydney looked behind him, trying to recall the distance the spot had been from the road and his car. 'There's more undergrowth since I was here.'

'Very likely, but do your best.'

Sydney advanced slowly. At a small clearing, or emptyish place, he stopped and looked at the ground. 'This could be the spot.'

The Inspector was looking at the ground, which showed no sign of having been dug up anywhere. 'All right. I'll put a marker on this and we'll come back tomorrow.' He tore a leaf from his notebook, and set a stone on it.

They made their way back to the Inspector's car. He drove in silence back to Sydney's house, and dropped him off with a good night.

That was the cool English way of doing things, Sydney thought. Let the murderer sleep in his own bed once more. Drop him at his house, bid him good night, the rope would jerk soon enough on his neck. Sydney imagined a corpse in the rug. Alicia barely recognizable, and himself, now, trying to sleep on this climactic night, writhing with terror, because Mrs Lilybanks had seen him with the carpet and put the police on to him. He had only hours more of freedom. A murderer, Sydney thought, a psychopath might go now to Mrs Lilybanks and strangle her while he could, in revenge and anger. It was a wonder, in fact, the police hadn't put a guard on Mrs Lilybanks's house, or advised her to leave, and this thought made him get out of bed and look.

It was so black, he could not have seen a parked car, or a standing man, if there had been one on the road. Mrs Lilybanks might be staying with a friend in the neighbourhood. Or a man might be inside the house, installed in Mrs Lilybanks's guest-room. Sydney went back to bed. He tried to do some more imagining, but since he was tired, he soon fell asleep.

The next morning around 8, Sydney saw Mrs Lilybanks pouring water as usual into the birdbath on her back lawn. He thought briefly of the police digging away, uncovering an empty and quite unbloodstained carpet, then started making his coffee. Before he sat down to work upstairs, he looked out of his window again at Mrs Lilybanks's house. Her windows sparkled, but there was no sign of her now. Ordinarily, she did a bit of gardening at this time. She was probably feeling very uneasy, Sydney thought, might even be in an agony of anxiety, and he ought to say something to reassure her. She would be thinking he was resentful of her talking to the Inspector, of her breaking her promise to him. But Sydney thought he would wait to speak to her until the police had told him they had found nothing in the carpet. Of course she would think him a fool for implying on Saturday night that there was something in the carpet, and he'd have to explain that by saying he had let his imagination run away with him, that he had been joking (a too grim joke, Mrs Lilybanks would dislike him for that, but so be it), or he could say he had been a victim of temporary aberration, hallucination, terror, worry, and he had really felt that night that he had done away with Alicia. All his explanations would be unsatisfactory, but the important thing was to tell her as soon as possible that there wasn't anything in the carpet. (What? I don't believe it, he'd say to the police. Somebody's stolen my corpse? I won't have it! Look again.) Sydney turned his attention to his new Whip idea.

The telephone rang a little after 10 a.m.

'Inspector Brockway here. There's no carpet buried in that area you pointed out last night. Can you come over now, Mr Bartleby? Maybe you'll do better in daylight.'

Sydney left the house within three minutes. What a pity, the poor boys digging all morning in that tough ground! They had probably been at it since 6 a.m.

He found the Inspector smoking a cigarette and talking to the young blond constable of Blycom Heath beside the Inspector's car. Sydney drew up behind them. 'Good morning, Inspector.' 'Good morning,' to the constable. 'I'm sorry I misdirected you. It might be a good idea if I walk up the road a little. Maybe I'll recognize something.'

'Just as you like,' said the Inspector.

Sydney walked on, along the left side of the road, paying attention to the woods, but every yard of them looked like the next. He began to walk back. When he reached the Inspector, who was now leaning against his car, he said:

'Sorry, Inspector, I don't think it's up there. I still think it's around here, so I'll walk in a ways.'

'Go ahead,' said the Inspector, and began to follow Sydney.

After twenty or thirty paces, Sydney saw the black figures of a couple of police, one seated on something, one knocking his spade against a tree to get the dirt off. Sydney headed towards them. 'No luck, I hear,' he said. 'I'm sorry for all the trouble.'

The ground was torn up as if they had started to make a square dugout. Both officers had unbuttoned their tunics.

'Ground's firm as anything here,' said the standing officer.

'But I'm sure it's around here,' Sydney said, and went on, a bit to his right and parallel with the road that was now out of sight. Clinging vines clutched at his trousers. He slipped on something, and saw with revulsion that it was a black slug five inches long. He reached a small clear area and hesitated. 'It could have been here,' he said to the constable who was just behind him.

The constable drew a penknife and made two downward

strokes in a young tree, then peeled off the bark so it showed white. The Inspector was looking at the ground and stamping on it.

Sydney cut in toward the road. He came to another spot that might have been it, but he favoured the last spot. 'It's a pity the grass grew up so much. That's why it's hard to find.'

'A lot of time passed. Nearly two months,' said the constable.

The body would be in foul condition, Sydney supposed he was thinking. 'I can't do any better than this,' Sydney said, stopping again at the place where the constable had marked the tree. He started as Inspector Brockway appeared through the woods in front of him.

'How deep is it?' asked the Inspector.

'About four feet, I think,' Sydney replied. 'That may be why they didn't find it at the first place. I'd like to see how deep they went.' He walked on past the Inspector.

The constable and the Inspector followed him.

At the first site, Sydney asked permission, and took a spade. He began poking at the soil near a big tree, and tossed several clods of dark earth to one side. But below where the officers had dug, the ground was firm, the roots looked undisturbed, and that was all there was to it. 'I can't understand it,' Sydney said.

The four men were standing about, watching him.

'Well, boys, I think we'd better go a little deeper here, just where Mr Bartleby was digging,' the Inspector said, 'and there's another spot farther on.'

The officers returned gloomily to their task, and the second spade was put to use.

Sydney watched them a few moments, then said to the Inspector, 'Is there any reason for me to stay? I have some work to do at home.'

The Inspector said there wasn't, and told Sydney he would give him a ring later.

Sydney made his way back to the car. By now, there was a faint trail in the grass to where the men were digging.

At 1 o'clock, the Inspector rang to say they had dug in the second spot also and found nothing.

Sydney pushed his fingers through his hair and thought, murderer imagines murder, carpet, corpse, burial, everything. 'That's strange. The carpet's at full length – a roll – it should be easy to find.'

The Inspector said they would try again after lunch, in the third spot Sydney had led them to.

Give them time, Sydney thought, they'd find it, because he was sure it was there. He went back to his synopsis. The Whip had been summoned by the police (who remained ignorant of his criminal activities) to help in capturing a Paddington-based gang of big-money robbers. Pretending to be a recently sprung jailbird, The Whip had joined the Paddington band in order to work from the inside, and was now making himself familiar with the band's fences, preparatory to turning some in to the police and keeping the cleverest one of them for his personal use.

By 4, there was no ring from Brockway.

His thoughts moved suddenly to Alicia. Where the hell was she? What was she doing? Who was keeping her? There must be somebody keeping her. She had rich friends, but would she ask them for fifty pounds in a situation like this? No. If a man were keeping her, she must be sleeping with him. Sydney frowned, wounded and puzzled. He got up then from his desk and did no more work that day.

Around 5 o'clock Sydney heard the telephone from the back yard, where he was mucking about in the compost heap, and went running into the house to get it.

'Hello, Sydney. This is Elspeth Cragge. How are you?'

'Oh. All right, thanks. And you?'

'Any news from Alicia? ...'

And so it went for five minutes or so. Elspeth Cragge had rung once before. She had just had a baby. She and her husband lived in Woodbridge, and they were rather boring people. Her questions and remarks were boring, and to liven things up, Sydney was tempted to say that the police were digging for an old carpet he had buried, with the idea that Alicia's body might be in it, but Elspeth didn't deserve this interesting information, and he might hold up a call from the police if he went into it with her, so he concluded the conversation as quickly as he politely could.

'Whew!' he said, after he had hung up.

The police telephoned just after 6. Inspector Brockway said:

'Well! We finally found it, Mr Bartleby. In the fifth spot we tried.'

'Good heavens. I am sorry.'

'Yes. Well, all in a day's work.' He chuckled. 'You're quite right, it's an old mothy carpet, more mildew than moths just now, I'd say.'

'Ha-ha. Yes. I can imagine.'

'You must have been in an energetic mood that day.'

Yes. Go a little deeper and you'll find the corpse, Sydney thought of saying. The carpet is just a blind. 'Yes. Actually – I wanted to dig as deeply as if I were really burying something, because I need it for one of my stories. How many roots does one strike, how long does it take? – you know.'

'The problems of a fiction writer,' the Inspector said.

'Yes. For television. Thank you very much for ringing me, Inspector.'

'You'll be in some time tomorrow?'

Tomorrow was Monday. 'Oh, yes. All day in principle, except for a little shopping.'

'I'll drop in some time in the afternoon.'

Sydney took a bath and changed into a better pressed pair of trousers and a clean shirt. He hurried, not wanting Brockway to

150

beat him in telling Mrs Lilybanks the news, a possibility that occurred to Sydney in the middle of his bath. Take her some flowers, a rose from the garden? A cauliflower? No, don't be silly about it. He had taken her some Brussels sprouts last week. Just a quiet visit, and he'd say he hadn't come over earlier because he had been helping the police and awaiting their telephone call.

He walked to Mrs Lilybanks's house with a serious, upright air, turned in at her front walk, tried to see from several yards away if she were in the living-room, then decided to go to the kitchen door. 'Mrs Lilybanks?' He tried the door, which opened. She was not in the kitchen. 'Mrs Lilybanks?' He walked on into the living-room.

Mrs Lilybanks stood in the living-room facing him with her back to the sofa, clutching her fist against her chest. For an instant, Sydney thought she was holding something in her hand, but her fist was only pressed against her body under her left breast.

'Mrs Lilybanks? What's the matter?' Sidney came towards her.

Her face was ghastly pale, her mouth open, as if she'd just had a terrible shock. She made a shrill, quavering sound, collapsed backward on the sofa, and slid off it to the floor before Sydney could reach her.

'Here. Let me lift you on the sofa.'

She was absolutely limp and he had difficulty raising her.

'Have you some medicine? Tell me where it is – your medicine, Mrs Lilybanks.' Sydney left her and went to the kitchen, wet a dishcloth and came running back with it. He thought of giving her water, but that might have been dangerous, as she looked in no condition even to swallow. He found some brandy in the kitchen, and brought some in a teacup, thinking the smell might revive her, and held it under her nose.

By then, he realized that Mrs Lilybanks was dead. The hand clenched under her breast had dropped to her side on the sofa, a hand curiously young and beautiful, its skin only very finely wrinkled. Sydney was tempted to take a sip of the brandy himself, but he set it down, pushed his hands down the sides of his trousers as if to wipe them clean, then started for the telephone. At the telephone, he turned and called loudly, 'Mrs Lilybanks!'

There was no response from her.

He picked up the telephone and dialled 999, then slammed it down again before the last 9 had time to register. What were they going to think of this? Bartleby reporting the death of a woman who had just reported his burying of a carpet? Wouldn't they think he'd done her in, perhaps just by scaring her badly, because he knew of her heart condition? Wasn't that exactly what had happened? Or, Sydney thought, turning to look at Mrs Lilybanks again, had Mrs Lilybanks chosen this moment to die, talked herself into being afraid or omitted some necessary dose of medicine, just so he would be blamed, so it would look as if he killed her in anger about the carpet? No, that was too much.

For a few seconds, Sydney felt unable to do anything. He took his hand from the telephone. His finger-prints were on the cup of brandy, the back doorknob. What was the matter with telling them the truth? With this thought, however, his mind slipped into fantasy again: yes, he killed Mrs Lilybanks by lifting an arm in a threat to strike her and scaring her out of her wits. Look at the picture. Wasn't it obvious? Even if the police had found nothing in the carpet, Alicia was buried somewhere, and Sydney Bartleby was out of his head. Some of his best friends would say that.

The telephone rang then. Sydney looked at it, and while it rang its double rings four times, he thought of telling no matter who it was that he had just walked into Mrs Lilybanks's house as she was having a fatal heart attack. Yes, he was just about to call the police himself, or a doctor, whatever was proper to do. Was it Prissie? Mrs Hawkins who rang every day? Inspector Brockway? Possibly. Sydney picked up the telephone quickly.

'Hello?' Then he realized he was speaking into a dead line. He pressed the cradle down, then let it up and dialled o. To the operator, he said, 'Would you ring Ipswich Police Headquarters, please?'

When he got them, he was told that Inspector Brockway had left headquarters just two minutes before. Could they take a message?

'No,' Sydney said nervously. 'No, thanks.' He hung up.

If the Inspector were on his way here, it would take him twenty minutes more, assuming he'd left a couple of minutes ago, Sydney thought. Should he wait? He preferred to go home, but that would look worse: was he retreating from a crime, and intending to deny it? He could, of course, call Ipswich and tell some other police officer. Sydney simply didn't want to do that. What was the matter with waiting? Even if a neighbour knocked on the door, couldn't he tell them the truth? Sydney avoided glancing at Mrs Lilybanks's horizontal form. He looked at his watch, and reckoned that the Inspector ought to be here by a quarter to 8, if he were on his way here. Sydney took a folded afghan from the arm of an easy chair, and spread it over Mrs Lilybanks, drew it almost up to her chin, though without looking at her face and without touching her.

Then he went quickly upstairs, simply to get away from the body. He went into the room where she painted, redolent of turpentine, as Alicia's study had used to be, but the room had such an air of life, as if Mrs Lilybanks had just stopped work and walked out of it, that Sydney turned from it and went through another open door. This was Mrs Lilybanks's bedroom. Pillows were piled high at the head of a comfortable-looking bed, under a vast crocheted bedspread. A book by Pamela Hansford Johnson lay on the night-table. On the lower shelf of the night-table were the brass-bound binoculars. Sydney turned and went out of the room. He stood for several minutes in what looked like Mrs

Lilybanks's guest-room which was clean, neat and less personal. He began to breathe more easily, and realized how tense he had been.

After a while, he went back into the bedroom and picked up the binoculars. It was the first time he had ever held them. He went to Mrs Lilybanks's window and focused them on the outdoors. They brought up his own house wonderfully close. He turned them on the back garden and the garage, and imagined himself that morning with the heavy – not so heavy as he was pretending – carpet over his right shoulder, emerging from the house with it, going the few yards to his waiting car, driving off in that dim dawn.

Sydney heard a knock at the back door.

'Mrs Lilybanks?' called a woman's voice.

Oh, Christ, Mrs Hawkins, he supposed. He heard her entering the kitchen. Old Hawkeye. He suddenly became cool as a cucumber, as she would say, as she did say, and he advanced towards the stairway. 'Is that you, Mrs Hawkins?' he called.

Her outcry, nearly a scream, might have obliterated his words.

'Mrs Hawkins?' Sydney came quickly down the stairs.

Mrs Hawkins swung around to face him and let out a terrible yell. She took a step back, and knocked over the little wine table on which the cup of brandy stood. 'Don't touch me! Don't come near me!'

'For God's sake, shut up!' Sydney roared back at her, suddenly furious at her noise.

Now she grappled, wide-eyed, her mind quite gone, for one of the porcelain dogs from Mrs Lilybanks's mantel.

'Jesus, don't throw *that*!' cried Sydney, horrified at the sacrilege of it.

She threw it as he spoke.

Sydney dropped the binoculars automatically, and caught the flying dog, which made a loud clink as it hit his ring. He glanced at it for a break or a chip, then glared at Mrs Hawkins. 'Calm down, you madwoman!'

'Don't come a step nearer!' Her hair looked wilder than ever, and her eyes were fairly crossed with terror. 'What're you doing here? Mrs Lilybanks is dead! What're you doing here?'

'Waiting for the police, and if you don't like it, why don't you get the hell out?' Sydney replied, all his intended politeness dashed by the termagant in front of him. He started towards the mantel to replace the dog, but Mrs Hawkins retreated another step and nearly sat down on Mrs Lilybanks's head. This made Sydney go hot with rage. He turned and carried the dog to a bookshelf on the other side of the room. Then he picked up the binoculars. 'Harpy,' he muttered.

'Get out!' said Mrs Hawkins. 'Get out of this house!'

'I'm waiting for the police,' Sydney said without looking at her.

There was the sound of a car outside. With a swooning move-ment and an 'Ooooooh,' like a Victorian maiden in beldam guise, Mrs Hawkins wafted herself clumsily to the front window and nearly fell against it. Her knees must have been weak.

Sydney opened the door. Thank God, it was Inspector Brockway in the nick of time. 'Inspector Brockway! I just tried to call you,' Sydney said. 'Come in.'

'What's up?' asked the Inspector, quickening his steps.

'Mrs Lilybanks has had a heart attack,' Sydney said.

'You're the Inspector?' said Mrs Hawkins. 'I come in five min-utes ago, I find this one 'ere' – pointing to Sydney – 'coming down the steps as cool as you please and 'e tells *me* to get out of the house, and 'er lyin' there stone dead!' She pointed to Mrs Lilybanks. ''E tells *me* –'

'My good woman, will you calm down? And we'll hear your story in a moment. Mrs Lilybanks is dead?' Inspector Brockway went to Mrs Lilybanks and gently raised the afghan, found her right wrist, and felt for a pulse. He shook his head once. 'What happened?' he asked Sydney.

Mrs Hawkins started up again like a cacophonous machine.

'Please—' said the Inspector, spreading his hands to her for silence, with more patience than Sydney could have shown under the circumstances.

Mrs Hawkins shut up.

'I came here about seven fifteen,' Sydney said, 'knocked and got no answer, so I came in the back door, calling to her. When I got to the living-room, she was grabbing her heart – like this.' He illustrated. 'I asked where her medicine was, but she was too far gone to tell me. She just sank down, and I pulled her on to the sofa. Then she died, I suppose. Just like that.' Sydney found his throat quite dry. 'I tried to give her brandy. Mrs Hawkins knocked the table over.'

'I'm sorry,' Mrs Hawkins squawked.

'When did you arrive, Mrs Hawkins?' asked the Inspector.

'Five minutes ago. I come in, and 'im 'ere, 'e's upstairs, comin' downstairs cool like, and 'er lyin' 'ere all the time. What's 'e doin' upstairs? What's 'e doin' 'ere?'

'Why did you come?' Inspector Brockway asked Sydney.

'I came to see Mrs Lilybanks, because I thought she might be thinking I was annoyed with her – for telling you about the carpet thing. I hadn't seen her since before then, you see, and ordinarily she'd have dropped over or rung me. I wanted to reassure her . . .' He hesitated.

And Mrs Hawkins took the opportunity to say, 'Hah!'

The Inspector looked at Sydney's hand, and Sydney realized he was holding the binoculars he had picked up from the floor.

'What were you doing with those?' the Inspector asked.

'I went upstairs – I couldn't stay down here, and I thought you might be on your way. I found them in her bedroom and I was looking out the window for a minute.'

The Inspector made no comment. He pulled out a notebook and took a statement from Mrs Hawkins, which she was pleased to give, then said that was all she would be needed for just now and he would get in touch with her later. Mrs Hawkins then left with an air of importance and of duty well done, but when she reached the kitchen, she turned and came back.

'Sir, what about Mrs Lilybanks?' she asked.

'Perhaps you can tell me her doctor's name, Mrs Hawkins. He'll have to issue a certificate of death.'

'It's Dr Thwaite. He lives just past the church in town, the house with the Poona porch.'

'Ah, yes, I know him. He's done some work for us. Thank you, Mrs Hawkins.'

Sydney relaxed as soon as she was out of the house.

The Inspector went to Mrs Lilybanks, and slowly pulled the afghan higher, over her face. Then he consulted the telephone directory, no doubt to ring Dr Thwaite, and Sydney walked out of the room, into the dining-room, unable to stand there and listen to it. He had liked Mrs Lilybanks very much. He looked at the binoculars in his hand, and successfully closed his ears to what Brockway was saying.

Then the Inspector came into the dining-room and said, 'Now. Sit down and tell me calmly what happened.'

Sydney sat down, and laid the binoculars on the table in front of him. Between him and the Inspector stood a pretty bouquet of mixed flowers in a vase, arranged by Mrs Lilybanks, fresh-looking as if she had just done it, 'I told you. It was exacdy like that.'

'You called headquarters?'

'Yes.' The Inspector could verify that, Sydney thought,

'Did you leave a message? That Mrs Lilybanks was dead?'

'No, I preferred to speak to you. I thought you might be on your way here.'

'Why did you think that?'

'I thought you might be coming to tell Mrs Lilybanks what was in the carpet – that she shouldn't be worried,' Sydney replied.

'That was exactly what I was coming to tell her. Then I was going to call on you.'

'Oh? What about?'

'To ask if you buried something else in the woods. Or some other woods?'

Sydney felt his face grow a little warm. 'No.'

'I think you might have done. Think again.'

'Do you think I would have forgotten?' Sydney asked with a smile.

'Possibly. If you wanted to. Or you might have got it mixed up with a story you're writing.'

Sydney was briefly embarrassed, and irked, too, that the Inspector's guess was so close. His notebook was at the back of a drawer in his worktable, and had been since last night. Now it occurred to Sydney he had better carry it on him at all times, because the Inspector might choose to search his house for just such notes as these. A crate-breaking cough from the Inspector jolted Sydney out of his thoughts.

'It occurred to me you could have staged the carpet burial elaborately, knowing Mrs Lilybanks might see it – or even just to pretend to yourself – when you'd really buried a body before or after.' Inspector Brockway smiled, showing teeth as rugged as his face, and as tanned also, from tobacco. His was the kind of face some writers called craggy. 'Nobody would bother burying a mothy carpet as deeply as you did unless they were pretending something.'

The Inspector let this sink in. Like Mrs Sneezum's comment on what society demanded, expected and would exact.

'Nonsense,' Sydney said.

'You can't dismiss it with nonsense.'

'Why can't I?' Sydney asked, though not insolently.

'Because I won't.'

Sink, sink, sink. Sydney shrugged a little. 'So you're still looking for a body in the woods?'

'Not necessarily in those woods. What happened the *next* morning, Mr Bartleby?'

'Didn't you ask Mrs Lilybanks? She had the binoculars. She was probably watching the next morning.'

'Did you go somewhere else the carpet morning and dig a hole? So the operation would be quicker the *next* morning?'

'What operation?' Sydney really couldn't figure it, if the Inspector was thinking he used the carpet to conceal Alicia's body as he carried it out of the house. What had he done with the body the night of the carpet morning? 'Why not the same day? Why waste time?' he asked quickly.

'Because it was getting lighter. You hadn't dug a second hole the day before, had you?'

'No, sir,' Sydney said emphatically.

'Must've taken you a good hour to bury the carpet.'

'More,' Sydney admitted.

'When did you realize that Mrs Lilybanks had seen you with the carpet?'

'The night you came over and asked me about it. Last night.' It seemed longer ago to Sydney.

'Not before?'

'No. – Mrs Lilybanks asked me for coffee and dessert just yesterday afternoon.'

Silence for a moment.

'Did you bury your wife, Mr Bartleby?' Inspector Brockway asked as calmly as if he were asking Sydney if he would like a cigarette.

Had to, dead you know, Sydney thought, but his face was tense. 'No.' He realized he had been playing with the binoculars, turning them slowly over and over above the table. He put them gently down.

'You'd probably like to have those, but I can't let you. They're part of the evidence now.' He got up from his chair. 'You're perfecdy free to say my theories are a lot of rot any time you wish.'

'I wouldn't do that. I like theories.'

'I'll have to stay until the doctor comes. I don't want to keep you, Mr Bartleby.'

Sydney stood up and said, 'Thank you.'

The Inspector walked into the living-room.

Sydney followed him, and went on to the front door. At the door, he turned for a last look at Mrs Lilybanks, only a soft-looking elongated form under the pink afghan, already a corpse under a shroud. Sydney said to the Inspector, 'You seem to be thinking that I caused Mrs Lilybanks's death, too.'

'Why do you say that?' Inspector Brockway asked, frowning.

'Why do you think I killed my wife?'

'I didn't say I thought that, I merely asked.'

Sydney watched the Inspector trying to peer into his mind. But the Inspector was awaiting some important sign or betrayal from him, and of course he had none, unless he pretended, and Sydney at that moment did not feel like pretending. 'Good night, Inspector.'

'Good night, Mr Bartleby.'

Sydney went out.

He heard the telephone, like an auditory hallucination, when he was several yards from his house, and broke into a run. He was right, the telephone was ringing, and it was Alex.

'I rang you before. I didn't know where you might be. Possibly in jail, I thought.'

'Oh? Why?'

'This carpet story. We heard it on the seven o'clock news tonight. Just a few minutes before, they said, the police found the carpet they'd been digging for all day. Good God, Sydney, what next? Are you enacting the next Whip? Let me in on it, the plot sounds promising.'

'Well, it's not a plot, chum, it's the truth.'

'Oh. You buried a carpet. But an empty one.'

'I buried a carpet.'

'Oh. Maybe they're hard up for news. They made a sort of a joke of it. A lot of trouble to find it. It was the last thing the news announcer wound up with, if you know what I mean.'

Sydney did. They always tried to wind up on a light note. 'Maybe the joke is still to come,' Sydney said ominously.

'Four feet deep, they said. Really, Syd, are you losing your mind? Or were you imagining the carpet was Alicia? Ah-hah-ah-hah-ah-*haah*!'

'Alicia's below the carpet. They just didn't dig deep enough,' Sydney replied, and returned the laugh more ghoulishly. 'Wait for tomorrow's exciting episode.'

'I have the strangest feeling you're not kidding. Tipped off by a neighbour, they said, who saw you through field-glasses. Would that be Mrs Lilybanks?'

'Yes, none other. She saw me along with a little bird. Well, Alex – what did you really call me up about? Surely not this trivial business.'

'You sound nervy, Sydney. Are you really in some kind of trouble down there? Don't be shy about telling me, you know. Hittie's worried, too.'

'Naturally, I'm in trouble. Alicia—' He dropped his voice to a whisper. 'Alicia was in the carpet, and Mrs Lilybanks thinks she saw her. Saw her feet sticking out. Or maybe an arm or a head.'

'Um. She took long enough to tell the police about it, didn't she?'

Sydney thought of Mrs Lilybanks dead, and his joking was gone.

'Syd?'

'I'm still here.'

'So you carried her out in the carpet.'

'But I buried her in a different place, and they'll never find it. There go the pips, Alex.'

Alex paid no attention to the pips. 'Where'd you bury her, Bartleby?'

'Why should I give them any more clues? I led them to the carpet.'

'Not very accurately, Bartleby. But can we quote you on that? You buried her somewhere else?'

'Yup. Rolled her out and buried her somewhere else.' Sydney loosened his tie in an agony of boredom. 'I've got to sign off. This has already cost you two half-crowns.'

'What did you really tell the police?'

'Alex, I'm tired—'

'Well, Syd, I rang up to say I'm staying at home this week to wind up this next script. Hittie's been at Clacton with the kids since Saturday. So if you want to ring me about anything, I'm here.'

'Okay, Alex, thanks. I'll remember.'

'Shouldn't be too difficult.' Alex said with a chuckle. 'Bye-bye, Syd.'

It was very noble of Alex to spend a week of his two-week vacation alone in London just to work on The Whip, Sydney thought.

He put on his old trousers with an idea of trying to work, but instead flung himself down on the bed in the bedroom. Mrs Lilybanks was dead, and he was sorry indeed that he had caused that. She had been killed by an attitude, he thought, an attitude on her part: she thought he had killed Alicia, therefore he had come into the house to kill her. This attitude had been caused by his attitude. Both things were quite false, yet had important and very real effects. Mrs Sneezum had an attitude, one of suspicion. Her conventions were attitudes, too, just as false as heathenism and the worship of pagan gods (or as true), yet since hers tended to maintain law and order and family unity, they were the attitudes this society endorsed. Religions were attitudes, too, of course. It made things so much clearer to call these things attitudes rather than convictions, truths or faiths. The whole world wagged by means of attitudes, which might as well be called illusions.

He got up and took his brown notebook from the drawer in his table, made a note of what he had been thinking, then took the notebook downstairs and put it in the inside breast pocket of his jacket, beside his wallet.

2 1

The next morning's *The Times*, Monday's, gave the carpet story four inches. Most of the item was devoted to a recapitulation of the circumstances of Alicia's disappearance. 'Her husband, Sydney Bartleby, 29, is an American and a freelance writer of fiction,' the column concluded dryly, which gave Sydney the feeling *The Times* thought him also a freelance inventor of fiction in private life. Never mind, Sydney thought. The carpet might have been empty, but millions of people would fill that carpet in their imaginations, because they wanted to fill it. For example, the readers of the *Daily Express*, who were often the same people as the readers of *The Times*.

He went off in the car to the Blycom Heath tobacco and sweet shop, which sold newspapers, to buy a *Daily Express*. The fat proprietor, who had the broadest Suffolk accent of any of the tradesmen, used not a syllable of it in his transaction with Sydney, only handed him his twopence change from his sixpence with his lower lip firmly clamped over his upper. Mrs Hawkins had already faithfully made her rounds, Sydney supposed, and reported Mrs Lilybanks's death.

Back at home, Sydney seated himself on the sofa and perused the *Daily Express's* write-up:

... The carpet story came out when Bartleby's next-door neighbour, Mrs Grace Lilybanks, 73, at last told police what she had seen through her field-glasses while bird-watching on the morning of July 3rd ... If a wife is missing, it would seem unwise for a husband to bury anything, even a mothy carpet. Big Brother may be watching!

Sydney sat down at his desk and went to work on his 'Paddington Snatchers' synopsis. Plummer had had the third finished script for nine days, according to Alex's last note, and a synopsis of the fourth and fifth stories. Sydney felt Plummer might make up his mind before Alex finished his current script, and Sydney wanted to have as many ideas as possible to show, if The Whip was bought. And in America, Sydney's agent had had *The Planners* for about a week, and it was probably at Simon & Schuster's by now. There might be news on that any day now, too, because Sydney had asked his agent to inform him of a rejection as well as an acceptance. He finished his synopsis, and began to break it down in scenes. His breakdown, he thought, couldn't have been better if Alex had been with him. When he finished it at 3, he put a new sheet of paper in the typewriter, and wrote:

ACT ONE

followed by a list of characters and sets, then:

SCENE ONE: A scrofulous exterior of Paddington Rachmanite dwellings. A series of innocent, everyday incidents, a woman shouts a message from a window to a small boy going off for a pitcher of beer from the local, exchanges gossip with a neighbour also leaning out the window. An old man tries to entice a cruising prostitute upstairs, prostitute refuses to climb stairs. Cut finally to GREEN-O, the sixteen-year-old member of Paddington Terrors, who leans like the others from a window, but gives a message of sinister import.

A robbery was being planned. Within seconds of script time, the Terrors struck in the heart of W1, using a stolen Rolls-Royce for their approach and getaway. Sydney was on Scene Two and banging away merrily, when a knock came at the door. The laundry, he thought at once, and he hadn't stripped the bed.

Inspector Brockway stood at the door.

'Afternoon, Mr Bartleby. Sorry not to have rung first, but I was on the road and didn't pass a call-box. Can you spare a moment?'

'Yes, of course,' Sydney said, opening the door wider.

'Dr Thwaite refused to give a certificate of natural death for Mrs Lilybanks last evening,' Brockway said. 'I thought I should let you know.'

'What does that mean?'

'That means there's got to be a post-mortem and an inquest. It means that Dr Thwaite thinks Mrs Lilybanks's death might not have been due to entirely natural causes.'

'Oh. She died of a heart attack – from what I could see.'

'The doctor thinks you might have scared her. Inadvertently, perhaps, but – what do you think?'

Sydney knew what the Inspector was driving at, and also knew the police probably hadn't finished looking for a body in the woods. The policemen were probably digging this minute, because Mrs Lilybanks's death had made a body in the woods more likely. 'I could have, of course. But I knocked on the door, then called her name as I came in.'

The Inspector drew up a straight chair. 'What exactly were you going to tell her?'

'That there was nothing in the carpet. And that I didn't mind that she'd told you about it. I told you that last night.'

'Yes.' The Inspector looked Sydney up and down quickly, and seemed to be pondering his honesty.

Sydney took a seat on the sofa.

'Well, the weeks go by, and your wife doesn't communicate.'

Sydney wiped his forehead nervously. 'I'm beginning to think she's with someone – a man – and doesn't want to admit it. She'd have to admit it, if she came forth now.'

'Or had you rather believe that – now?' the Inspector asked in a kindly tone.

'I don't know what she's doing for money unless she's with someone. Or working under another name, but I don't think that's likely.'

'M-m. I had a look through the binoculars from Mrs Lilybanks's window also,' said the Inspector. 'At dusk one evening. It might be possible to make a mistake about what was in a large carpet – something or nothing.'

'Well – what did Mrs Lilybanks say she saw?'

'Oh, if she'd said she saw anything, I'd have told you,' said the Inspector, showing his teeth briefly. 'She said later, she supposed something could have been in the carpet. But she was that kind of woman, you know, reluctant to tell me of the carpet in the first place, consequently very reluctant to tell me of any unpleasant doubts she may have had.'

Sydney was calm now, listening.

'You might have carried a body out in the carpet, and buried the body somewhere else.'

'I suppose that's possible. But not the same morning, as I said before. I'd have been too tired. Two holes, you know.'

Inspector Brockway smiled patiently. 'Why do you say, "I suppose that's possible"? Your answers are strange.'

'The story is possible. But not for me physically. Are they still digging in the woods?'

'We're still digging, yes. I'm afraid from the police point of view, that's the logical thing to do. We're still looking in Brighton and vicinity, of course.'

'And maybe the logical thing for me to do is look in Brighton and vicinity, too. If she's changed her hair-do, I think I'd be more likely to recognize her than anybody else.'

'That is a point.'

Sydney felt disappointingly uninsulated by the Inspector's attitude. He was reacting with impatience rather than guilt and impatience was useless for his murderer's notes, he thought. Or was it? 'Would you have any objections if I went to Brighton for a few days?'

'Not if you kept in touch with the police there. Give me a ring first. If I'm not in, I'll leave a message at Ipswich Headquarters. By the way, we should have the result of the post-mortem tomorrow at eleven, if you're interested.'

Sydney really wasn't, but he nodded politely. 'Thank you.'

Sydney went back to work after Brockway left. At 6.45, just before the newspaper shop closed at 7, he drove to Blycom Heath to see what the *Evening Standard* had to say about the digging. If they were still digging, the reporters should be interested, he thought.

He was right. There was an article on page four, with a large picture of a police officer in shirtsleeves digging in the woods, and an unflattering picture of the Bartleby house, so dim and drab, it could easily be imagined the setting of a murder. The dustbin in the foreground was a particularly sordid touch. Much was made over the depth at which he had buried the carpet, as well as the fact the police were unsatisfied and still digging. The *Daily Express* would no doubt carry on tomorrow morning. Sydney thought it strange the Sneezums hadn't rung up about this, and then supposed they were leaving it entirely in the hands of the police.

The telephone was ringing when he got home.

The man's voice on the other end said that he represented the

Daily Express, and could he come to see Sydney? He was ringing from a call-box near Blycom Heath.

'Sorry, not this evening and not tomorrow either.'

'If you're innocent, sir, and I have no doubt you are, then a good newspaper story would help you. The *Daily Express* would like to be the first—'

'I have nothing to say besides what I've told the police.'

'The situation now doesn't look so – comfortable for you, sir. I've spent the afternoon with the police in those woods.'

'Then make up a story from what they told you.'

'Have you any statement to make on the death of your neighbour, Mrs Lilybanks, sir?'

Sydney put the telephone down.

He was up early the next morning, and went to the village for a *Daily Express*. This time, three early risers, one man and two women, stared at him in the shop as he waited to pay. The women edged away from him, but the man stood his ground boldly. Sydney knew them all only by sight, and perhaps he'd said good morning once or twice to all of them in the past, but there was no question of that now. Though one of the women smiled timidly, Sydney imagined her thinking with the others, 'Murderer ... The police are digging this minute for his wife's body ... The gravedigger of Blycom Heath ... ' Once more the buttoned lip from the fat proprietor. Sydney had forgotten his change in a pair of trousers at home, and had to break a ten-shilling note. A lad on the pavement, parking his bike, looked at Sydney with straightforward interest from under his tousled hair, however, and almost smiled. Sydney smiled at him, and then the boy smiled in return.

He went home before he opened the paper. He found an item five inches long aoout Mrs Lilybanks's doctor refusing to sign a certificate of natural death, because 'in the best of my opinion, she was in quite good health, even so far as her heart went, on

Sunday, August 14th, and I see no reason for her to have dropped dead without some external cause.'

'Sydney Bartleby,' the item continued, 'her next door neighbour, stated that he called on her on Sunday evening for the purpose of informing her that the police had found nothing in the now famous buried carpet ... Police authorities are still digging in the vicinity for a possible body, as Mrs Alicia Bartleby has been missing since July 2nd. The sixty-hour search of the woods has so far revealed nothing.'

Sydney spent the rest of the day and evening on his script of 'The Paddington Snatchers'.

On Wednesday, Sydney drove to Ipswich, left his car in a car park, got twenty pounds from the bank, and took a train to London. He carried an overnight bag which actually belonged to Alicia, but was not too feminine for a man to carry. He thought he might be away two or three nights. In London, he realized he hadn't rung Brockway, so he did this. The Inspector was not available at the Ipswich station, but the message was awaiting him: Call at the police station in King Street, Brighton, and speak to a Mr Macintosh. An appropriate name for a police officer, Sydney thought, and the Mister before it implied a high rank indeed in the English system, or at least it did in regard to doctors, Sydney knew.

Sydney had to go from Liverpool Street to Victoria Station, which he did by bus and very slowly in traffic snarls, because he didn't care when he got to Brighton. As much chance of spotting Alicia in a restaurant at 8 p.m. as there was on the beach in mid-afternoon, but Sydney didn't think she was in Brighton proper, not with the police concentrating there. At Victoria, with a forty-five minute wait until the next fast train, he telephoned Alex to see if there was any news about The Whip.

'What're you doing in London?'

'I'm on my way to Brighton to join the search for Alicia,' Sydney answered. 'I'm calling to see if you heard anything from Plummer.'

'Yes, old chum! It came in this morning. They bought it.'

'Good. And the price?'

'Eight-hundred quid per story.'

'Um-m. Average, but I'm not complaining. I hope you're still working madly?'

'Madly. Uh – you haven't a few minutes to spare, have you?'

'I'd rather not. I want to get going. What's on your mind?'

'Well – this whole police business. You know, Syd – it's a wonder it went down so well at Granada.'

'What do you mean?' But as soon as Sydney asked, he knew.

'Your name's on the script, too. What if you land in jail, old man?'

'I'm not going to land in jail. After all, suspicion isn't jail,' Sydney said defensively.

'No, maybe not, but suppose it gets worse?'

'It's not going to get any worse. That's why I'm going to Brighton, to spot my errant wife.'

'Oh. Ring me from Brighton, would you? Reverse the charges, if it's not convenient from where you are.'

'Okay,' Sydney said without enthusiasm. Then his spirits rose at the thought of their sale. 'We're set now, Alex. Have you told Hittie?'

'Oh, yes.'

'Bye-bye, Alex.'

'Bye-bye.'

Of course, Alex had rung Hittie. But he hadn't rung him, though Sydney had been at home until nearly 11. Sydney suspected what was on Alex's mind. Alex was thinking that if he got into worse trouble, The Whip could be stopped, or The Whip would belong entirely to Alex. Or was it true Alex was thinking that? Sydney frowned. Take it easy, wait and see, he told himself. He walked slowly, with his overnight bag, towards platform nine, from which the Brighton train would depart. So this is what it felt like to be successful, to have made a big money sale – comparatively speaking. Alex was certainly chirping about it. Sydney felt awful. The city drew him as if by force of its own mass, and he turned round. Who else could he telephone? Carpie and Inez, of course. He had to get more pennies from a news-stand. It took a long time.

Within two minutes, he had arranged to go to Inez and Carpie's. Inez was out. Sydney took a taxi, because their place was such a long way from any bus stop.

Carpie, in sandals and a shapeless housedress, opened the door for him. 'Welcome, Sydney! Come in and sit. It's the children's hour on the living-room floor. You won't mind, will you?'

'Oh, no,' Sydney said pleasantly.

Two blankets were spread on the floor, reminding Sydney of the picnic, but now the babies were pushing plastic toys around instead of food.

'Can I get you some coffee, Syd?'

'Oh, no, thanks.'

'Sit down.'

He did, to get out of the way, sit down on the studio couch.

'Or a sherry? That's all the house boasts just now. Boasts? You should taste it, yet.'

'Nothing, thanks. I won't stay more than ten minutes,' Sydney said, though he thought he'd nearly missed the next train, anyway, and have another hour's wait.

Carpie sat down on a square hassock of yellow leather. 'How long will you be in Brighton?'

'Two or three days, I imagine. Enough to give it a good look. I think I can do a better job of looking than the police.'

'Tell me. About this digging. What's up?' Carpie chuckled

172

throatily. The hassock sagged under her great weight. It was astounding that anyone could be so mature in a womanly way at twenty-four, which was all she was. In fact, Carpie preferred to say she was a little older.

'They dug for the carpet, which I buried pretty deeply,' Sydney said, 'and now they're wasting time digging for Alicia. As for Mrs Lilybanks, she had an attack just as I was walking in her door Sunday evening to tell her there was nothing to worry about in the carpet, you see. The police had just found it, so I had official information.' Sydney shrugged. He accepted the cigarette that Carpie offered. 'Thanks.' He took a deep pull on the cigarette, 'I think I'll stay around Brighton over Friday and Saturday night. If Alicia's with a boy friend, he might not get down till Friday or Saturday. I might not see them.' He felt utterly depressed.

Carpie looked a little stunned by all the information. She was watching Sydney carefully. 'I liked Mrs Lilybanks.'

'So did I.'

'You haven't heard a thing about Alicia? Not a hint from anywhere?'

'Not a hint. In fact, the reason I came to see you is to ask you – again – if you have any ideas as to boy friends.'

Carpie's full, lipstickless lips remained in solemn repose, closed. Her wide dark eyes were fixed on Sydney's face. 'Inez and I even talked about it. The answer is no, Syd. I'm sorry.'

'You see—' Sydney got up. 'I have the feeling – just a feeling – it's somebody she met here. We don't know so many people who give parties like the ones you give. Not the Polk-Faradays, for instance, not any of the people down in Suffolk. Up, sorry. That last party – when was it? In March?'

Carpie thought, pressing a heavy hand against her temple. 'Oh, lordie. Around then. I remember. People standing up around the walls. I certainly didn't know everyone who was here. People brought people. You know.'

If any man at that party had struck up an acquaintance with Alicia, Sydney thought, he wouldn't likely have come back to Inez and Carpie's, even if invited. That was another handicap in naming him. 'Wait.' Sydney stood up and faced the wall beside the door. 'There was a fellow standing over here talking to Alicia that night. On the make, I remember. I was over here on the couch and never met him. Do you remember anybody sort of well-dressed, brown hair, not too tall, about thirty? I can't remember the eyes. Very neat?'

Carpie chuckled again. 'Ought to. Neat and well-dressed. That doesn't turn up here too often.'

Sydney smiled. 'Oh, I don't know. Could you ask Inez if she remembers anybody like that? Very Savile Row?'

'Sure, Syd.'

'And I'll call you tonight. On the off chance she remembers.' He picked up his bag. 'I'll just make that train if I taxi to the station. Sorry to be so rude, Carpie.'

'That's all right!' She came with him to the door. 'Best place for a taxi is turn left and left again.'

Sydney found a taxi quickly and caught the train. Today was the first time he had been among the public for a long while, he realized as he sat in a compartment with five other men. None of them stared at him. His picture had been in the papers only once, in early August, when the search for Alicia had begun.

At Brighton, he stepped into a sunny, open world, where it looked as if nothing and no one could hide. Men wore sport-shirts without ties, women were in sandals and slacks or bright cotton skirts. Sydney walked down to the seafront. Utterly useless to look for her at 3.30 p.m. on the promenade, he supposed, yet the temptation to try the obvious places first was irresistible, and he visited three hotel lobbies briefly and walked back the way he had come with his eyes on the beach and the promenade. He paid a sixpence admission and went on to the Palace Pier. Here were hot-dog stands, caramel popcorn, your-photo-in-three-minutes booths, mechanical fortune-tellers, bingo parlours, and the noise of mingled juke boxes. For another sixpence, one could rent a deckchair from 9 a.m. to 2 p.m., but Alicia was not sitting in any of them. Sydney went back to shore, and asked the direction to police headquarters.

Mr Macintosh was not on hand, but a pleasant man called Constable Clare spoke to him and explained, using a map of Brighton and the district, how they had been conducting the search.

'Two weeks ago, we covered all this,' said Constable Clare, indicating a wide circle around Brighton, full of roads on which inns' and hotels' names were written as well as towns'. 'We even knocked on doors. Naturally, we're looking in a much wider area – all over England, you might say.'

Here they were joined by Mr Macintosh, a dark slender man. 'I understand from the Ipswich office you want to join the search.' His lips smiled at one corner.

'Yes, I do. For a few days,' Sydney replied.

'I'd appreciate it if you'd check in here every morning and evening to tell us what you might have discovered. Or heard. A telephone call will do. Where will you be stopping in Brighton?'

'No idea as yet. I might not even stay in Brighton.'

'Would you mind giving us a ring tonight then, Mr Bartleby, when you put yourself up?'

Sydney walked out into the sunlit street again. For what it was worth, he supposed he should be at the railway station at 7 and also at 8 this evening.

He was, and it netted him nothing, neither Alicia nor the elusive face of the dapper man Sydney was trying to recollect. He had a drink in three restaurants after that, at the height of the dinner hour. No luck, either. Then he reclaimed his bag from the depository at the railway station, walked with it to the bus station, and took a bus to a tiny spot ten miles away called Sumner Downs. It was as good a place as any, Sydney thought. He put himself up at an inn, where bed and breakfast was twenty-six shillings, and called Brighton police headquarters from a kiosk outdoors on the road, so as not to be overheard by anyone in the inn. However, the name Bartleby hadn't aroused interest in the woman proprietor.

'I'm sorry, I don't know the name of the inn,' Sydney said in answer to the police clerk's question. 'But it looks like the only one in town.'

In the next two days, Thursday and Friday, Sydney toured the countryside in buses which stopped everywhere, Bognor Regis on the west, Arundel, Lancing and Worthing, then Seaford and Peacehaven to the east of Brighton. Sometimes he got out and walked about, looking, and sometimes he asked questions at general stores and post offices. No one had heard of a blonde young woman, a summer guest, or of a young woman a little on the tall side and slender, whose hair was blonde or reddish or brown (Sydney couldn't imagine Alicia dyeing her hair black), but everyone asked, 'What's her name?' and Sydney always said, 'That doesn't matter, because I'm sure she'd be using a false name.' Two or three of the people he asked said, 'They were looking for the Bartleby woman a couple of weeks back. We think she's dead, poor girl. It wouldn't be her you're looking for, would it?' 'No,' Sydney had answered, for what good would it have done to say yes?

On Friday, 19 August, Sydney was back in Brighton in time for the 5 p.m. train. There were trains every half-hour now. Hurrying businessmen poured off them, many with expectant smiles, many crashing happily into the arms of waiting girls – but no girl was Alicia and no man was Dapper Dan. If the fellow was as well-heeled as he looked, Sydney thought, he might well drive down in a car. Sydney filled the intervals between trains with tea or a drink in the buffet of the station. At 7, back on the platform to watch the detraining passengers, Sydney saw a man who looked very much like the man he remembered.

He was hatless, hurrying, with his head a little ducked, as if he didn't want to be seen.

Anyway, Sydney gave chase. The man wasn't looking for anyone, that was plain from the way he kept his head down. He wore a grey business suit, neatly pressed, jacket open, carried a rolled umbrella, a black brief-case, and a bulging paper shopping bag from Sainsbury's. He looked for a taxi outside the station. Sydney did the same. The man got his, and Sydney managed to get one, by being rude to a woman, about fifteen seconds later.

'Just turn right here – first,' Sydney said, sitting forward on his seat in order to keep the man's taxi in view.

'Into town?'

'I don't know yet.' A moment later, Sydney said, 'I'm with a friend in another taxi, the third up on the right. I've got to follow him.'

The driver was rather lost, but courteous, and Sydney promised to direct him as he watched the other taxi. They went down to the sea road and turned right. Like a jockey, Sydney urged his driver to pass a couple of cars so the man's taxi was in better view. Sydney sat up still more as the town thinned out. Suppose it wasn't the right taxi? Suppose the man were meeting a fat, dark-haired girl, or going to a house full of people where he was expected, a house where Alicia wasn't, and where the people had never heard of Alicia?

The man's taxi made a right turn, away from the sea, and slowed.

'Not too close behind him, please. Okay, drive on past,' Sydney said in a suddenly choking voice.

Sydney had seen Alicia standing at the left side of the road beside a motor scooter, her hair short and auburn in the light of the setting sun, a summer skirt of blue billowing out. He looked left as he passed the two, who were so absorbed in each other – hands held, a kiss on the cheek and on the lips – they might not have known if a parade of lions was passing them. Sydney even heard a high note of Alicia's voice through the open window.

'Those are my friends,' Sydney said. 'I want to surprise them later, so – could you make a turn up here, turn around and go back?'

The driver did so. The scooter was out of sight now, but there was a smaller road off to the right. Sydney asked the driver to take it. The scooter was in sight for a moment, then disappeared as it descended a hill. It was not going fast. The man was driving, Alicia was behind. The sea was on the left, and the road narrowed. Sydney did not want to be seen following them.

'All right, turn around again, if you will,' Sydney said somewhat breathlessly. 'I'd like to go back.'

'Go back?'

'I'm early,' Sydney said limply, not caring what he said.

He had the driver go back to the station, because he couldn't think of any other place to tell him to go to.

After he had paid off the taxi, Sydney stood in a daze in the station without direction or purpose for a full half minute. Alicia looked very happy. That was perhaps the most shocking thing of all. However, one had to be practical and efficient; names, addresses, dates and all that. Telephone numbers. He forced himself to remember Inez and Carpie's. Then he got a lot of shillings from a ten-bob note, and went to a telephone booth.

Inez's voice came first, yelling over her shoulder to someone, and behind it the heavy rhythm of calypso music. 'Hail-o!' said Inez gaily.

'Hello. Inez. Sydney here. How are you? Besides musical.'

'*Me* musical?' And she giggled as if someone were tickling her.

'I wondered—' Sydney began and stopped. He couldn't tell them he had found Alicia, and under what circumstances. 'I saw

Carpie Wednesday for a few minutes, you know. Asked her about a – a certain man I saw at one of your parties.'

'Oh-h, yes,' said Inez, suddenly sobering. 'Carpie! What was that man's name again? – Oh, yeah. She thinks – *we* think – it might be Edward Tilbury, but don't quote us on that. He's a lawyer, friend of Vassily's. You know Vassily, from the picnic at your place.'

Sydney remembered Vassily with the station wagon. 'You think. Is he about five eight, well dressed? Rolled-umbrella type?'

'He is. And I remember him, too, a little, but I didn't know his name until we both sort of came up with it.'

Sydney could easily ask them to check on what Edward Tilbury was doing with his spare time lately, but he couldn't bring himself to. 'Thanks a lot, Inez.'

'You're welcome, Syd, but I only think this is the guy you're talking about, and I don't know a thing about him seeing Alicia. Naturally.'

'Sure, I understand, Inez. I'm very grateful. And don't worry. It's only an idea. On my part. She could be seeing – anyone else, for that mattter.'

'You think she's alive, Syd,' Inez said like a statement. 'You don't think she's killed herself or anything.'

'No, I don't.'

'Well, all this talk about *you* killing her – makes you think somebody did, because they're acting like she's dead.'

'Hogwash,' said Sydney.

Inez shrieked. 'Hogwash! You tellin' me! I can just see you buryin' a carpet, you old nut, with nothin' in it. Hah-ha-ah!'

Inez's good spirits picked Sydney up suddenly. 'Inez, I sold The Whip series with Alex. Just heard a couple of days ago.'

'No kidding! Well, isn't that great! I'll spread the news, Syd. Funny Alex didn't tell us. Carpie called them last night for a wine party tomorrow. You back tomorrow night, Syd?'

'I don't think so. Thanks, Inez.'

'That's too bad. What're you doing in Brighton? Just cruising the streets?'

'More or less.'

Their conversation trickled off and they hung up with no further words about Edward Tilbury.

Sydney patiently waited for a bus to Sumner Downs for ten minutes, still in a kind of fog, then realized he had another fifteen minutes to wait, and that he was supposed to ring Brighton police headquarters for his usual check-in. He went to a kiosk.

'I'm still at Sumner Downs,' he said, and almost said he'd be going back home tomorrow, but didn't.

'Did you turn up anything today?'

'Not a thing – sorry to say.'

22

In his room in the inn at Sumner Downs, Sydney sank down
tiredly in the one upholstered chair, and reached in his pocket for
the brown notebook. Not finding it, he pulled out his wallet in
panicky haste, and felt again. Not there. Hadn't he had it when
he left Blycom Heath? Still sitting in the chair, he looked around
the room, but he knew it wasn't in the room, because he hadn't
made any notes since he had been here. Now the note he had
been going to make danced in his head.

I have seen A. and feel on the brink of schizophrenia.

And he had been going to elaborate on this. He could elaborate still further because of the missing notebook now. Had he
ever had a notebook? Which half of him had had it? Where was
that half now?

Where was the notebook? Sydney had changed into his best
suit before leaving Blycom Heath, but he had brought along his
old tweed jacket. He leapt up and went to the wardrobe, felt in
the old jacket, and found nothing. Could he have left the notebook absent-mindedly at home on the bed where he had spread

his things when he packed? That was possible. Left it in some store? Today? He had broken a pound for cigarettes at a tobacconist's. His name wasn't in the notebook, and he wasn't worried now about any implication of guilt the notebook might give rise to, he was only sorry to have lost his jotted thoughts.

He looked around for some paper, found none, and took from the drawer of the night-table a rather soiled piece of tan wrapping paper on which he wrote his schizophrenic observation, which he continued:

Perhaps we are a quartet, Alicia a corpse and I a murderer somewhere, and Alicia all suntanned down here and I an anxious and cuckolded husband. *The Schizophrenic We* would make a rather good title.

Then he suddenly remembered that there was a name at the front of his notebook on a page by itself: Cliff Hanger. He had proposed it to Alex once as the name of their next television sleuth.

Sydney smiled grimly, and muttered, 'God's *teeth!*'

He looked at the map he had bought of Brighton and the district. In the direction in which Alicia had been going lay Shoreham, Lancing and Worthing. Then Goring, Ferring, Angmering, Rustington and Littlehampton. Hadn't Alicia once mentioned Angmering? Sydney had been to Lancing and Worthing. He supposed the thing to do was to go to them again and to the four towns beyond. He had a small bitter and a Cheddar sandwich downstairs in the inn, went to bed and slept badly.

He got up at 7, and after shaving and dressing, went downstairs and asked for a London telephone directory. The inn had none. Sydney went to the kiosk outside, and from London information learned that there were several E. Tilburys, and that a middle initial would be helpful. Sydney asked them to ring the number of an Edward J. Tilbury in Maida Vale. There was no answer, though he let it ring many times. He wished he had thought of ringing Tilbury last evening, when he had been in Brighton, and could have taken a look at all the E. Tilburys in a London book.

A little after 10 a.m., Sydney got a bus that went in the direction of Worthing. He stayed on it until Angmering, where he got off. He had been here before, too. He remembered the Angmering post office, and also the thin, freckled man behind the window. Sydney walked on along the seafront. There were four or five cottages in view, and Sydney looked them over for a scooter parked outside, for a glimpse of Alicia or of Tilbury at a window or outside the cottages, but without success. He wondered if they were cautious enough to take the scooter inside the house when they got it home.

Sydney went into the post office. 'Morning,' he said to the man at the window.

'Afternoon,' replied the freckled man, smiling.

'Yes. I'd like to ask if you know anyone around named Tilbury? Summer guests?'

'Tilbury? – No, but I'll take a look to make sure.' He referred to a list that he pulled from a drawer, and shook his head as he looked it over. 'No Tilbury.'

'All right. Thank you.' Sydney felt suddenly tired and discouraged.

'You were asking about a girl before. That's her name?'

'I'm not sure.' He smiled a little, shrugged, and went out. Then he came back. 'I wonder if you know any people with scooters? A grey one with a seat in back? If you know a girl with short red hair who rides one?'

'Oh. That sounds like Mrs Leamans.' The freckled man frowned. 'Would you be looking for her?'

'She lives nearby?'

'Cottage down this way.' He gestured towards the sea, the opposite of the Brighton direction. 'She's there with her husband. He comes down weekends.'

'She's a summer visitor? New here?'

'That's right. She's the purple house about four down the other side of the road.'

'Thank you,' Sydney said, and went out.

Sydney looked once, a long minute, at the house the man probably meant, a pale lavender cottage of which Sydney could see only one back corner. He had no desire to go any closer. Mrs Leamons? Leamans? A clever name, if it were Alicia and Tilbury. It didn't sound like a phoney name, not as phoney as Tilbury.

It was 3 p.m. before Sydney got back to Sumner Downs and his inn, where he paid his bill and went upstairs to get his few belongings. Today's newspaper was under his arm, and on the night-table lay the newspapers of the past two days. Mrs Lilybanks's inquest had been adjourned *sine die*, and the funeral had been Wednesday morning. The post-mortem had disclosed no poison or medical dose whatsoever, but her heart showed the dilation or whatever it was that had caused its failure, and this in Dr Thwaite's opinion had been caused by a severe shock of some kind. And that would not have happened, Sydney thought, if Inspector Brockway had telephoned Mrs Lilybanks just a few minutes before and told her there was nothing in the carpet. The Thursday paper also reported that Sydney Bartleby had gone to Brighton to assist the police in the search for his wife. No wonder Edward Tilbury had ducked his head on Friday evening. It was a wonder he had come at all.

Downstairs, Sydney engaged the inn's taxi to take him to Brighton. With The Whip money coming, he felt he could afford the guinea cost.

He called in at the police station. Mr Macintosh was there. Sydney told him he had had no luck, and that he was going back to Suffolk.

'Would you sign something for us before you go, Mr Bartleby?' Mr Macintosh gave him a sheet of paper on which he had to fill in several blanks, his hour of arrival in Brighton and hour of departure. The paper stated that he had come with the purpose of assisting the police in their search for his wife ALICIA, and below this he was to write in his results. Sydney wrote, 'No success.'

In the Brighton station, he looked at a London directory and thought that an Edward S. Tilbury in Sloane Street looked the most promising. There were only four E. Something Tilburys, after all. Sydney got some change and risked a call. No answer from Tilbury in Sloane Street.

He could stand outside the house in Sloane Street Sunday night and Monday morning to see if Dapper Dan came in, Sydney thought, but he balked at such snooping. He could also ask Inez and Carpie to find out where their Edward Tilbury lived, if he could swallow his pride. That jerky, muck-faced square! Alicia had fallen for that!

Sydney had twenty minutes before his train, so he rang Alex on the off chance he might be there, though Sydney expected that he had gone to Clacton by now. Alex answered.

'I'm arriving in London at five, and I wonder if I can see you for a few minutes,' Sydney said.

'Ugh. I was going to catch a six o'clock train, old pal.'

'Can't you take a later one?'

'Did you hear anything about Alicia?'

'Not a thing, I'm sorry to say. Alex, I'll get there as soon as I can. We've just sold The Whip and after all—' Sydney checked himself, realizing he was pleading. 'What about contracts, for instance?'

'It's here.'

Sydney said he was coming, and put the telephone down before Alex could start protesting.

He dozed on the train up to London, though it was the last thing he had thought he would be able to do. Just before Victoria, he splashed non-potable water on his face in the lavatory and combed his hair. Then he took a taxi to the Polk-Faradays' flat in Notting Hill. It was the first floor of a white house. Sydney half expected no answer when he rang the bell, but Alex came down the stairs to open the door.

'Hi,' said Alex.

'Hello. I won't keep you long. It's only five twenty and you might even make the six o'clock.'

Alex showed no interest in the time, and Sydney suddenly felt he had been faking the 6 o'clock train.

They climbed the stairs.

'Do they want any changes in the first script?' Sydney asked.

'Quite a few little things, but I'll do those.'

'Changes in the plot?'

'No.' Alex opened the door of his flat, which led immediately into a large and now quite untidy living-room that gave on the street.

A suitcase lay open on the sofa, only half filled. Their main closet was in the living-room, a great white wardrobe in the corner. There was a hobby horse and a soiled buff-coloured giraffe on its side on the floor.

'Let's see the contract,' Sydney said.

Alex got it from the pocket in the lid of his suitcase. 'I haven't signed it yet.'

Sydney read through its three sheets. The contract gave a fifty-fifty split. The series was to run for a minimum of six weeks, with a proviso for extension and increased payment in case of extension. 'It looks all right, doesn't it?' Sydney asked. 'Nothing great, but they're not cheating us anywhere.'

'No,' said Alex in a troubled way.

'What's the trouble?'

'The trouble—' Alex fumbled with something in his suitcase, then straightened. 'The trouble, Syd, is the trouble you're in.'

'Oh, come off it, Alicia's hale and hearty. Probably got a boy friend. I'm sick of it.'

Alex studied him, and took a step back, around the foot of the sofa.

Sydney realized he had walked a step towards Alex. He wondered if Alex were pretending to be afraid of him. 'What's on your mind, Alex?'

'What's on my mind is – the series could be stopped, if this thing gets any worse.'

Sydney felt suddenly angry. He was angry because he thought Alex was faking. 'Maybe what's on your mind is, you'd like to have the series all to yourself. Especially as the first six stories are already invented and on paper. Already accepted, from the plumber story down to Paddington.'

'Don't be mad! Want the series for myself!' Alex gave a laugh. 'But Syd, there is a problem and you know it. Where's Alicia? It's all very well to say she's alive and got a boy friend, but where is she? Do you think the public's going to look at your name coming across the screen every week with mine without thinking about this or doing something about it?'

'Doing something about it?'

'Boycotting us. Writing in complaints.'

Sydney smiled. 'Enjoyed the play, but I object to the author. Ha!'

'Don't you know they can cut us off in mid-stream?'

'Don't be vulgar, Alex.'

'Don't be funny. Do you see any reason why I should run that risk? Just for you?'

Sydney frowned. 'So what do you propose?'

'I think I ought to get sixty per cent, and you forty. I think

187

that's only fair, considering the work I've put in and will put in. Considering it could be cut off any minute.'

Sydney sighed. He remembered Alex's appetite for money, instilled in him by his family, who prodded him constandy less he forget. 'I'm running the same risk. I've put time in on it, too.'

'But your work is finished. And you caused the risk.'

'Without me you wouldn't have any of it. Oh, hell, Alex, I'm sick of the argument and I don't agree to your terms.'

Alex gave a tight smile and walked to the coffee table for a cigarette. 'You're free now, relatively speaking, but how long do you think it's going to last? What if the police knew what Hittie and I know, Syd, about your bumbling mistakes when you were trying to tell us where Alicia was? You couldn't even remember the story you intended to stick to. All those—'

'That she was with her mother? That's what she told me to tell people.'

'All those jokes, after you'd had a few drinks, about putting her six feet under and living on her income. All those fights you had with her. When we were there.'

'I don't need a few drinks to make up stories like those. I can make up stories like those any time.'

'How do I know they were stories? Suppose they're true?'

Now Sydney was merely irritated. Whether Alex was being stupid, or trying blackmail with a heavy hand, Sydney was bored. 'All right, Alex, do you believe they're true?'

'I dunno!' Alex replied.

Sydney watched him. Was he lying? 'Get to the point, do you? Or do you just want a bigger cut?'

'Syd, I don't know what's going to happen. *Did* you kill Alicia?'

He looked like an emoting character in one of his own plays, Sydney thought. 'No, dear,' said Sydney. 'Are you trying to blackmail me?'

'I don't call it blackmail. I simply—'

'You probably don't. Blackmail's a plain word, it's very clear what it means. And you don't seem to care to be clear.' Sydney again took a step towards Alex without thinking, and Alex again retreated. 'Are you afraid of me? Have you convinced yourself that I kill people?'

'Since you put it in the plural, we shouldn't forget Mrs Lilybanks. The doctor wouldn't give a certificate of natural death. What sort of conclusion do you think people'll draw? That you scared her to death, of course. Maybe deliberately.'

'If the police were drawing that conclusion, I'd be arrested. Come off it, Alex. If you don't like the word blackmail, let's call it greed. It's greed you're showing now.' Sydney took one of Alex's cigarettes from the package on the coffee table.

'Thanks,' he said, lifting the cigarette.

Alex was checked for a moment, but not defeated. He came back to the attack with a new will. 'I'm holding out for sixty per cent, Syd, for my own security. Take it or else, and you know what the else is.'

'No, I don't.'

'I can tell the police a great deal. A great deal that isn't nice, and a great deal of what went on before Alicia disappeared. Those nasty quarrels you used to have—'

'Oh, throwing a teacup?' Sydney laughed. 'If you believe what you're saying, you should say these things anyway – to the police.'

'I don't really know what to believe,' Alex said. 'And I'm trying to protect my interests. It's as simple as that.'

His logic reminded Sydney of some of Alicia's, but Alicia's was always naïve, and Alex's was full of self-interest. But Sydney could see that Alex was sincere. Alex had simply blinded himself, like a squid behind its own ink.

'You're in no position to laugh.' Alex walked towards his suitcase. 'I'm tired of arguing, too, and I'm going to take off.'

'Not waiting for my answer? My answer is that I don't accept.'

'That's not at all wise of you,' Alex said. 'I'll give you till Monday to make up your mind. By Monday you might be in custody, anyway, but if you're not, my address is Clacton-on-Sea, the Sea Winds Hotel.'

'My love to Hittie,' Sydney said, then crossed the living-room with his overnight bag and went out the door.

On the train to Ipswich, Sydney had planned to think, to decide what to do, but as soon as he tried, his problems seemed like one huge mountain hurled at his brain, and he collapsed under its weight – figuratively speaking. His brain was benumbed, and sought escape in sleep. He recovered his car in Ipswich, and drove home in the gathering darkness.

23

On Saturday, Alicia and Edward were relieved to see a tiny item in the *Evening Argus* saying that Sydney Bartleby had left Brighton after a search for his missing wife which had netted him nothing.

By now, they were in Lancing, where, still as Mr and Mrs Eric Leamans, they had rented very cheaply a house much too big for them. The house was called a villa. Since the death of Mrs Lilybanks, Edward was more than ever for stopping the game, since he thought it cast an unfair suspicion upon Sydney in regard to Alicia. Edward wanted to go quietly back to London and stay there, and wanted Alicia to go quietly to her parents' home and announce herself, but Alicia couldn't face admitting to her family and to Sydney that she had been living with a man for more than a month under another name. It was Edward's idea to marry her, once she got divorced in an ordinary manner, and Alicia wanted this, too, but each day, for all her efforts to think and act, bogged her deeper in guilt and embarrassment, as if the whole situation were a quagmire. She had said many times to Edward, in the earlier part of their liaison, and when Mrs Lilybanks had rather mysteriously died, 'Syd's not really right in the head, Edward. I've known it for a long while. Look at the way he acted with Mrs Lilybanks. Acted is the word. That carpet performance! And then his nervousness about the binoculars, the papers said. He doesn't know what's truth or fiction any longer.'

'Then it's time you acted, darling, before he gets himself in any deeper. They can't arrest you for what you've done. You're not the first woman to have an affair extra-maritally.'

Edward's words, meant to be bracing, only made Alicia feel more frightened and cowardly. 'I can never face him now,' she said flatly. 'He'll kill me on sight, or at very least think I'm a ghost. He's lost his mind, Edward. I certainly can't face him the way things are now.'

'I don't think he's lost his mind,' Edward murmured nervously. 'I think he's somehow waiting – for you to come back.'

'Why do you think that?'

Edward didn't know, but he felt he had a glimmer of what Sydney was all about. He could hardly have put it into words. It was quite in character for Sydney to come down to Brighton and spend four days looking for Alicia – and not find her. 'I can't imagine,' Edward said and not for the first time, 'that if he really roamed around in this area, he didn't see one of us at some point. In the street or in some shop.'

Alicia was silent for a moment, afraid that Sydney might have seen her and done nothing about it. That would have been like him – rather mad. 'It wouldn't have mattered if he'd seen you. He wouldn't have remembered you from that party that night, I know.'

Then Edward would be silent (they had had this conversation three times), because he was not so sure Sydney didn't know about him and Alicia, while if he told Alicia this, she'd lose her last shred of courage and say good-bye to him for ever in a chaos of shattered pride. Vassily had said something to Edward about Inez and Carpie asking what he had been doing lately. Vassily had repeated to them Edward's answer, that he had been visiting friends in Surrey quite a bit. Good old Vassily. Vassily could be trusted to keep his White Russian discretion, even if he suspected the truth. But Edward had the feeling Sydney would quiz Inez and Carpie and get them to make enquiries for him, and that therefore Inez and Carpie might know the truth now, too. And they might tell it, Edward thought. Departures from London were increasingly torturous to Edward. He felt he was definitely being spied upon, spied upon when he set foot on the Brighton platform, spied upon as he pressed the first kiss on Alicia's cheek, if she were there to meet him. It was making him horribly nervous, and he had to take a sleeping pill almost every night in London. And he felt that an axe was due to fall, if he didn't get back to his customary, respectable bachelor's routine in London, where he spent his weekends reading and playing music and perhaps going to a little dinner party – to which he usually escorted no one – on Saturday evenings. That was the kind of life Alicia said she wanted, too.

'We'll never budge from where we are now, if you don't make a move, darling,' Edward said to her. 'You've got to get in touch with Sydney eventually, if only to get your divorce.'

Alicia only looked into space and bit her lower lip. Why did things have to be like this, in such a God-awful muddle? Well, mainly because of Sydney. If he hadn't stupidly, asininely buried the carpet, and probably asininely, like a clown, pretended to be nervous and guilty when their friends or the police asked him where she was, she and Edward wouldn't be in the position they were in. She'd just have gone away for a few months, as she told Sydney she was going to do, and as he agreed to let her do. She could have seen Edward, enjoyed his company for a while, and quietly come back and told Sydney she wanted to divorce him. Now she had a faint desire to get back at Sydney, to let him sink as deeply into a mess as he wished to, and perhaps more deeply.

'I think, too,' she said to Edward, 'it's very likely Sydney saw me somewhere, even though I was being careful those days, naturally. But I had to do a little shopping for us – anyway, you said you didn't see him at the station on Friday.'

'I wasn't looking around, naturally. That only attracts attention. He might have seen me.' Edward was sitting on the shabby straw chaise-longue on their terrace, putting white on his shoes.

'Well, if he saw me, he can say he saw me, can't he? What's stopping him? It's not as if I were contributing to getting him blamed for murder.'

Now she sounded more sure of herself, but her logic was faulty. 'No, dear, if we know he saw you. But we're not sure of that. It's no good saying there's a fifty-fifty chance he did, or more than likely he did. How do we know? I'm bound to say it's more logical to assume he didn't see you and therefore can't save himself by saying he did.' Edward left this on an expectant note, and Alicia looked at him.

Her eyes filled with nervous tears. 'I know what you're going to say, that I ought to go back and face things. Well, I can't. I'd really rather kill myself.'

'Nonsense,' Edward said in a solid tone. 'But look, darling, whether you like Sydney or not, whether he's treated you well or ill, he's going to lose even his professional standing if this goes on.'

'Professional standing? A silly television series?' Edward had heard through Vassily, who had heard through Inez and Carpie, that Sydney had sold The Whip.

'You told me he wrote books.'

Alicia was not thinking about Sydney. She gazed miserably across the room at her best painting, the best and biggest she had ever done in her life – six by eight feet, an abstract of sea and flowers. With Edward, she could paint. Somehow his solidity, his very conservatism, brought out her imagination more than

Sydney's kinkiness ever had. She knew the kind of life Edward led, knew the kind of friends he had, the kind of house he kept, with good antique furniture in it and a daily who kept things waxed and dusted. She hadn't seen his flat, but she could imagine it. That was the kind of life she wanted, the kind she had been brought up to lead, after all, just as her mother said. Now, because of Sydney's antics, that lovely future with Edward was spoilt, could never start smoothly, if it ever started at all. What excuse could she make for herself? That was the main thing. That she had been afraid of Sydney? That was the only half-honourable way out. What she most of all dreaded was that the police would insist on knowing where and how she had hidden herself away for two months, under what names and with whom. Her parents would never forgive her. And it would ruin Edward's career.

'I can't go back, Edward,' Alicia said, and put her face down in her hands on her lap. 'I can't face it.'

24

Of the two problems, Alicia and Alex, Alicia seemed the bigger. When Sydney tried to think about Alex, Alicia intruded, and forced Sydney to think about something he had always shrugged off, taken for granted, and tried not to think about. That was the relationship between Alicia and himself. He had been loyal to Alicia during the year and ten months of their marriage. Because he had not thought about it before, Sydney did not know if he had been loyal because he really loved Alicia, because there had been no temptation, or because he was naturally loyal. Sydney had always supposed natural loyalty was an attribute more of women than of men. He had seen lots of pretty girls, even met them at parties, and had thought briefly of how it would be to go to bed with a few of them, but it had never crossed his mind to make any efforts in that direction. He had even said to Alicia a few times, 'Gosh, isn't so-and-so a knock-out?' and Alicia hadn't been jealous, and Sydney hadn't expected her to be. Alicia had said now and then, 'Don't you think so-and-so's attractive? He's what I'd call my type – if I had a type,' and she'd smiled at Sydney, and that had always been the end of it. Sydney had taken it for granted Alicia was loyal, because she was very conventional really, and had been rather primly brought up. Women like her just didn't have extra-marital affairs, he thought, unless something went awfully wrong with their marriage, or with them. Since Alicia seemed fairly all right in the head – though a bit neurotic – Sydney had to conclude something had gone horribly wrong with their marriage. They had certainly used to make love more often than they had in the past six months, but that was of course a result not a cause of anything. Sydney had been worried about money and about his writing. *The Planners* had piled up five rejections in England, and that hit not only at the bank account but at the ego, which hit the bed department. He couldn't muster much passion, or even affection, for anyone, if his ego was low. And one of his theories was that murderers had little or no sex life. Well, he wasn't a murderer and he certainly had a sex drive and a sex life, but since he had been trying to imagine that he had killed Alicia, he'd had no stirrings towards her or anyone else. Not even towards Prissie Holloway; he had simply appreciated her, he felt. He thought of making a note about all this, then remembered the lost notebook. He went upstairs and looked around the bedroom, then his study, even in the desk drawer where he used to keep it. He looked under the bed. Definitely, he had lost it somewhere outside the house. He went into his study and made the note about Prissie and himself on a piece of paper which he put into the drawer.

Then he went downstairs and opened his bag, which was still in the middle of the floor, and carried his three dirty shirts to the laundry basket in the corner of the junk room beyond the living-room. It was 11.20 p.m. on Saturday night. He got the London directory for the Ts from the telephone table, and tried Edward S. Tilbury of Sloane Street.

No answer. He hadn't expected any, and yet it bothered him, that meaningful emptiness of the flat in Sloane Street. It was bound to be the right Tilbury, Sydney thought, because the other three Tilburys were a dentist, a resident of a Camden Town street, and the Maida Vale dweller who hadn't answered when Sydney rang from Sumner Downs. It could be the Maida Vale Tilbury, but Sloane Street was more likely. Sydney felt as he listened to the futile rings in Sloane Street that he really loved Alicia, and maybe loved her all the more because he had taken her for granted – just as perhaps she had taken him for granted, and Sydney didn't mind that she had. He had taken it for granted that they loved each other, despite their quarrels, and they still did love each other, he felt. He hung up. Maybe Alicia was thinking the same thing he was at this minute. Maybe her happy face had been an act she put on for Tilbury, or to try to convince herself.

But what were her intentions now, he wondered, to keep on hiding out until he got into a worse mess? Was that her way of getting back at him? And meanwhile, what should he do? Tell the police he had seen her, and where he had seen her? Should he tell them now, or two days from now, or in a week? Should he write to Mrs Leamans, Angmering, and tell her he knew all, and would she like to come back to him or not? He could write that he forgave her, if she'd forgive him, forgive his foul quarrelling and his practical jokes, and would she like to come back? Yes, he wanted her back, if she wanted him, and he could swallow his pride enough to ask her. Sydney was staring out the window, and suddenly the scene of unkempt lawn, picket fence (mended by him, painted white by Alicia), the old croquet mallet poking out from below a bushy hedge, the maligned dustbin with its lid askew, seemed to writhe with a life of its own like a Van Gogh landscape, and it was at once filled with Alicia and with her absence.

Sydney decided to let the Alicia situation go for twenty-four hours, and if possible to solve the Polk-Faraday dilemma. For twenty-four hours, he could imagine he had killed two people, Alicia and Mrs Lilybanks, and imagine what the world thought of him, or suspected. And after twenty-four hours, he would have wrung that idea dry of what it might furnish in the way of story material; then he would decide what to do and act on it. If Alicia said she didn't want to come back to him, he could at least help her to start divorce proceedings, which he was sure she was too afraid to begin herself.

He took some coffee up to his study and sat thinking. He tried to imagine Hittie's attitude. She ought to disapprove of Alex's stand, if Alex were honest enough to tell her what he'd said. On the other hand, one could never overestimate the loyalty of a wife, be her husband pimp, picklock or priest married on the sly. Hittie might rationalize and join forces with Alex. Or she might really believe, as Alex was pretending to believe, that he had done Alicia in, and Mrs Lilybanks, too, and might believe The Whip stories would be interrupted or even never get started. The first show would be some time in October, Plummer had told Sydney and Alex weeks ago, if the series was bought. The thing to do, Sydney supposed, was talk to a lawyer, or directly to Plummer. The situation didn't seem to be bothering Plummer now, and Sydney wished he'd had the wit to point that out to Alex in London. Alex giving him a deadline, an ultimatum! Of all the cheek, as Alex would say. Sydney got up from his desk and prepared for bed.

The tranquillity of Sunday morning and the newspapers was broken by a telephone call from Inspector Brockway. He had heard from Brighton that Sydney was back, and he 'wanted to check' with Sydney.

'I heard you had a fruitless search,' said the Inspector.

'I'm afraid so,' said Sydney, a little amused by the word fruit-less.

'May I come by and see you for a few minutes some time this afternoon?' the Inspector asked.

They agreed upon between 2.30 and 3.

Sydney decided to serve tea, though it was early for tea. Tea would give a relaxed, domestic atmosphere to the unrelaxed and undomestic Bartleby household.

Inspector Brockway, in flannel plus fours and the blue and brown tweed jacket today, began pleasantly by congratulating Sydney on the sale of his Whip series.

'Thank you,' Sydney said. 'How did you hear about it?'

'Your friend Mr Polk-Faraday rang me up – oh – Friday morning, I think it was. Your collaborator, it seems.'

'He's sort of a playwright, yes. More than I am, anyway.'

'He was a little worried about whether you'd be able to continue with the series, in case the situation worsens.'

Sydney looked at the Inspector, who was rubbing his chin and staring at the floor as if he were talking of the weather worsening, of something uncontrollable. 'Well – has it worsened?' Sydney asked.

'No, but it is out in the open now, you might say. Even though there's not something about your wife or you or Mrs Lilybanks in the papers every day – not in all the papers, that is – the subject is not going to be dropped until your wife is found, dead or alive.'

'Haven't there been cases of people who successfully disappeared for ever? We have a couple of famous ones in the States. Judge Crater. Never found, dead or alive.' He heard the kettle prepare to shriek.

'Yes, of course. We have them, too. But in this case we may need – simply closer investigation. Harder looking, if you like.'

They could use a bit of that, Sydney thought. The kettle's note was ascending. He jumped up. 'Excuse me, Inspector. I thought you might like a cup of tea.'

'Thank you,' said the Inspector. He brought his hand up to his mouth and gave a crate-breaking cough.

Sydney scalded the pot, measured the tea in teaspoons, just as Alicia would have done, except that there was no lemon to slice. He carried the tea in on a tray. After a proper interval, Sydney poured a cup for the Inspector and himself. Sugar. Milk. The Inspector took both.

'Your friend Mr Polk-Faraday implied – or rather said, that there were some things that worried him. Have you any idea what he means?'

Sydney looked at the Inspector and shrugged slightly. 'No.'

'If you think he means anything specific, I'd rather hear it from you than from him.'

Sydney rather doubted that. Why should he? 'I don't know what he could know that I haven't told you. I mean about where my wife said she was going. It could be that she talked to Alex and said something else. Is that what he means?'

'I don't know what he means,' said Inspector Brockway, watching Sydney closely.

Here Sydney permitted himself to register concern, nervousness. Or rather, he did register nervousness automatically, rattling his teaspoon in his saucer, sitting forward on the edge of the sofa. 'Did he say Alicia had said something to him?'

'No. That he didn't. It was more like a situation, I gathered. The situation here at home before she disappeared.'

Sydney passed a hand across his forehead and reached for a cigarette.

'The Polk-Faradays were frequent guests when your wife was here, I gather.'

'Oh – once a month, something like that.'

'Even when you and Mr Polk-Faraday were collaborating?'

'Yes. We did a lot of that by post. Still do.'

'Um. But if he heard you make any threats towards your wife, or overheard any quarrels, it'd be better if you told me about them.'

Oh, come, Sydney thought. Not better at all, possibly worse. The Inspector wanted to compare his story with Alex's, that was all. 'I'm sure the Polk-Faradays overheard a quarrel or two,'

Sydney said. 'There was one night I remember when Alicia dropped a glass and I shouted at her. Pretty loudly.'

'Did you ever strike your wife?'

'Yes,' Sydney said solemnly. 'Once or twice. But not severely.'

'Did Polk-Faraday ever see you strike her?'

'No. At least I don't think so. I don't think we ever had any serious quarrels while the Polk-Faradays were here.'

'What do you mean by a serious quarrel?'

'One in which I hit her. Or one that goes on for a few days.' Sydney gripped his hand with the cigarette with his other hand. His trembling was genuine, but he was not trembling because of what they were talking about. He was thinking of Alicia with Edward Tilbury.

'I wish you'd talk to me about what's worrying you,' said the Inspector in a kindly tone.

Sydney absolutely couldn't have done that, and the thought almost made him smile. 'Naturally – I'm worried about what Polk-Faraday might say to you. He wants the Whip series. He asked me yesterday to agree to a forty-sixty per cent split in his favour. Or else he'd tell some stories to the police, he said.'

'Really? True stories?'

'I don't know, I doubt it.'

'What stories could he tell me that are true?'

'I don't know – except a couple about quarrels I had with my wife.'

'If he tells me anything, you may be sure I'll check it with you before I believe it or pass it on,' Inspector Brockway promised, and set down his cup. 'There's one other matter which turned up while you were in Brighton. A notebook you left in the newspaper shop here in Blycom Heath.'

Sydney's start was practically a shudder, and his tea slopped into his saucer. It wasn't the notebook, but the *place*, and that suspicious proprietor. He remembered now, breaking a ten-bob note there the morning of the day before he left for Brighton. Sydney pushed his fingers, damp with tea, through his hair, and said, 'Oh, yes, I wondered where I'd lost that.' And the proprietor must have seen him *not* pick it up from a stack of newspapers, Sydney thought, and had decided not to call his attention to it, because he wanted to have a look at it.

'Mr Tucker said he would have returned it to you that day, but you weren't home.'

'No,' Sydney said, but he had been home that day, and left for Brighton the next day. 'It's— Well, it's not important, just some note. Notes for stories.'

The Inspector smiled understandingly. 'Mr Tucker thought it was a diary. Of course, it looks like a diary, with the dates in it.'

Sydney glanced at the pockets of the Inspector's jacket. He didn't see the notebook.

'Notes for fiction, you say?'

'Yes. Imaginary, all of it,' Sydney said, realizing once again that the truth sounded guilty as sin.

'Some sounds like fiction and some doesn't. However, considering you're a writer, it could all be fiction, I suppose. That's not the way the average person would take it – like Mr Tucker – the account of the murder, pushing her down the stairs and all that.' The Inspector smiled quickly, and pressed his large, knuckly hands together.

'Yes. Well, as you probably gathered, I was trying to imagine all of it.'

'Some of it, yes, certainly sounds imaginary. Well, for safety's sake, we have the notebook at headquarters in Ipswich. No one has seen it but me up to now, except Mr Tucker and his wife. Nevertheless, considering the nature of it, Mr Bartleby, I'm afraid I must show it to Inspector Hill who's coming down from London next week. The Sneezums have insisted on Scotland Yard looking in.'

Sydney grimaced and stood up. 'May I pour you some more tea, Inspector?' he asked, reaching for the pot.

'No, thank you very much. I must be off. Golf appointment at four o'clock over at Aldeburgh.' He stood up also. 'I'll say good afternoon, Mr Bartleby, and thank you for the tea.'

'Good afternoon, Inspector.' Sydney watched him walk along the short stretch of driveway to the road where his conservative black car stood, a bag of golf clubs visible in the back seat. Sydney closed his own door.

An hour later, Inez called. 'I had a hunch you'd be home. When'd you get back?'

'Last night. In answer to your first question, I had no luck,' Sydney said, feeling he had to ward off the question.

'Oh, Syd,' she said sympathetically. 'Well, my gosh, if the police can't find her and they've got a whole platoon at work—You didn't happen to see Edward Tilbury?'

Sydney laughed. 'If I'd seen him, I'd have followed him.'

'Because Carpie and I found out he's not home much lately. Especially weekends.'

'Really. Tell me, is he the Tilbury in Sloane Street?'

'Yes, I think so. I remember Vassily mentioning Sloane Street. Carpie and I didn't make a big point of it, but we asked a couple of people how he was, because we hadn't seen him in quite a while, and we heard he's away every weekend. He told Vassily he's visiting friends in Surrey or Sussex somewhere. It's like playing detective, you know?' Inez chuckled. 'And as Sherlock Holmes would say, maybe it isn't logical to draw a conclusion just from this, but there's something you could do, Syd, if you're really interested, and that's trail him from his house one weekend, see what train he catches and maybe go with him. Or trail him from his office. They can't arrest you for trailing somebody.'

'No.' Sydney hated the conversation. 'Inez, if the police talk to you and Carpie again, I'd just as soon you wouldn't mention Tilbury. First of all, we don't *know*, and it isn't at all wise to—'

'But they could find out if it's true. Easier than we could. It'd help you.'

'I realize that, but— It's hard to explain over the telephone, and I don't mean to be telling you what to do, but—' Now he was almost in a sweat. 'I'd just appreciate it if you say you still don't know any more than you did a month ago.'

Inez reluctantly promised, and a few seconds later their three minutes were up.

Sydney went out for a walk. He walked towards the setting sun, and wondered if Alicia and Tilbury were walking together on some beach now. Good Lord, he thought, they could have been together nearly two months now. That was long enough for them to get to know each other well. What on earth were Alicia's intentions? Why didn't she write to him and have it posted from London, if she didn't want him to know where she was? Sydney had an almost overpowering desire to write to Mrs Leamans in Angmering and simply ask her what she wanted, let her know he could explode her game any time he chose. But he shrank from it with a feeling akin to the qualms he might have about invading someone's privacy. Pride was mixed up with it, too, and now he didn't want Alicia to know her actions bothered him enough for him to ask her intentions. Alicia would go to pieces, anyway, if she knew the world knew about her lover. And the other thing that held him back was the fact that the situation was becoming more interesting because of its duration. He was curious, too, to know how far Alex Polk-Faraday would dare to go.

On Monday morning at 7.15, with a cigarette and a cup of coffee beside him, he rang the Sea Winds Hotel in Clacton-on-Sea.

'Would you ring the Polk-Faradays' room, please?'

Hittie answered, sounding more sleepy than the operator.

'Hittie, I'm sorry to wake you at this hour,' Sydney said, and he really was, 'but I wanted to be sure and catch you in. Could I speak to Alex?'

'Oh, yes, Syd, just a minute. Wake up, darling. It's Syd.'

Sydney heard Alex mumbling, then he came on. 'Hello, Alex. I just wanted to tell you that I don't accept your forty-sixty split. I accept a fifty-fifty. Is that clear? You asked me to tell you today.'

'Very well,' Alex said more crisply. 'We'll see about that.'

'Have you told Hittie? About the forty-sixty?'

Alex didn't answer for a moment. 'Sydney, I don't mean to be unfriendly, but I think you'd better do some serious thinking.'

'That's all I wanted to say, Alex. Good-bye.' Sydney hung up.

So Alex didn't want to be unfriendly. That was a nice line, of course, for Hittie to hear. Sydney concluded that he hadn't told her of his plans. Sydney stood on tiptoe in the living-room with his coffee cup and laughed out loud. The sun was already shining through the window, and it promised to be a lovely day.

Moreover, the post a few minutes later brought a letter from Potter and Desch, the London publishers to whom Sydney had sent *The Planners* three weeks ago. They would buy the book. Sydney felt redeemed. He stood holding his breath and staring at the short, typewritten note. 'We are pleased ... Could you come in to our offices soon to discuss a few ... Our contract will be following after ... ' He walked to the junk-room end of the house, then turned and walked back, in a daze, into the kitchen. He was smiling foolishly. He'd have a book out. And a good one.

And he had no one to tell the news to. Or rather, no one he wanted to tell the news to. He wouldn't tell anyone, he thought, until someone asked, 'Well, Syd, what's new these days? What're you working on?' Then he'd say casually, 'I have a book called *The Planners* out soon from Potter and Desch. It's a good book. Or they seem to think so.'

And certain brilliant paragraphs and sentences went through his mind as he bathed and shaved.

25

Around 2 that afternoon, as Sydney was attacking the junk room with an objective of throwing away and tidying, Inspector Brockway rang up and asked if Sydney could come to Ipswich at 4.

'Well—' It was the last thing Sydney wanted to do.

'It's rather important, or I wouldn't ask you. Inspector Hill is coming down from London. Mr Polk-Faraday has spoken to him, so if you don't mind, Mr Bartleby . . .'

He set out at quarter past 3, in order not to antagonize Inspector Hill by being a bit late. He half expected to see Alex, who must have whisked himself to London that morning to speak to the higher-ups, and so might have come up with Hill to Ipswich, but Alex was not in view. Sydney was introduced to Inspector Hill, a tall, slender, handsome man in his late forties. Inspector Brockway introduced them, looking stiff and serious and on his best behaviour for London. The three of them went into an office that might have been borrowed for their conversation, or might have been Inspector Brockway's, Sydney could not tell, as Brockway did not choose to sit behind the desk.

Inspector Hill began with a few minutes of relaxing comment

on the difficulties of finding people who wanted to hide, and expressed disappointment that Sydney's four-day search in Brighton had not been successful. Inspector Hill lit a cigarette, and so did Sydney.

'Mr Polk-Faraday spoke to me this morning in London. He mentioned several things that I thought I should take up with you.' Inspector Hill's tone was pleasant, and he gathered three or four small pages of notes together in one hand. 'This carpet story ...' he began with a smile. 'It seems the Polk-Faradays visited you one weekend shortly after your wife left. Mrs Polk-Faraday noticed there was a new carpet in the living-room. And they said – rather, Mr Polk-Faraday said, you reacted strangely when his wife mentioned it.'

'How strangely?'

'You looked worried – according to Mr Polk-Faraday.'

'I don't know what they mean. I told them I bought the new one very cheaply, and got rid of the old one.'

'Did you tell them how you got rid of it?'

'No,' Sydney said.

'The next point. Mr Polk-Faraday says that you acted strangely on the telephone with him, when he rang you from London one day, after the weekend. You were talking about the way you'd got rid of your wife. Mr Polk-Faraday says you might have been joking. Or maybe you weren't. "Pushed her down the stairs," he said you said. "Never felt better in my life."' Inspector Hill smiled.

Sydney did not smile. 'Yes, I said that. Is Alex trying to make something serious out of it?'

'We don't know. He's reporting it. And it's correct, is it?'

'Yes,' said Sydney. He had no doubt Inspector Hill had seen his notebook, probably in the last half hour, so it was very fresh in his mind.

'He speaks also,' Inspector Hill went on, and Sydney had the feeling he wanted to throw everything at him at once for a reaction, 'of an atmosphere of hysterical gaiety about you. On that weekend. Bachelor life was agreeing with you and all that.'

'That was Alex's comment.'

'You were talking about living on your wife's income – or that you soon would.'

'Another remark of Alex's. I joked about it later. We make up plots like this, you know. We're always making macabre jokes.' Sydney's voice cracked on his last word. His palms, pressed together between his knees, were actually moist now. 'I've done nothing about trying to get my wife's income. I'm not at all sure I could. I should think her parents could stop that.'

'No, they couldn't. Not the fifty pounds a month part of it,' said Inspector Hill, 'if she were dead. They could of course not pass on to you what would have gone to Alicia once they're dead.'

Sydney drew on his cigarette. He glanced at Inspector Brockway, who was leaning against the desk, listening.

'And . . .' said Inspector Hill musingly, sitting very still in his chair with his legs crossed, 'the Polk-Faradays think you went out of your way to tell people that you didn't know when your wife would be back, and that it would be a very long time. Six months or so.'

'I told people that when I was asked.'

'You didn't make a point of saying it?'

'No.'

'The Polk-Faradays say you did.'

Sydney wondered if Hittie had come to London, and decided she hadn't, because of the children. Alex had probably just been reporting 'what my wife and I think'. 'The Polk-Faradays are wrong,' said Sydney.

'Another point.' Inspector Hill looked at his notes. 'Your friends Inez Haggard and Carpie Dunne. Mr Polk-Faraday seems to know them, too. He says he spoke to them, and they described a Saturday afternoon on which they came to your house for a picnic. Your wife had then been gone about three weeks. According to Mr Polk-Faraday, you told them and everyone that your wife was at her mother's house in Kent, and that afternoon, Mrs Haggard told you that she had not been able to reach your wife at her mother's house, her mother didn't know where she was or even that she was away from home, and this took you by surprise. Or you were rattled.'

'Rattled? I was surprised. Since my wife told me she was going to her mother's.'

Inspector Hill leaned back and watched Sydney.

Sydney also leaned back, and folded his arms. He saw a babbling, maniacal Alex, eyes bulging, yakking away at Inspector Hill in London that morning, but silent, like a television picture with the sound turned off. 'Didn't Mr Polk-Faraday talk to you about The Whip series for Granada television?'

'No,' said Inspector Hill.

'He should have. That's what all this is about. We've just had a series of six stories accepted, and Mr Polk-Faraday proposed a forty-sixty split in his favour instead of the fifty-fifty the contract calls for. I think, too, that Mr Polk-Faraday thinks if he can throw enough suspicion on me, he might squeeze me out entirely. I would've thought Inspector Brockway would have mentioned this to you.' Sydney glanced at Inspector Brockway.

'No, he didn't. Neither did Mr Polk-Faraday,' said Inspector Hill. 'Yes, I can see why you're piqued, but – you tell me Mr Polk-Faraday's statements to me are essentially true. Or do you not?'

Sydney shifted in his chair. 'They are exaggerated – the jokes. Alex reports them all as statements from me, it seems.'

Inspector Hill smiled and rubbed his chin. 'I appreciate writers' fantasies. I've just seen your notebook – which I will assume is a notebook of ideas – not truths.'

Truths? Ideas? Sydney passed a hand across his forehead. 'The narrative – description in the notebook is not true. You might say the ideas in it are true. I mean, it's not a diary of facts.'

'It's a dangerous kind of thing to write just now – for you.'

'I had no idea anyone but me would see it. That's why I carried the notebook with me. I pulled it out by mistake with my wallet.' A murderer's Freudian slip, Sydney supposed. He looked down at the floor. He was thirsty.

'We'll take your word for it for the time being. But we must keep the notebook until this matter is cleared up,' Inspector Hill said. 'Now if these things were said by you – to Mr Polk-Faraday – and by the way, did you say such things to anyone else?'

'No. I only joke that way with Alex.'

'It was still a strange situation, your wife leaving for such a long time. Much longer than any of her previous trips. Isn't that true?'

Did they expect him to break down, Sydney wondered, just by pointing out obvious facts? 'Yes,' said Sydney. *Did you kill her?* Sydney could practically read the question in Inspector Hill's calm eyes, and Sydney imagined his brain busy with the suspicions the Sneezums had put there. Meanwhile, Alicia was sleeping with Edward Tilbury. 'Why don't you find her, if you think I killed her? Underground or overground?' Sydney said in a tone as calm as Inspector Hill's.

'We are looking. It's not easy, as you see.'

'Meanwhile, I'm exposed to attacks such as Polk-Faraday's putting on. It's not easy for me, Inspector.'

'The attacks won't be in the newspapers, at least. That's not the way we do things here.' Inspector Hill glanced at the motionless, attentive Inspector Brockway. 'On the other hand, you could hardly do better at incriminating yourself, and I don't mean only the notebook – which by the way Mr and Mrs Sneezum don't know about. What about the binoculars? Your neighbour Mrs Lilybanks told Inspector Brockway you reacted with what seemed to her extreme uneasiness when you saw the binoculars in her house, and when she told you she had seen you the morning you buried the carpet.'

'But you dug up the carpet.'

'Answer the question, please, Mr Bartleby. Why were you uneasy when Mrs Lilybanks mentioned seeing you through the binoculars?'

'Because – I knew what she was imagining. Thinking.'

'Really?' Inspector Hill asked earnestly. 'Why did you think Mrs Lilybanks would think a thing like that?'

'Well, I didn't – at first. But when my wife didn't write to Mrs Lilybanks, which Mrs Lilybanks mentioned to me, I began to see what she was thinking.'

Inspector Hill said, 'M-m,' and glanced at Brockway, who was still leaning quietly against the desk. Hill stood up. 'I have nothing more to ask at the moment, Mr Bartleby, except – have you ever had any treatment for mental disorder?'

'No.'

'No breakdown ever?'

'No.' Sydney stood up also. Alex had probably told them he was cracked, Sydney thought. Dear old Alex.

'I'd like to go back with you to your house for a few minutes, if you don't mind,' said Inspector Hill.

Of course Sydney didn't mind.

'We can go in one of our cars,' said Inspector Brockway, 'Are you going home now?'

Sydney had thought of going to the library, but he obligingly said he was going home.

'I'll drive him,' Inspector Brockway added. 'You won't have to lead the way.'

Sydney drove home at his usual rate of about forty miles per hour. The Inspectors arrived in Brockway's black car less than five minutes after Sydney.

They came into the living-room, and Inspector Hill looked

around, at the staircase and at its top, as if measuring its lethal distance with his eyes. It was covered with a rather thick carpeting that would have been a help in any fall. Or rather a hindrance for a murderer. They went upstairs, and Sydney showed them Alicia's painting room with its old dried palette becoming dusty now, though Sydney hoovered and dusted the room like any other, when he cleaned. They looked into the room where he worked, and into the bedroom. They went outside, and Inspector Brockway pointed out Mrs Lilybanks's house from the front, and then they walked to the back of the house. Sydney had not been asked to come with them, so he stayed behind, and re-entered the house through the front door. Inspector Hill of course wanted to see how far the driveway and back door were from Mrs Lilybanks's windows.

Sydney looked out his workroom window and saw Inspector Hill gazing at the ground as he walked around the rectangle of the garden. He also went into the garage, opened the doors wide to let light in, and disappeared in the garage for several minutes. Then the two men stood between the garage and the garden, talking together for so long that Sydney stopped watching them and sat down at his desk. A milk bill had come that morning, so Sydney got out his cheque book and wrote a cheque for one pound three shillings and ninepence to be put into an empty bottle tomorrow morning.

When he heard the men come in through the back door, Sydney went down.

Inspector Hill smiled at him and said, 'Thank you. Mr Bartleby, for letting me look round. May I ask what your plans are about the house? You intend to stay on here?'

'Yes,' Sydney said.

'You don't find it lonely?'

'A little. But I don't mind being alone. Not as much as most people.' He was annoyed with himself for his pleasant tone. He was talking to a man who had swallowed everything Alex had said.

The Inspectors left.

It was after 6. Sydney got into his car and went to Blycom Heath for the *Evening Standard*. Mrs Hawkins was in the newspaper shop. But Sydney had decided to face them all for his paper, and not drive four extra miles to Framlingham for it just to avoid Buttonlip. Mrs Hawkins drew back deep among the sweets at the far end of the shop, darting glances as if for support to the two other people who stood between her and Sydney, but they were musing over the long glass counter of sweets. Buttonlip rolled towards him, and Sydney got four pennies from his change, reached for the *Evening Standard*, and was surprised to see the old picture of himself – cut to just the head and shoulders – on the front page, one column wide. It was a picture of him in a white, open-collared shirt that Alicia had taken at her parents' house shortly after they came to England, and Sydney supposed the Sneezums had given it to the Press.

'Good evening,' Sydney said semi-pleasantly to Buttonlip, and got a sort of grunt in reply.

He did not look at the paper until he was home. The write-up beneath the picture was extremely short and vague.

MYSTERY MAN?

Authoritative sources said today that a close acquaintance of Sydney (missing wife) Bartleby has shed a good deal of light on the personality of the young American. No details were given, but Bartleby was reportedly called 'far out in every respect'.

Damn them all, Sydney thought, and it occurred to him that the mess could cross the ocean and spoil *The Planners* as well as The Whip. He tossed the newspaper down on the floor, where it sprawled with a faint plop. Alex had very likely said that he made up most of The Whip plots, that he had to steer Bartleby's cookie (kinky, Alex would say) mind back on the track time and time again in their plotting.

Sydney went out to the garage with a sudden idea. He turned on the garage light, and dumped a tall paper bag of waste paper on to the ground by the open garage doors. Fortunately, he hadn't burned any paper in nearly a month. Now he picked out certain used typewritten sheets on the backs of which, folded once across, he invariably made his notes for Whip synopses, and for chapters in his books when he was writing. He found fourteen such folded papers, all scribbled over in his small handwriting, with diagrammatic outlines and numbered scenes. Of course, he had his synopses carbons in the house, but these papers were the real beginnings, and they were all his. He went into the house to sort them out and see what he had to go on, in case he had to fight.

26

Sydney found that he had notes for the third, fifth and sixth Whip stories, and they were very much the same in his scribbles as they were when the synopses had been typed out. Story number four had somehow got lost, or thrown away in a different place, and Sydney didn't want to go through the sloppy dustbin on the chance it might be there. The notes for the first two stories, alas, were burned weeks ago. He paperclipped his synopses notes and put them carefully away.

On Tuesday, 23 August, a note came from Cecil Plummer of Granada, saying that under present circumstances the purchase of The Whip series would have to be postponed 'until the situation is clarified'. The contract, Mr Plummer said, would be reissued and redated. Sydney remembered it had borne Plummer's signature and a date when he saw it.

The postponement was a financial blow. It could mean a couple of months' delay, Sydney supposed. No money from Granada until the contract was signed, and no money from anywhere until the end of September, when $300 would come in on his quarterly arrangement of his dead Uncle Herbert's legacy. Sydney wished he hadn't paid the twenty-eight pound grocery bill in Framlingham last week, because the store was very nice about its credit. Sydney had paid it, because he had felt sure of The Whip's money.

Sydney picked up the telephone and rang Potter and Desch for an appointment to discuss *The Planners*. A very pleasant female secretary spoke to him.

'Miss Freemantle is free at four o'clock today. Could you come in?'

Sydney said he could.

The appointment made him feel better.

Sydney bathed, shaved for the second time, and drove off to Ipswich to catch a train for London.

The Potter and Desch offices were in New Cavendish Street, one flight up in a large old building a bit threadbare but clean. He met Miss Freemantle, a bespectacled, slender woman of perhaps forty-five. The points she mentioned were ones Sydney might have stuck on, he thought, if he had been editing *The Planners* for someone else. Fuzzy thinking in some of Ernesto's politics (ex-communist, now Trotskyite), and an anti-ex-lover speech by one of the women was a little heavy-handed, and eloquent for her character. The work wouldn't take him long, not that he cared how long it would take. He signed the contract in Miss Freemantle's presence, having made sure there was nothing in it giving a percentage of any movie money to the publishers. There was nothing about movies in it.

'We'd love to see your two earlier books that you mentioned in your letter,' Miss Freemantle said. 'Would that be possible?'

Her telephone buzzed.

'Of course. I can post them this week.'

Miss Freemantle answered her telephone, then told Sydney that Mr Potter would like to meet him, and would he step into his office, the second door to the left down the hall.

Sydney bade adieu to Miss Freemantle in a glow, his manuscript under his arm. He knocked on Mr Potter's door. Mr Potter stood up to greet him, a big, dark-haired man with glasses.

All went well for two minutes, until Mr Potter said:

'We definitely want your book, Mr Bartleby, but I hope you'll understand that we can't publish until this matter of your wife is cleared up. I'm sorry about it – but I think you'll agree that a new book shouldn't be blighted by something quite extraneous like this.'

Sydney had a sensation of blushing, which flustered him all the more. He pressed down his pride, and said, 'But you do want the book. There's no question of your not publishing.'

Mr Potter hesitated. 'I have to admit there is.'

Sydney was not in such a glow when he walked out of the building. Despite the contract, he knew he would lose if he tried to force Potter and Desch to publish – say, six months from now – and who would want to be on such a hostile footing with a publishing house, even if he should win his case.

He got some shillings from a shop, found a call-box, and rang the post office in Angmering, Sussex.

'Hello,' Sydney said when a man's voice answered. 'I'm calling to ask if the Leamans are still – if they still have an Angmering address?' He knew the town was so small, merely Angmering would reach Alicia, if she were there.

'Oh, the Leamans. No. Just a minute.' And in a leisurely manner, as if it weren't a trunk call, the postmaster absented himself from the telephone, and returned a minute later. 'They said they were going to Lancing.'

Sydney knew the town by name, from his map. 'Any street?'

'Just Lancing.'

'Thank you very much,' said Sydney.

Then he caught the first train he could back to Ipswich and his car.

At home, he checked the spelling of Lancing on his map, then wrote a letter on his typewriter:

218

Tues. Aug. 23, 19—

Dear Alicia,

For some time I have known where you are, and though I still consider it your affair and your privilege to hide yourself, I would appreciate it very much if you announced that you were still alive. Afterwards, if you wish, you may go into hiding again. Please believe that I bear no ill feelings against you, and hope that you do not against me. I suggest that you go to your parents' house. You do not have to see me, if you don't wish to. But your staying away is making it increasingly difficult for me to live and to work. With very best wishes and love,

Syd

He re-read the letter, put it into an envelope and sealed it. It was certainly mild enough, he thought. Threats would get him nowhere with Alicia, though on the train to Suffolk, he had composed threatening and angry letters in his mind, letters that mentioned Edward Tilbury. He knew what was happening inside Alicia: she was ashamed of having shacked up with Mr Tilbury, and was having more trouble facing her family than the world probably. Yet it was impossible to imagine Alicia facing up to the police first, ringing them or dropping into a station and saying. 'My name is Alicia Bartleby, and here I am.' Therefore, Sydney had had to suggest that she break the news through her family. The family was still a sort of nest, where she would be protected. Unless, of course, she decided to go into a police station on Tilbury's arm, but Sydney doubted if Tilbury had the courage to do that. He didn't look the type. Sydney drove to Framlingham to post the letter, because they had a later collection than Blycom Heath, and he wanted her to get the letter tomorrow.

The next morning, there was a letter from Dreifuss, Scott and

Co., Sydney's American agents, on the floor under the letter slot, and he opened it eagerly. It was from Jim Dreifuss, and said:

Dear Syd,

S. & S. seem quite interested in THE PLANNERS (I like it too, need I say, a great improvement) but they are worried about the publicity you're getting here. Sharpshooting in one gossip column, that's the latest, and of course there was a lot of stuff in July when your wife disappeared. S. & S. want to wait before committing themselves, but I think we can clinch it after . . .

Sydney felt a little faint. He went into the kitchen and automatically started making coffee.

And was Alicia opening her letter at this moment? Sydney hoped so. He wished now that he had said, if you don't go to your parents in the next twenty-four hours, dear, I'll have to come down and get you. But he hadn't said that, and he could easily imagine Alicia sitting in a blue funk for the next week. Sydney drank coffee, but couldn't prepare any breakfast.

Inspector Brockway dropped in at 11 that morning. His message was that Sydney might be asked by Scodand Yard to come to London to answer a few more questions. 'I gathered they might want you there for a few days,' the Inspector said. 'They'd like to ask you some questions with Mr Polk-Faraday.'

Sydney had in his hand a letter to Jim Dreifuss which he had just been going out to post, saying he was positive the whole affair would be cleared up within three days, though he could not tell Jim why just now. Sydney said, 'I'm sorry, Inspector, but I don't care to go.'

The Inspector smiled slightly. 'If you don't, they'll come to see you. It's not a question of their taking you to London forcibly, but you can't avoid answering the questions they put to you. We're all of us bound to answer questions put to us by the police. That's reasonable, isn't it?'

Sydney felt he no longer knew what was reasonable and what wasn't. But he felt he would have to prod Alicia again. His letter hadn't been strong enough. 'Yes, it's reasonable,' Sydney said.

'Have you had any news of any kind?' asked the Inspector, glancing at the letter in Sydney's hand.

'No, I'm sorry to say.'

When the Inspector left, Sydney waited until his car had turned around and disappeared, before he drove to Blycom Heath and posted his letter to America. In the post office, indifferent now as to what Mrs Naylor at the window might think, he composed the following telegram and handed it to her:

PLEASE CONTACT YOUR PARENTS BY TOMORROW THURSDAY OR
I SHALL HAVE TO COME FOR YOU. SYD.

In the afternoon, instead of an answering telegram from Alicia, or a joyous telephone call from her parents, to say she was on the way to Kent, or a call from the police saying the same thing, there was a blast from Alex, a two-page letter with as many underlinings as an epistle from Queen Victoria.

... So now you've done it, old chum, got The Whip
'postponed', which as you know means *out*, rejected,
corpsed. Exactly as I foresaw ...

I mentioned to the police that your *own wife* had once
spoken to me on the subject of your sanity, asked me if I
thought you were a bit off. I think this is *important*. You're in
no mental state and haven't been in some time to compose
anything but maniacal, illogical farce (I've had to
manoeuvre our plots back to common sense a million times,

if you recall) or melodrama spun out of thin air, like a spider web. But you'll be caught in your *own* web, Syd, and you are now. For your own sake, I advise you to hang on to what shred of sanity you may still have and make a clean breast of things to the police. Plead insanity, it'll go easier for you. I believe that you did Alicia in and that you have convinced yourself *somehow* now that you didn't, after cockily admitting it, even proclaiming it at first. But now you'd prefer to think it was all a dream, like something you made up for a story. Hittie agrees with me, so don't think she may be on 'your side' or that I've coerced her into being on mine. She simply feels as I do about you ...

Because life would be pretty hellish for her if she didn't, Sydney supposed. He only skimmed over the last page, a thunderous peroration about defending his work (by which Sydney gathered he would have to haul out those synopses notes) and his *family*, and about justice, the clean and normal mind, and the sanctity of law-abiding society. It had a strong Sneezum flavour.

Alicia had received the telegram by 1 or 2 in the afternoon, certainly by 4, Sydney thought – unless of course she had moved from Lancing or never been there. But the telephone did not ring Wednesday evening, and he at last went to bed in a rage of impatience and frustration that kept him from sleeping for hours.

27

On Monday afternoon, when Alicia read in the evening papers that 'a close acquaintance' of Sydney's had called him more or less a psychopath, she became quite jittery, imagining Sydney's rage against Alex. She was sure the close acquaintance was Alex Polk-Faraday. Up to now, she had heard of Alex's comments via Vassily, who got them from Inez and Carpie and told them to Edward. But Alex's statements now were to the police and the Press. Sydney must have got into a quarrel with Alex over their Whip series, Alicia thought. It was like Sydney to fly into a temper and ruin things when he was on the brink of succeeding.

Then on Wednesday, when Sydney's letter arrived, followed by his telegram a few hours later, Alicia got into a near panic. Sydney knew where she was and even knew her name! He must also know that the man she was with was Edward Tilbury. He'd been spying, and of course doing a clever job of it. Alicia drank several Scotches to steady herself, but she was in such a state by 3 p.m., she could neither sit nor stand still. She was alone, and had been alone since early Monday morning. She had the feeling now that Sydney would barge into the house at any moment and knock her senseless before he summoned the police. Around 4, she did the unprecedented, and rang Edward in his London office. She had to wait a long time while they extricated him from a conference, and when Edward came to the telephone, he was angry.

'I had to ring you, Edward. I'm in a terrible state.'

'I'm very busy. Can I ring you back?'

'Can you come down tonight? Will you? Something's happened, but I can't tell you about it over the phone.'

'All right. I don't know if I can make it before nine,' Edward said grumpily, and hung up.

Edward arrived at five minutes to 9. Alicia, hoping he would take the 7.30 train down from London, had been concentrating on the clock for the preceding hour, and when she at last heard his quick step on the stone walk, her relief was like an inward collapse. He tried the door, used his key, then looked surprised to see her huddled in the corner of the sofa.

'Why didn't you let me in? What's the matter, Alicia?'

'Oh, nothing. Now that you're here,' she answered, and got up. 'Fix a drink?' She found herself unsteady from what she had drunk, more than a third of a bottle of Scotch, which had done her no good at all.

'Come, come now, what's up? Somebody say something to you?' Edward tossed down his brief-case and hat and followed her into the kitchen.

Alicia was determined not to tell Edward she had heard from Sydney, no matter what he asked her. Just where she went from there, however, she didn't know. She had burned Sydney's letter and telegram. 'In a way,' she said finally. 'I just got horribly nervous on the street today. I went out to buy something – and I came back with nothing.' She splashed Scotch into two glasses.

'That's all right, dear. Did you see someone? – Did a policeman speak to you?'

'No.'

'Did you see someone you know?'

'No, none of that.' She handed him his glass, smiling. 'Maybe I'm pregnant.'

'But you said –'

'I know. No, I don't really think so.'

They sipped their drinks in silence for a few moments, standing. Edward studied her with a worried expression.

She knew he was going to launch into another speech about her going home to her parents, as soon as he'd drunk half his drink. Where did one go from there?

When the speech came, she barely heard it. The same old argument, even the same old words. Alicia only knew that she had to have Edward with her, or she'd go under. Here or London or anywhere, but with her. 'I'm not going back, so don't talk about it,' she said finally, interrupting him, and with more force than she thought was left in her.

'But obviously you can't stand the strain, and neither can I – much longer.'

'Would you – go back with me to my parents?' she asked.

'No. That I can't do. It's not fitting. It's impossible.' He lit a cigarette. 'But I think I should start things moving by going back to London. You'll never make a move unless I do. I feel I should go back and stay there. And I should go now. I should go back tonight.' He moved restlessly about the room.

'Oh, Edward, don't *leave* me,' Alicia wailed with the start of tears.

He smiled and patted her shoulder. She was standing by the sofa. 'Darling, I'll be waiting for you. You know that. Whatever we have to face, we'll face together. But don't make me run the risk of losing my position – and finding it damned difficult to get another, if I do.' Edward spoke passionately now.

'Then stay here,' she pleaded.

'That I can't, darling. Forgive me, but I cannot. I must go.'

Hesitantly at first, then more purposefully, Edward began to gather his belongings, preparatory to packing his suitcase that was in the bedroom closet.

And absurdly, it crossed Alicia's mind that she owed Edward seventy-two pounds, because he had paid all the bills, almost, since they had been together. She could easily repay him out of the hundred pounds that would be at the bank in Ipswich by 2 September. She remembered, only a month ago, when finances had been her most embarrassing problem. Now money seemed a triviality compared to the total wreckage around her. She lifted her glass and tried to drink it all down at once, almost succeeded, but choked on the last couple of inches. Edward came back into the room as she was bent over, coughing, and she turned and darted for the door.

It was cool outside. She ran into the dusk, ran faster at the sound of Edward's voice behind her, calling her name.

28

Thursday dawned sunny and clear, and with the pleasantest of temperatures. It was the kind of day to put an optimistic cast on any work or any problem a person might have, Sydney thought, and he began to feel optimistic about Alicia. Around 8.30, he imagined her waking up – still in Lancing – and feeling cheerful herself about going to her parents today. Well, he wasn't quite sure she'd be cheerful about it, but he felt that she'd go, and that it was all the more likely she would go today, because the sun was shining. If it had been a rainy day, she might have retreated, or postponed it, or simply balked.

Sydney sat in a patch of sunlight in the living-room, writing in one of his notebooks. He had the germ of an idea for a new book and wanted to get something down on paper before, perhaps, the idea evaporated in the atmosphere of Scotland Yard. He did not get very far in the five minutes he wrote, but still the germ was on paper, like the beginning of a dream or a poem, and it would grow eventually. The telephone startled him with its loudness. He felt sure it was the police, telling him Alicia was home. Or perhaps her mother.

'Hello?' Sydney said.

'Mr Bartleby? – Inspector Hill here.'

'Yes?' eagerly.

'Can you come up to London this afternoon around six, Mr Bartleby? I'd like to see you earlier, but I'm busy until then.'

'Well – I'm busy also and expecting a couple of important telephone calls today. Would tomorrow—?'

'I'm sorry,' Inspector Hill interrupted in a tone that brooked no refusal.

That, at 10 a.m., ruined Sydney's day.

The telephone did not ring again before he set out, early and restless, for Ipswich a little after 3. He was in the foulest of moods – depressed, discouraged and angry. Alicia had better surrender today or else, Sydney thought. And he had a vision of himself storming into the Lancing cottage or whatever they had there, dragging Alicia out by the hair, and throwing a punch *en route* at Tilbury with his free hand. He might go down to Lancing after the police interview today. Or if they got unpleasant enough at Scotland Yard, he'd give them the address of Mr and Mrs Leamans, Lancing, simple as that. Let the police do the rest.

In the Ipswich station, Sydney wandered over to the newsstand after buying his ticket. He looked at the headlines of the *Standard*, MYSTERY WOMAN FOUND DEAD, and at the picture of a cliff with an arrow pointing to a light-coloured blob at the bottom. The cliff was near Lancing, Sydney read below. He bought the paper. The story was on the front page also.

It had happened late last night, the police believed, but the body had not been noticed until mid-morning.

Then with a terrible pang in his chest, Sydney read the lines that confirmed his guess:

Inhabitants of Lancing identified the dead woman as Mrs Eric Leamans, who had recently taken a furnished villa with her husband in the town. Mr Leamans was not at the villa.

Inspection of the villa disclosed only Mrs Leamans's clothing, none of her husband's, and no papers that might have established her identity, which is now in question. Mrs Leamans's hair was blonde but tinted red, and this fact plus the initials A.B. on a keyring in her skirt pocket has led police to believe she may be Alicia Bartleby, 26, missing from her Suffolk home since July 2nd last. No handbag was found near her body or in the villa. Police are continuing inquiries as this goes to press.

The story must have been broadcast on the radio since noon, and they must know by now that it was Alicia – even if her face had been badly damaged, Sydney thought, and winced.

Had she jumped? Or had Tilbury pushed her?

Mr Leamans was not at the villa. He had evidently cleared himself out. Or had Alicia had a couple of drinks on a lonely night, in a blue funk about whether to go home to her parents or to stick it out a little longer, and thrown herself over the cliff? Sydney couldn't imagine Alicia getting herself into such a state. But he could imagine Tilbury wanting her to give it up before she was found out – rather, before he was found out and sacked from his posh job, and Sydney could imagine Alicia resisting that. They might have been having some fine battles. If Tilbury had pushed her, and was trying to get away with it, it was absolutely hopeless. Sydney gloated grimly over the welter of things that would trip him: fingerprints all over the house, the description of him by Lancing people, his steady absence from London lately on weekends, worst of all his attempt to clear the house of identifiable items. Since no handbag was found, it sounded as if Tilbury had been around last night, and he must have been in an absolute panic to be so stupid as to run. Sydney wondered if he had gone back to London last night and reported for work today as usual.

Tilbury might have got through the day a little nervously, but still a free, unquestioned man. Sydney looked at his watch. Ten past 4. In an hour or so, Tilbury might be on his way from his office to his flat in Sloane Street, if the police didn't get on to his trail by then, and why, particularly, should they so soon? It was even conceivable that they wouldn't get on to his trail at all, if Vassily and Carpie and Inez didn't choose to talk.

Sydney cursed Tilbury as he boarded his train. Whatever had happened in Lancing, Tilbury had mucked it up. He was suddenly glad to be going to London. He might be just a little late getting to Scotland Yard.

On the train, he planned and re-planned. Ideas built in his mind like clouds piling up in the sky, and just as quickly blew themselves away. It was lovely, planning, and his thoughts shot like lightning through the nebulous visions.

His final plan was not quite safe – what plan was? – but a little daring would carry the day, he thought. He felt he had a nine out of ten chance to succeed, which was, to say, to accomplish what he wanted to do without interruption, if he acted immediately. If he were interrupted before he began, then he was safe also. To be interrupted during it was not so safe, and would come under the heading of bad luck.

He was in London by 5.20, and took a Kensington bus outside Liverpool Street station. In Knightsbridge, he stopped at a chemist's shop and bought, casually from a counter display, a large bottle of sedatives called Dormor. They were probably not strong at all, but it was the best he could do without a prescription, and he was hoping Tilbury might have something stronger at home. The chemist's shop was busy, and he thought he wouldn't be remembered. Sydney hoped he wouldn't have to cut Tilbury's wrists into the bargain, if Tilbury didn't have anything stronger at home. Sydney wasn't sure he could.

By now, it was nearly 6. Sydney walked into Sloane Street, and began to look for the number. It was a medium-sized building of four stories with two small formal stone pillars flanking the front door. Five names on the bell register, and one of them was E. S. Tilbury. Sydney walked out on the pavement and looked in both directions to see if Dapper Dan was possibly in view, but he wasn't. Sydney pressed the bell.

No answer, and Sydney waited a good long while.

He rang again, two firm blasts.

At last, the release button came, and Sydney went into a polished, ornate foyer with carpeted stairs beyond. It was possible the police were with Tilbury now, Sydney thought, in which case, he'd just have dropped by to speak to Tilbury, because of rumours he had heard. The pills were out of sight in Sydney's jacket pocket.

Tilbury leaned over the stairwell. 'Wha— Who is it?'

'Me. Sydney,' Sydney said pleasantly. Tilbury was on the third floor. 'Good evening, Edward.'

A woman came out of a doorway on the second floor with a dog on a leash, glanced as Sydney, and went on past. Bad luck, Sydney thought.

Tilbury straightened and stepped back. His door was open behind him. He looked frightened and startled, and Sydney saw that he was drunk, or else in a very bad state of nerves. Tilbury's jacket was unbuttoned, also his collar, and he had slid his tie down.

'Got time for a few minutes' talk?' Sydney asked.

'Yes – I suppose so. My goodness, yes. In fact – I wanted to speak to you.' Tilbury's not very tall figure swayed a little as he walked through his apartment door.

Sydney followed him into an impeccably neat, formal living-room with oriental carpet, books, and table lamps that looked like the Victoria & Albert Museum. A coal fire was laid primly in the black-and-grey marble fireplace and hardly looked burnable. A half-finished highball stood on the coffee table beside an ashtray in which were a dozen cigarette butts.

'Of course you know about Alicia,' Tilbury said, glancing at Sydney with desperate, pinkish eyes.

'Of course,' Sydney said.

'Would you care to sit down?' Tilbury asked, gesturing towards the green satin sofa.

'No.'

Tilbury looked at him uneasily, started toward his highball glass, stopped, and opened his hands. 'I – Excuse my—' He slid his tie up and adjusted his collar on his rather plump neck. 'I came home from the office today about three. Couldn't stand it any longer. I'm afraid I've had a few drinks.'

'O – think nothing of it,' Sydney said. He was standing about five feet from Tilbury.

Tilbury picked up his glass. 'Oh, forgive me. Would you like a drink?'

'No,' Sydney said with a slight smile. 'Go right ahead.'

Tilbury picked up his glass. 'Oh, forgive me. Would you like an explanation, of course. It's very nearly done me in – last night. You see, last night—' He glanced up at Sydney. 'I went chasing out into the night after Alicia. She was in a dreadful state, and I tried to get her to go home to her parents' house. I mean, I'd tried to get her to before. Many times. She'd had too much to drink last night before I got there. She was unusually upset. Something had happened, she said, but she wouldn't tell me what. Then she dashed out. I lost her for a while in the darkness, she was on the road that goes along the shore. I caught up with her – once – and actually had her by the hand, but she broke away again. She ran and threw herself off the cliff before I could do anything about it.' Edward's free hand opened limply as he finished and looked at Sydney.

Sydney did not know whether to believe him or not. If Tilbury had had her by the hand, why had he let her go? Because he wanted to let her go? Or was the story a cover-up for Tilbury's having pushed her?

'I don't know what they'll think of me at the office,' Tilbury mumbled, loosened his tie once more, and drank from his glass.

The office was, of course, uppermost in Tilbury's mind. 'So you ran away. Last night,' Sydney said.

'Well—'

'Oh, I can understand, really. You tried to remove all the signs of yourself from the house.'

'I was in a state of shock last night. It – might not have been the right thing to do, but I really didn't know what I was doing.' Tilbury's eyes seemed to plead for Sydney's approval, or his forgiveness.

'Well – the police haven't questioned you yet, have they?'

'No, and I – well, I hope they don't. I'm horribly sorry about all this. I loved Alicia, you know. I never wished any harm to come to her. On the contrary, I – I tried to convince her we were getting you into trouble. Rather, she was, because she wouldn't go back to her family. But Alicia's death was none of my fault. I'd have saved her, if I could have done. Whereas if I'm dragged into it now, my career is ruined. Quite unnecessarily, you see.' Again the pink eyes looked at Sydney.

'Oh, I don't think you're going to be dragged into it.'

Tilbury looked at him in a puzzled, dubious way. Fatigue had made little puffy bags under his eyes, forerunners of what he would have in middle age, if he had been going to reach middle age. Tilbury was pale, his forehead glossy with a fine sweat. He went to replenish his glass from a bar cart in a corner of the room.

'Does anyone else know about you and Alicia?' Sydney asked.

'I don't know,' Tilbury said with a glance at Sydney over his shoulder. 'Some people might suspect. I'm not sure they'd say anything.'

'You need a sedative, Edward. Put a sleeping pill or two in that drink.'

'What?' Tilbury turned with his drink.

'Sleeping pills. Have you some?'

Edward smiled foolishly. 'Yes, but – I don't need them now. I take one before I go to bed. Didn't do me much good last night.'

'Try one now. I insist,' Sydney said, walking towards Tilbury.

Tilbury didn't know what to make of it. He stepped to one side as Sydney advanced.

'Where are they? In the bathroom? Get them,' Sydney said.

'Yes.' Tilbury walked obediently towards a door that led off from the living-room. 'I don't really need them now.'

'Yes, you do,' said Sydney, following him.

In the bathroom, Tilbury opened the medicine cabinet door, hesitated, and said, 'Looks as if I took the last one last night.' He closed the cabinet.

Sydney opened it, and saw three or four plastic containers of pills among many little bottles. One with yellow pills in it looked promising, because it was in front. 'Aren't these sleeping pills?' he asked, lifting the container out,

'No,' said Edward, in a way that told Sydney they were.

Sydney gave him a look.

'Well, yes, they are,' Edward said with a fuzzy, frightened smile.

Sydney shook one out on his palm, extended it, and said, 'You need it.'

'Oh, no.' Tilbury shook his head.

Sydney grabbed him by the front of his jacket. 'Take it or I'll smash you to a pulp.'

Trembling, Edward took it from Sydney's palm, and put it into his mouth. He drank it with his highball.

'Take another. Two're better than one.'

Tilbury demurred at the second on Sydney's palm, but Sydney shoved his palm closer, his fingertips touching Tilbury's chest, and Tilbury took it and swallowed it,

'There.' Sydney smiled. 'You'll feel better now. Much better for you than Scotch.' He walked out of the bathroom with the container of pills.

Tilbury came back into the living-room.

'Sit down,' Sydney said.

Tilbury was looking at the telephone. Sydney stood between him and the telephone. Then Tilbury turned and ran for the door.

Sydney caught him before he touched it, and jerked him back with a strength that surprised himself and made Tilbury's neck snap. 'You see how nervous you are. Take a couple of these right now.' Sydney put his back to the door, and poured two more pills on to his palm.

Tilbury scowled at him.

'Come on, no nonsense, take them,' Sydney said.

Then Tilbury shrugged and said with an eerily successful attempt at unconcern, 'You'll only make me sick and I'll throw them up.' He took them from Sydney's palm.

'Go sit down on the sofa,' Sydney said.

Tilbury took a minute to cross the room in a slow, weaving way, as if he were debating every step. He picked up his glass from the coffee table, glanced as Sydney who had followed him, and swallowed the pills. Then he sat down on the sofa with a resigned, amused air.

Sydney held the container up to see how many more pills were left – about thirty, he thought – and Tilbury got up and made a wobbling dash for the telephone. Sydney grabbed Tilbury's wrist and twisted it, then put the telephone back in its cradle.

'Nine nine nine will get you nowhere,' Sydney said, and shoved Edward back towards the sofa. He had a desire to beat Tilbury to a pulp now, but he realized that wasn't the way. He also realized his finger-prints were on the telephone, but he was going to use the telephone in a few minutes. 'Sit down,' Sydney said.

Tilbury sat down uneasily on the sofa.

Sydney went to the bar cart and returned with a cut-glass bowl of canapé biscuits. 'A little titbit,' Sydney said. He was afraid Tilbury might be sick.

Tilbury took a handful, as if they might help him.

Then Sydney sat down and waited a minute, while Edward looked increasingly worried.

'I don't know what you're trying to do,' Tilbury murmured with an attempt at a cheerful smile.

'Calm down. You know you need these – God knows, Alicia was difficult,' Sydney said in a soothing voice, pouring more pills out. 'Now take these slowly one by one.' He gave Tilbury one, and went to the bar cart and got the soda dispenser. He put some soda into Tilbury's glass and handed it to him.

Tilbury took his pills. 'I'm qui' sure I'll be sick.'

The telephone rang.

Sydney ignored it, and Tilbury might not have heard it, and finally it stopped ringing. Tilbury was making an effort to sit upright and keep his eyes open. Sydney shook out more pills, offered them on his palm, and as Tilbury looked reluctant, Sydney grabbed his throat, not tightly but in a crucial place. Tilbury opened his mouth wide for air as Sydney released him.

'Don't scream. If anybody comes in, I'll tell them you're taking the pills because you pushed Alicia over the cliff. You understand? – Of course you do.'

'I'm not taking any more,' Edward said, and struck Sydney's hand, knocking the pills off Sydney's palm. Tilbury struggled up.

Sydney caught him again by the throat and administered a light blow to Tilbury's nose, not hard enough to make it bleed. 'Didn't you push Alicia? Didn't you?'

'No,' Tilbury said in a voice so shaking with fear, it was not possible to tell whether he was lying or not.

'You can't get any help, Tilbury, and you'll damned well take these pills,' Sydney said, still gripping him with his left hand by the throat, hard enough to hold him, but trying not to cause any

236

bruises. 'Come on, knock yourself out. It's the easiest way. It's an honourable way, Tilbury. A suicide pact between lovers. Or would you rather I said you told me you pushed her? I came in at six fifteen and found you well on the way, taking an overdose, and you told me you were taking the pills because you pushed Alicia.' And two things encouraged Sydney now: he believed Tilbury had pushed her, and he didn't think he would have to cut Tilbury's wrists, because he thought the pills were rather powerful. He pushed Tilbury back on to the sofa.

Tilbury bounced and sat still, his hands hanging. He looked up with eyes suddenly full of fear again. 'I'm not taking any more!' Then twisting, he flung himself off the sofa, on to the floor.

Sydney picked him up as if he weighed no more than a life-sized doll, fixed him upright against the sofa arm, and got some more pills from the bottle. He crammed the pills into Tilbury's mouth, and held the glass of weak Scotch and soda for him – so quickly Tilbury might not have known what was happening. At any rate, the pills were in his mouth and Tilbury was drinking from the glass. Sydney sat beside him, holding him firmly by the shoulder and one arm against the arm of the sofa.

Tilbury did not struggle now. His eyes were beginning to look glassy. Sydney let four minutes pass, by his watch, as he held Tilbury back against the sofa. Sydney shook out some more pills, and Tilbury took them as if he were too sleepy to know what he was doing. He hiccuped once, but the pills stayed down.

'That's a good fellow,' Sydney said softly.

In the next six or seven minutes, Tilbury took all but one of the pills that were left. He took them very slowly into his mouth from Sydney's fingers, like a sleepy child or a bird, and at last slumped sideways on the sofa, his lids open only a slit, his mouth ajar, as if he tried to say something and hadn't the energy. When Tilbury seemed very quiet and his eyes were closed, Sydney looked around on the floor for the three pills that had fallen. The third one was under the sofa. Sydney retrieved it and dropped the three pills into what remained of Tilbury's Scotch and soda.

Tilbury was so far gone, Sydney could get only an inch or so of the liquid down him before it started spilling on Tilbury's chin. Sydney then lifted his feet on to the sofa, pulled Tilbury's neatly folded handkerchief from his breast pocket and wiped his finger-prints from Tilbury's glass and, holding the glass by its rim with the handkerchief, wrapped Edward's limp hand around the glass, and pressed his thumb and fingers on it in a few other spots. Sydney performed the same operation with the soda dispenser, and the container of pills. He made a trip to the bathroom to erase prints on the medicine cabinet door, and finally he went to the telephone and called Scodand Yard.

He asked to speak to Inspector Hill.

'Inspector Hill, I'm sorry, but I got delayed,' Sydney said in a harassed voice. 'There were telephone calls and people at my house today. I'm sure you can understand. But I've just got to London and I'll see you very shortly.'

Inspector Hill did not sound at all annoyed.

Sydney wiped the telephone, then carried it towards Tilbury, but it didn't reach. He had to lift Edward off the sofa to the floor, and press Edward's hand around the telephone there. Then Sydney replaced the telephone with the aid of Edward's hand-kerchief, removed it from the cradle and left it lying on the desk. At last he left the handkerchief wadded on the coffee table beside the drink. He'd have to let himself out by touching the door-knobs, but doorknobs were notoriously fuzzy when it came to finger-prints, Sydney knew, and it would look worse to wipe them.

He left the apartment. He would drop the Dormor bottle into a rubbish bin or down a drain in the street, and not in this neigh-bourhood.

29

In the taxi to Scotland Yard, which Sydney providently caught at Hyde Park Corner instead of Sloane Street or Knightsbridge, it dawned on him that he hadn't remembered to think what it felt like to commit a murder while he was committing it. He had not thought at all about himself. Of course, the murder was not committed yet. It was still being committed. Tilbury was still alive, and might live if he were found in the next hour or so and had his stomach pumped. *A suspension of mercy*, Sydney thought. An absence of something. And yet he had not even been aware of that at the time. No, his action had been merely a brutal, unthinking retaliation for Tilbury's deceit and heinousness in fleeing from Alicia after she was dead or dying

The taxi stopped, and Sydney paid him off.

He was passed by a sentinel constable, who escorted him to another policeman inside the building, who accompanied him to Inspector Hill's office on the second floor.

Inspector Hill was with two men in plain clothes, both of whom remained in the office, though Inspector Hill gave his attention to Sydney as soon as he entered, 'Ah, Mr Bartleby, good evening. Sit down, if you please.' His telephone rang. 'Hill speaking ... Oh ... Excellent. Well, find him and bring him here.' He hung up, passed a hand over his hair and said to Sydney. 'We're making, progress finally. I'm sorry indeed about your wife, Mr Bartleby. The identification was established this afternoon beyond a shadow of a doubt.'

'I know. I knew,' Sydney said.

'You knew?'

'I knew when I saw the photograph in the paper. The photograph of the cliff.'

'And for the record, Mr Bartleby, where were you Wednesday night?' Inspector Hill asked briskly.

'I was home that evening and that night.'

'Can you prove that, if you have to?'

Sydney thought a moment. 'No.'

'Well, you may not have to. We're just now on the trail of the man your wife was with, the Eric Leamans. We have an excellent description of him. Does the name Edward Tilbury mean anything to you?'

'Yes,' Sydney said.

'What?'

Sydney glanced at the two interested listeners on his left, one a middle-aged man, the other younger. 'I knew since last Friday that my wife was with him, but I wanted to give her a chance to come back herself. On her own. That's why I didn't mention it to the police.'

'And – how did you find out?'

'I saw them in Brighton. I didn't know the man's name, but I found it out later.'

'How, may I ask?' asked Inspector Hill.

Sydney knew the police must have got Tilbury's name from Inez and Carpie. 'I asked a couple of London friends. Inez Haggard and Carpie Dunne.'

'Um-m. We've just spoken to them. Have they known all along?' the Inspector asked with a frown.

'No. Only as long as I have. You see – I described to them the man I saw in Brighton. And if anyone's to blame for their not telling the police, it's me, because I asked them not to. I didn't tell them I'd seen my wife or Tilbury, either, but I remembered Tilbury paying attention to my wife at a party they gave. I didn't know his name, but I remembered what he looked like.'

'I see. Well, they're bringing Tilbury here tonight.'

Sydney was wondering if he should tell the Inspector he had written the letter and telegram to Alicia. Alicia might have destroyed them. Tilbury hadn't mentioned the letter or the telegram. The telegram might come out, since the post office kept a record of them for a while. Or if by some wild fluke, the police decided to think Tilbury had not been on the scene the night of Alicia's death, the telegram could be seen as a ruse: he had sent the telegram Wednesday morning, jumped on a train and gone to Brighton and Lancing Wednesday night, pushed Alicia over the cliff in a fit of jealousy, cleared Tilbury's things out of the villa to make it look as if Tilbury had killed her and fled, and returned home. Sydney blinked. It really couldn't happen. He wouldn't be able to make it happen even in a piece of fiction. 'You spoke with my wife's parents, I suppose?' Sydney asked, breaking into several seconds of silence in the room.

'Yes, around noon today. We corroborated the identity, in fact, by asking her mother if she had a birthmark on the inside of her forearm.'

Sydney knew the birthmark, a strawberry mark like a tiny map of France, Alicia had always said. He thought again that her face must have been damaged beyond recognition. 'Where is she now?'

'Her body is being taken to Kent after the post-mortem,' Hill replied, then answered his telephone on the first ring. 'Oh? . . .

Well, break in then, of course. And call me back.' He hung up. 'Telephone's off the hook in Tilbury's flat, the lights on, and he doesn't answer the door. Interesting.'

Sydney said nothing.

'Where did you see your wife in Brighton?' Inspector Hill asked.

'I'd been waiting in the railway station to see if I could see Tilbury,' Sydney said, 'or rather someone who looked like him.' He told about following Tilbury in a taxi to where he met Alicia, who then had red hair, and how he had visited towns to the west of Brighton and traced her to Angmering by means of the post office. 'I thought it would be a matter of time until she came back herself. Or communicated. I didn't want to embarrass her by exposing all this.'

'We traced them to Angmering, too,' said one of the officers on Sydney's left.

'But just today,' said Inspector Hill with a tight smile, and answered his telephone again. 'Sorry, I can't talk about that now, Michael, I'm expecting a call and I want the line free.' He had hardly hung up, when the telephone buzzed again. 'Oh? . . . Yes, I agree. Right. See you.' He pressed the cradle, then dialled a single number. 'Inspector Hill speaking. I'd like a car right away.' He hung up and said. 'Tilbury's taken an overdose in his flat. They're getting a doctor. I think we should go over.'

They all moved, took hats and macintoshes, and went down-stairs to a black car that was already waiting.

There were a couple of people in Tilbury's foyer, and a few more on the landing outside his flat door, which was closed. Sydney recognized the woman who had seen him, but she did not seem to pay any particular attention to him. Hill knocked, and was admitted to the flat. Sydney followed with the other two men.

Tilbury was still on the sofa, and a long rubber tube hung from his mouth and led to a grey enamel cooking pot on the floor. His eyes were closed, his face pale and flaccid.

'Not getting much,' said the doctor to Hill.

'Is it a fatal dose, you think?' asked Inspector Hill.

'Depends on how many of these he took,' said the doctor, picking up the plastic pill container, in which one pill remained. 'It's whole-grain Seconal.' He put the container back on the coffee table.

Inspector Hill took it and read the label, which gave a doctor's name, the chemist's shop, and said 'one or two as needed'. Hill opened the container and sniffed. Then he set it on the coffee table.

'Can't get any more out,' said the doctor, and removed the tube from Tilbury's throat. 'Next step is the hospital.' He went to the telephone.

Hill looked at his watch and made a wry face. 'It'll be hours before Tilbury's fit to talk. Mr Bartleby, can you spend the night in London? We'll want to talk to you if and when Mr Tilbury comes to. Unless you prefer to go home and come back tomorrow.'

'No, I'll stay,' Sydney said.

'Would you give us a ring tomorrow between nine and ten?'

'Yes.' Sydney said good night to the Scotland Yard men, and left.

The woman who had seen him was not on the landing, but the two men were still there.

'How is he?' one of the men asked. 'Is he alive?'

They'd heard about the overdose, no doubt. 'Yes, he's alive,' Sydney said, and the message was passed down to the men standing in the foyer.

Sydney rang Inez and Carpie from the first call-box he came to. He emphatically didn't want to be alone, and they were just the people he wanted to see.

'Sydney, darling!' Inez sang out 'Are you in London?'

Inez said they would love to see him, and that they were alone, though their telephone had been ringing all evening.

They had not been quite alone, Sydney saw as his taxi turned into their mews street. Alex Polk-Faraday was walking away from their house, his head down, though Sydney knew he was aware of the taxi and of him, because taxis didn't go often into a dead-end street. Alex was avoiding him.

'Sydney! Come in, darling,' Inez said at the door.

He was welcomed by restrained embraces from both the girls, and words of sympathy about Alicia. They gave him a Scotch, which Inez said Carpie had just run out to buy especially for him, and then they questioned him. Had he seen Tilbury? What were the police doing to him?

'I just saw him,' Sydney, said. 'He's taken an overdose and they're getting him to the hospital.'

'What?' from Carpie.

'I'll bet he pushed her, that son of a bitch,' Inez said. 'Don't you think he pushed her?'

'I don't know,' Sydney said.

'Did he take a fatal dose?' asked Carpie.

'I don't know that either.'

'Just that he cleared all his gear out of the villa down there,' Inez said. 'Even got rid of Alicia's pocketbook, didn't he? Nobody found it. He's guilty, and no wonder he tried to kill himself.'

Sydney found himself wordless and slightly shaky, even with the Scotch. Carpie replenished his glass generously from the bottle. 'Can I stay the night?' he asked. 'On your couch? I've got to talk to the police again first thing in the morning.'

'But of course, Syd. Say, have you eaten?' Carpie got up. 'We haven't, because we had a visitor till now.'

'Your old pal Alex,' Inez said. 'I knew he'd shoo when he heard you were coming. We didn't have to ask him to.'

Sydney nodded and smiled faintly, no longer interested in what Alex had to say about him. Their series, he supposed, would run its length of six instalments and stop. Then Sydney realized he could carry it on himself, or at least try to.

'He had to change his tune a little,' Inez said. 'Now he says you're not a wife-killer, just a nut.'

'As if he isn't,' Carpie put in from the kitchen, which was partitioned from the living-room.

'Gosh, Syd, we shouldn't be joking,' Inez said. 'It looks like poor Alicia was the one who was out of her mind. Staying away for so long—'

'We didn't tell Alex you knew about Tilbury for a whole week,' Carpie yelled over the sound of running water. 'That'd have made him even more furious.' Her voice was cheery.

'I just told the police I did,' Sydney said.

'Well, so did we, today,' Inez said. 'I hope you didn't mind, Syd. With Alicia—'

'I don't mind,' Sydney said. 'Let's talk about something else. I sold *The Planners* to Potter and Desch this week.' He announced it rather lugubriously.

There were proper congratulations, and a refill of drinks.

The dinner was good, though Sydney could not eat much. The girls put him to bed very soon afterwards on the couch, and Sydney fell asleep listening to their chatter that came faintly from the upstairs regions.

He awakened to the morning feeding of the two kids. It was a quarter to 8. Sydney realized with a jolt that Tilbury could be alive and talking at this minute. The police, of course, didn't know where to reach him. Sydney had only coffee and orange juice for breakfast.

'What do the police want you for now?' Carpie asked.

'They want me to talk with Tilbury probably.'

Inez nearly dropped a plate as she turned to face Sydney.

'Gosh, he might be dead, mightn't he? Do you know what hospital they took him to?'

'No.' And he wouldn't call up to ask, if he did know, Sydney thought. Had Tilbury blabbed everything? What kind of sentence would they give a man who'd tried to make someone take an overdose? The same as for murder, of course. Or would Tilbury live and be remarkably, unbelievably noble, and not say anything to the police about his visit from Sydney Bartleby? Would Tilbury possibly try to redeem himself that way? If he was writing it in a story, Sydney thought, could he dare to make Tilbury that noble? Not without a little indication of nobility beforehand, and Sydney had yet to see any in Tilbury. Sydney spent an anxious and sickening hour until 9 o'clock, relieved by a couple of nips of Scotch which Carpie pressed on him. Inez had taken the kids out for an airing. Sydney could not bring himself to turn on the radio for the news, and it didn't seem to occur to either of the girls to do it.

Sydney rang Scotland Yard. Inspector Hill had not come in yet, but a man he was passed on to said in answer to Sydney's question that Edward Tilbury had died at 4 a.m.

'His heart gave out,' the voice said. 'It always depends on the heart whether they pull through.' The man possibly thought he was speaking to a relative. 'Inspector Hill ought to be in any minute.'

'What's the news?' Carpie asked from the kitchen.

'Tilbury died last night,' Sydney said.

Carpie turned with a dishcloth in her hands. 'Goodness. Oh, Christ. A real fatal dose. That sounds like he did push her. Doesn't it?'

'I don't know,' Sydney said. 'I don't suppose it matters much. I imagine Tilbury was worried about his job – wasn't he?'

'Oh, sure. I know that. I talked with Vassily around six. My God, I wonder if Vassily knows he's dead?'

Sydney barely heard her. He was thinking that he ought to call the Sneezums. 'May I make a call to Kent, Carpie? I'll get the charges.'

'Oh, of course, Syd. Alicia's parents, you mean?'

Sydney nodded, and started putting the call through. He had to get the number from information, as he could not recall it exactly. Carpie went upstairs so he could be alone. A servant answered, and Sydney asked to speak to Mrs Sneezum.

'Just a minute, please. I'll see if she's free.'

Sydney waited more than a minute. Then Mrs Sneezum said: 'Hello?'

'Hello, Mrs Sneezum. This is Sydney. I wanted to say how sorry I am about Alicia. I'm—'

'Oh, Sydney –' Mrs Sneezum's voice seemed to give way. But she regained it quickly, and said, 'We're all sorry. I had no idea what was going on. None of us did. Not even you – did you?'

'No,' Sydney said. 'I'm sorry it had to end like this.' He was really sorry, and Mrs Sneezum, for all her stiffness – and her stiff side was the only side Sydney had ever seen – seemed more human and real now than anything he had encountered in the last many days. 'Edward Tilbury is dead. I just heard a few minutes ago. He took an overdose of sleeping pills.'

'Oh, heavens! Oh, good Lord! – It's like some horrible tragedy – on a stage. I keep thinking all this has nothing to do with Alicia. It can't be real. Do you know what I mean?'

'Yes.' Yes. As if his murder of Tilbury wasn't real, either, because Tilbury might have done it himself, if he had lost his job, and there wasn't much doubt that he would have lost it.

'Sydney, may I say I think you've been extremely patient? Patient also with our wayward daughter. She drove herself to an extreme, to the brink of death – until she just couldn't take any more. I know it's difficult to talk, but will you come to see us at some point? Drop us a note, Sydney.'

'That I will. I certainly will,' Sydney said, grateful that Mrs Sneezum was winding up the impossible conversation. 'Give my love to your husband.'

'Oh, my goodness – the funeral. The funeral service will be tomorrow at eleven, Sydney. At the little church here.'

'Thank you, Mrs Sneezum. I'll be there.'

'Come to our house tomorrow,' she said in a tremulous voice.

It was over. Sydney wiped his forehead, and fished two half-crowns out of his pocket to leave for the call.

Carpie came down the stairs.

'I'm off to Scotland Yard now,' Sydney said. 'Thanks so much, Carpie. And for the razor, too.' Sydney had shaved with soap and Inez or Carpie's safety razor.

'Will you come by later and see Inez? Ring us anyway.'

'I'll ring you,' Sydney promised. He wasn't sure what Inspector Hill had in store for him, and if he were quite free, he wanted to get back home immediately, and think what to do about the house, his life, everything. Sydney came half-way up the stairs to meet Carpie, and pressed a kiss on her cheek. 'Thanks for being the best friends in the world.'

'Oh, Syd, we adore you. You're going to be on our list of celebrities, you know. *The Planners* has got to be a best-seller.'

Inspector Hill met Sydney in the hall outside his office, smiling pleasantly. 'Sorry to have delayed you this morning. I went to fetch a lady and she was a bit late. A woman who thinks she saw you going into Tilbury's house last evening. Around six?' The Inspector looked at Sydney expectantly.

Sydney's reaction was the blandest possible, he felt. An 'Oh?' which admitted and denied nothing, and certainly showed no alarm.

The plump woman of about forty-five, whom Sydney remembered with her dog, was seated in Inspector Hill's office.

'This is Mr Bartleby,' said Inspector Hill. 'Mrs Harmon.'

'How do you do?' Sydney said.

'How do you do?' she replied. 'Yes. This is the man I saw.'

'Mr Tilbury admitted you,' said Inspector Hill, still pleasantly. 'Mr Tilbury was in at six. Is that right?'

'Yes, that's correct,' Sydney said.

'That's why you were a little late yesterday?'

'Yes.'

'I think that's all, Mrs Harmon,' said the Inspector. 'I thank you very much for coming in. If you'd like, one of our drivers will take you back to your house.'

Mrs Harmon stood up. 'No, thank you, Inspector. I've an errand not far away. I'd just as soon take a bus.' She gave Sydney another look, a nod of good-bye, then left the office, graciously seen into the hall by the Inspector.

'Why did you go to see Tilbury?' asked the Inspector as he came in and closed the door.

'I was interested in getting the true story from him – if I could. What really happened to Alicia.'

'Sit down, Mr Bartleby.'

Sydney sat down.

So did Inspector Hill, behind his desk. 'And what did Mr Tilbury say?'

And what if Tilbury weren't dead, Sydney thought. What if the man he had spoken to this morning had been told to say he was dead – the police could later call that information a mistake – to see what Sydney's story would be? 'He told me that Alicia was upset Wednesday evening. She ran out of the house and Tilbury tried to catch her. He said she headed for some cliffs by the sea, or the sea road. And he couldn't stop her from throwing herself over.'

'Did you believe him?'

Sydney hesitated a moment. 'Yes, I did.'

Inspector Hill studied him. 'Did you expect Tilbury to confess or admit to you that he'd pushed her, something like that?'

'No. I just wanted to hear the real story. I assumed Tilbury knew, because he'd been there.'

Inspector Hill's gaze still rested quietly on Sydney. 'How long did you stay at Tilbury's?'

'I suppose about ten minutes. Maybe fifteen.'

'Did you ring me from his house?'

'Yes,' Sydney said, not wanting to admit this, but if he had rung from a call-box, the noise of the push-button and falling coins would have been heard by the Scotland Yard operator, and just might have been remembered. Anyway, now he'd said it.

'What kind of mood was Mr Tilbury in? Surprised to see you, I suppose.'

Maybe Mrs Harmon had said that, Sydney thought 'Yes. Frightened at first, I think. He'd also had quite a bit to drink. He said – after he told me the story – that he was afraid of losing his job if all this came out, and of course he knew it would come out.' Sydney was aware that he had no feeling, therefore no look, he supposed, of guilt now. Far less than when he had spoken to people in the early days of Alicia's disappearance. Perhaps that was due to practice.

Inspector Hill pressed his lips together in what looked like a resigned smile. 'He didn't say anything to you then about taking pills? Taking his life?'

'No.'

'Did you make any threatening remarks to him? About telling the story to his law firm, something like that?'

'Oh, no. I knew it'd come out without my doing anything.'

'I see. And why didn't you mention yesterday that you'd been to see Tilbury?'

'Well – I'm sure I would have mentioned it finally, but I thought Tilbury was going to be brought here yesterday. I wanted to compare what he'd say to you with what he said to me – if I'd been allowed to hear it, or if you'd told me.'

'Do you think it would have been different?'

'Probably not. No. Tilbury denied pushing her. He wouldn't have admitted it ever, if he did push her.' Sydney spoke calmly. He felt calm.

'Hm.' Inspector Hill opened a drawer and pulled out Sydney's brown notebook. 'I suppose you'd like this back.'

Sydney stood up to take it. 'I would. Thank you, Inspector.' As he touched the notebook, Sydney thought that he would write a description of the Tilbury murder in it, while his recollection was still very clear, because the notebook was now, after all, the safest place in which to write it.

'A curious little book. Well, Mr Bartleby, I think that's all I have to ask you or say to you this morning.' Inspector Hill stood up and walked around his desk, looking at Sydney all the while with a remote and thoughtful smile.

An accuser who cannot prove, Sydney thought, because the Inspector certainly suspected he might have forced Tilbury to take the pills. Sydney could feel the Inspector's thought like a radar beam, definite as the hand of the law on his shoulder, only the hand wasn't physically there. The hand was extended, in fact, and Sydney took it. The Inspector's attitude was a friendly one – and everything was a matter of attitudes.

PATRICIA HIGHSMITH

sphere